Praise for
THINGS THAT PASS FOR LOVE

"The people in Allison Amend's transporting stories—a teacher less inured to human suffering than her fifth-graders, a little boy and his father who are meeting for the first time, an investigator of cults—are smart, funny, and achingly vulnerable. I read this book in a single sitting, unable to resist going on to the next story and then the next and then the next."
—**Judith Claire Mitchell, author of** *The Last Day of the War*

"Allison Amend's witty and sharply observed stories never fail to surprise. Her collection demonstrates both impressive range and a deep curiosity about the world."
—**Sarah Shun-Lien Bynum, author of** *Madeline is Sleeping*

"I love this book. The stories in Amend's *Things That Pass for Love* are such good company that I found myself reading more and more slowly so that the collection wouldn't end. Amend's voice is so compelling, easeful, and polished you feel that the stories almost rise up off the page and tell themselves. And, as we all know, the hardest thing a writer can do is make it look easy."
—**Alison Smith, author of** *Name All the Animals*

"Amend is one very strong contemporary writer. I have been reading her stories for many years. This book has an organic feel that I love; it speaks to something new."
—**Peter Orner, author of** *Esther Stories* **and** *The Second Coming of Mavala Shikongo*

D0172891

"Quick-witted and observant, rife with startling detail, these stories do what good stories should: they compel our attention, demanding to be read. Amend's characters inhabit their unusual worlds with a scientific precision, and one wonders at the sheer variety of human experience that unfolds."
—**Sheri Joseph, author of** *Bear Me Safely Over* **and** *Stray*

"*Things That Pass for Love* is an ambitious, challenging, and wonderfully strange collection that speaks not only to the struggle we all have simply to exist, but to the struggle we equally have to connect with others and make sense of it all. Amend is a storyteller without fear whose characters feel the shudder of the world acutely, with passion and a mordant humor that surprises you even as it breaks your heart."
—**Tod Goldberg, author of** *Simplify* **and** *Living Dead Girl*

"In the tremendous, fulfilling variety between these covers you are guaranteed to learn something you don't already know as Ms. Amend examines some ordinary and extraordinary lives."
—**Samantha Schnee, Editor & VP, book projects of** *Words Without Borders*

"For those of us who love and worry for the short form, Allison Amend's startling and fresh new voice is a Godsend."
— **Helen Schulman, author of** *P.S.* **and** *The Revisionist*

"Allison Amend is a gifted storyteller—no, more than gifted. Her writing is powerful enough to create its own kind of weather. Her characters are so real it's as if you could reach between the pages and shake hands with them. If you want to read good stories, read this book."
—**Hannah Tinti, author of** *Animal Crackers* **and editor of** *One-Story Magazine*

THINGS THAT PASS FOR LOVE

THINGS
THAT
PASS
FOR
LOVE

stories by

Allison Amend

an imprint of Dzanc Books
3629 N. Hoyne
Chicago, IL 60618
othervoices@listserv.uic.edu

"Dominion Over Every Erring Thing" appeared *Prairie Schooner*, Summer 2008. "Carry the Water, Hustle the Hole" appeared in *Other Voices 36*, Spring 2002. "The World Tastes Good" appeared in *Black Warrior Review*, Fall 2003. "A Personal Matter" appeared in *River Styx*, Fall 2003. "Bluegrass Banjo" appeared in *Atlantic Unbound* (*The Atlantic Monthly*'s online journal) Fall 2000. "The Cult of Me" appeared in *Bellevue Literary Review*, Fall 2003. "Good Shabbos" appeared in *StoryQuarterly 35*, Fall 1999. "The Janus Gate appeared in *Other Voices 32*, Spring/Summer 2000. "What Was Over There is Over Here" appeared in *Rattapallax*, Fall, 2002.

Published 2008 by OV Books, an imprint of Dzanc Books
Book design by Steven Seighman
Cover photo by Nancy Racina Landin

08 09 10 11 5 4 3 2 1
First Edition October 2008

ISBN-13: 978-0-9767177-4-4
ISBN: 0-9767177-4-3

Printed in the United States of America

CONTENTS

DOMINION OVER EVERY ERRING THING

I am teaching my fifth graders to add fractions when the body falls. Only one of the students looks up. I have placed Kendrick next to the window at a desk by himself, away from the table clusters because the previous Friday, as I walked by his desk, he said, audibly enough so that José, sitting closest to him, snickered: "I smell white pussy."

Today he is ignoring his paper, purposely avoiding drawing in the bars that measure 1/5 and those that measure 2/5. I see the body fall out of the corner of my eye, and Kendrick stands up and shoves his head so far forward that I hear it hit the glass just after the body thumps to the ground.

"Oh my God," I say. I go over to the window, and through the soiled glass I can see the body, toes up and eerily straight, in the dirt of the playground. In the background, two planes land and take off from the airport in symmetry.

"What?" Tisha wants to know.

"Nothing," I say, and I hurriedly close the blinds. "It's nothing."

1

"Just another body," Kendrick says.

"Kendrick," I warn him.

There is a bored sigh, and then the class settles back into its worksheets. I stick my head out the door and ask the floater to watch the class.

"Come on." I put my hand behind Kendrick's head to steer him downstairs.

"What, what'd I do?"

"Nothing," I say. "We're just going to see Ms. Sabarowski."

"Awwww," Kendrick says. "Why? I didn't do nothing."

Ms. S is the guidance counselor. Her office is next to the overworked principal's, and she has become the disciplinarian. Inside, Ms. S is standing at the window, watching the paramedics drive over the dirt field to the body, her hands on her broad hips.

"Another one," Ms. S says without turning around.

"He fell feet first," Kendrick says. "And no blood."

Confused, I strafe my gaze from Kendrick to Ms. S and back again. I feel like there is a joke that I'm not getting.

"They probably didn't tell you," Ms. S says. "About the bodies. They climb up in the landing gears of the planes and then freeze in the air. When the landing gears get lowered, the bodies fall."

It has taken me a full two months to get used to the roar of planes taking off and landing at the airport nearby. Now I have almost come to appreciate it, the rhythm they give the class. Three seconds every minute to catch my breath, to pause and let the lesson sink in. It is almost like a camera flash, where every movement seems clearer because of the darkness between images. It reduces every lesson to its essentials.

"Who?" I ask, stupidly.

"Guatamalans, mostly. Some Cubans, El Salvadoreans."

"It ain't no thing, Miss Gold," Kendrick says. He says it almost kindly, and I wait for him to add an insulting epithet, which he doesn't.

"Can you go sit outside, Kendrick?" I ask.

When he leaves, I ask Ms. S how she could let the students in the school think that bodies falling out of airplanes "ain't no thing"?

"It just is," Ms. S says. She looks down at her clean desk as though there is a paper requiring her urgent attention. She sticks out two swollen fingers and rearranges some pencils. Her nails are long and manicured; the thumb has a rhinestone embedded in the tip. "How am I supposed to explain a thing like that? Bodies get shot sitting on their front porches, bodies overdose on drugs, bodies die from trying to get a free ride to America. They've seen it. They're OK," Ms. S pauses. "Do you want to talk about it?" she asks.

That night I tell my fiancé what happened at school.

"Yeah," he says. "I read about that."

Jake does market analysis and consulting for a hedge fund. I have absolutely no idea what this is, though he has explained it to me a few thousand times, and I am not stupid. His office has a small window that looks over the avenue into another tall building across the street. The company on the floor opposite Jake's sells athletic equipment to health clubs. The employees all wear workout clothes and occasionally they demonstrate new equipment in the conference room. Jake's always coming home with new exercises.

As far as I can tell, Jake spends the day surfing web news and business sites. He always knows everything that's happening. As a result, he is great to have at dinner parties. "You know . . . ," someone will start, and Jake will inevitably say, "Yeah, I read about that," and proceed to pepper the conversation with factoids.

"Apparently, it happens all the time," I say. "It doesn't even faze anyone anymore."

"We're so inured," Jake agrees. That's another of his habits, automatic empathy. When I first met him, it made me think he was listening intently.

"What kind of world . . ." I let the thought trail off. Even I'm sick of my what-kind-of-world speech.

"Come cuddle," Jake says, and pats the couch cushion next to him.

"Can't, I have homework." I am taking Hebrew classes in preparation for my conversion before our wedding in May. I have already taken Jake's name at school for simplicity's sake.

Because I go to Hebrew school twice a week, I now know more than Jake does about his religion and his cultural heritage. I celebrate the minor holidays, Israeli state days he's never heard of. And I've started muttering small prayers to myself, the way nervous Catholics say their rosaries while waiting for the bus.

In our bedroom, I sound out this week's dialogue:

— *Abba, where has Grandfather gone?*

— *He has gone to Gan Eden, my son.*

— *And when will he return?*

— *When Olam Ha-ba is upon us.*

— *I will miss him. He takes me to the park. He reads to me and explains mysteries.*

— *I will miss him too, Son. That is why we rend our garments, cover the mirrors and invite his friends to come and tell us how much they esteemed him.*

— *Good-bye, Grandfather.*

It is odd being a teacher all day and a student at night. Sometimes I understand how my students must feel. Other times, I have no sympathy at all. "Why is your homework not done?" I demand of a tall, chubby girl named Marta. She is wearing a large T-shirt that has the name of a popular rapper. She shrugs her shoulders and looks at the ground. She picks at a chip in the desk until she catches me watching her hands, and then she curls them together at her stomach.

Marta is Amazonian—my height at age ten and already in need of a large-cup bra. She has tried to get out of class more than once by claiming "girl troubles," which succeeded in embarrassing me enough to send her to the nurse two months in a row. Still, she is meeker than my other students, easily manipulated by her peers, and for that I dislike her, though I know I am not supposed to admit that I have favorite students, even to myself.

"Come on," I say. "Give me a reason. Any reason. You didn't feel like it. You played video games instead. You got stuck in traffic. You had to cook dinner for your seven little brothers and sisters . . ."

She cracks a quick smile and then looks back at her feet. Her right shoe is untied.

"I didn't get it," she says.

"Weren't you in class when I handed it out?"

"I mean, I got it, but I didn't really get it, like, understand how to do it."

"What part of it?"

"I don't know. Like, fractions. I don't get them."

"OK." I try to hide my exasperation. We have been doing fractions since the beginning of the year, something they should have learned last year anyway. We should be multiplying by now! Dividing! I can hear a slight whine in my voice, though, and I know that she can tell I'm frustrated.

"I'm sorry," she says. "I'm dumb."

Don't be stupid, I almost say, *you're not dumb*. Out loud I say, "No, you're not. We'll just go over it again."

At the blackboard I draw a pie and split it up into pieces. Next to it I draw a knife.

"What's that supposed to be?" Ennis asks.

"A pie, stupid," Da'nelle answers him. Da'nelle is the favorite student I'm not supposed to have. She is popular, tall, and she carries a small purse with a picture of a boy band. In it are a couple of dollars for lunch, a small brush which she uses frequently, and some lip gloss, cherry flavored, which she likes to eat, putting it on, licking her lips and then reapplying. I can usually smell it from the front of the classroom.

I really should support the underdogs, the children who remind me of me: Jannette, whose nose is always running, or Callie, who is something of a runt—little and scrawny and dressed in clothes that are not now, nor will ever be, in style. But it's Da'nelle, strong-willed, tell-it-like-it-is, take-no-bullshit Da'nelle who makes me smile. She has a posse of girls who share her cluster of desks. They wait for Da'nelle's cue before speaking or acting.

I pause while a plane passes overhead and let my gaze rest on the playground outside.

Something catches my eye, a large object falling.

"Damn," Kendrick says, admiring.

I catch an uncommon enthusiasm in his voice. All my students jump up from their chairs and go to the window like the signal for a fire alarm has just sounded.

This accident is bloody—messy and gory—like the overreaction produced when someone miscalculates the amount of baking soda that should go into the science fair volcano.

"A woman," someone says.

"Is not," Callie answers.

"Is so," Kendrick says.

And indeed, if I squint I can see her dress. The wind gusts and raises the skirt, exposing crooked knees. Ambulances are already barreling toward the site, their silent flashing lights signaling urgency. I close the blinds and send everyone back to their desks where I ask them to take out their Language Arts notebooks. I get the floater to watch them while I go downstairs.

Ms. S is not at her window, but rather at her desk. She sighs as I walk in. "How did they come so quickly?" I ask.

Ms. S shrugs. Her suit jacket is trimmed with fur.

"This one was a woman."

There is a pause. "Is that all you have to say?" I ask.

"I didn't say nothin'," Ms. S says. She looks over a document and then stamps it with her signature.

"This is ridiculous," I say. "I can't teach with bodies falling from the sky."

"I hear you," she says. "But I'm not sure what I can do about it. Obviously, no one would choose to have these . . . accidents, but in the scheme of things—"

"Am I the only one who thinks this is bizarre?" I ask, hands on hips. "Am I the only one who questions this?"

"Stick around awhile," Ms. S says wearily. "In five years it'll be as troublesome as a bad snowstorm."

When I tell Jake about the woman, he says, "Yeah, I read about that." He is driving me to Hebrew. He'll go to the gym while I go to class, and then he'll pick me up on the way back.

"Don't you think that's weird?" I ask.

"Weird, yeah," he says. He squeezes my knee.

"And everybody at school; it was like I was the crazy one, like women fall from heaven every day."

"Mmm," Jake says. "There's some strange stuff in this world."

We pull into the Temple driveway. "See you in an hour," he says. "*Mazel Tov.*"

Mazel Tov means congratulations. It's one of the few Hebrew expressions Jake knows.

My class is not strictly a conversion class. It is a regular Hebrew class for adults, and as a result, I am one of the few people under fifty. There is another convert, like me, but she is quiet, bordering on unfriendly, and she does not look happy to be here, mumbling her dialogues and keeping her head down. I wonder who she is marrying.

The other class members are mostly women in their late fifties. They are not brilliant students. They do their homework but have trouble remembering vocabulary and spend a lot of the class gossiping about people they know in common. A few of them volunteer at the Sisterhood. They've been trying to get me to join, but I claim that I have too much on my plate with school and the wedding, which is not exactly a lie.

The other students are a handful of retired men whose wives signed them up to get them out of the house.

And there is one Christian named John, a Protestant, who wants to learn the language of the Bible so he can read it for himself.

Our teacher, Mr. Lipshitz, is a wizened man who, despite his advanced age and shrunken mien, is a feisty and enthusiastic teacher. I want to ask him why he teaches Hebrew adult education classes, but he scoots out of class as soon as he dismisses us, and the opportunity has never come up in our class discussions. He is patient and firm with the middle-agers. He has excellent classroom management skills.

"Who wants to start us off with this week's dialogue?" When no one raises their hand, Mr. Lipshitz calls on me. "Elizabeth? John, you go opposite her."

John the Protestant stands up and goes to the front of the room. We're supposed to recite the dialogues without books. I never know what to do with my hands.

— *Teacher* (I start in Hebrew), *how many mizvot are there in the Talmud?*

— *There are 613* (John answers. I have never been this close to him. His face is whiffled with acne scars and he gives off a faint, though not unpleasant, sesame odor).

— *And why should one bother with good deeds, when bad deeds often make one rich?*

— *Because it is your duty to be a righteous woman, Daughter.* (Here John has switched the gender so that he is using the correct pronouns and verb endings for talking to a woman. I am impressed, because in the book the dialogue is between two males, and I don't think I could conjugate fast enough to pull this off.)

— *But where is my reward?*

— *Your reward is in the knowledge that you have respected the mandates of your religion according to the laws of tradition.* (The word "mandates" is hard to pronounce. When I looked it up in the dictionary, it was the same word for "rules," and I wonder why the textbook didn't use the more common English translation.)

— *But what if no one sees me?*
— *God sees you.*
"Very good, *yeladim*," Mr. Lipshitz says. He calls us children. "Elizabeth, watch the words that begin with vowels. The first sound is the most important. John, excellent job. Who wants to go next?"

I sit back down in my seat as two women make their way to the front of the class. I wipe my forehead and realize my face is red. John smiles at me. He reaches over and pats my head twice, as though I were the obedient child from the dialogue.

Jake laughed yesterday as he tested me on the dialogue. "This is really deep," he said. "God sees you? What about getting into heaven? That's a good reason."

"Heaven doesn't necessarily exist," I said. Mr. Lipshitz had told us this the previous week, when we read through the dialogue about death. "Judaism is more about the here and now."

"Very Zen," Jake nodded.

When Jake picks me up tonight, he remembers to ask how class went.

"Fine," I say.

We sit in silence for a while. Jake decides to take the highway home, and it has started to rain slightly. I hope it will clear away the blood from the playground.

"Why would someone think they could survive in the landing gear of an airplane?" Jake asks suddenly.

"I don't know," I say. "Maybe things were so bad that she wasn't really thinking straight."

At home Jake and I make love. He enters me from behind and I bend over our sofa, burying my head in the pillows. With each thrust my head goes deeper into the cushions until when I open my eyes all I can see are the wide green and white stripes.

In the morning he comes into the kitchen for coffee just as I'm leaving.

"Have a good day," I say.

"She had to have heard about the others who tried it, right?" Jake pours himself a cup and sits down.

I don't understand what he's talking about.

"The woman from yesterday, who fell. Did she think she was different—that the laws of physics wouldn't apply to her?"

I lean over and give him a kiss on the top of his head. "I don't really want to talk about it," I say.

Today during faculty meeting I bring up the fact that two bodies have fallen from the sky in the past month. A senior teacher sighs heavily. I look around the table. Teachers grade papers, write lessons, and examine their nails.

"Shouldn't we be having funerals for these people? Shouldn't the students be grieving, learning the value of life, accepting death?"

Mr. Thew, the assistant principal, leans forward. "If we had a ceremony for everything . . . ," he lets the sentence trail off.

"What kind of a world . . . ," I begin, and I let the speech leave my mouth about how callously and insensitively we are raising our youth.

"What do you want?" Mr. Thew cuts me off.

"A guinea pig," I say, before I can think of a different answer. I have been thinking about a dog I had as a child. He was an old carnival mutt who could do tricks. "Play dead!" I told him, and he would roll over onto his back with his legs straight in the air. Then, like a revival tent preacher, I would command him to "Live!" and he would sit up and wait for his treat. That's what we need at school; something that can be resurrected. But a guinea pig will have to do.

"Take it out of petty cash," Mr. Thew says, before going on to the next item on the agenda.

When I bring the guinea pig to class on Monday, the kids squeal.

"Ewww, a rat!" Geena says.

"A guinea pig," I say. "It's a completely different species. See?" I turn him around. "No tail. We'll do rotations to care for him, feeding him, changing the cage . . ."

"It's squirmy," Keisha observes.

"Yeah, well, he's nervous," I say. "Remember your first day of school?"

"What's his name gonna be?" Jannette asks.

"I don't know," I say. "We'll have a contest. Brainstorm quietly at your desks, and I'll come around with him so you can get a closer look."

I put the guinea pig in my left hand and walk between the desks. I can feel his little heart beating against my palm like fingers thrumming on a desk. Callie extends a tentative finger and screams when she touches his fur.

Ennis asks, "Why is it called a pig?" When I tell him I don't know he says, "Ima get me a coat made from pig fur."

When I go over to Kendrick's seat, he reaches forward with both hands so violently that I pull the guinea pig to my chest to save him. Kendrick smiles, looks me in the eyes and says softly, "Ever put one up your honky ass?" I turn away, feeling a rise in my chest as though I might cry.

I would take away his recess as punishment, but then I'd have to make an issue of his language, and I don't think I can repeat this comment to anyone. I don't think I can say those words out loud.

The guinea pig roots around his cage all during Math Block and on into Language Arts. Just before lunch, I collect the name suggestions. I go to the teachers' cafeteria and buy a ham sandwich.

I sit by myself at a table and read over the names. Though they were submitted anonymously, I recognize my students' handwriting. "Wiggly," Da'nelle suggests. There are a bunch of copycat suggestions of "Wiggly" by Da'nelle's posse. "Furry": Ennis; "Mr. Rat": Jannette. George, a nerdy, brainy kid, suggests "Denominator," which I love (someone is paying attention!) but I'm sure the class will hate.

Kendrick suggests "Wart Cunt," and I slide the paper into my purse before anyone else can see it.

The most promising names are "Pepper" and "Boo." I could also live with "Mike" and "Spot." But I know my students, and they'll vote for "L'il Piggy," the suggestion put forth by Morris, who is repeating fifth grade. It could be worse.

Sure enough, "L'il Piggy" wins the next day, and I ask Jennyfer to make a sign for his cage.

There is only a week before break and I cross my fingers that we will make it through without another incident. L'il Pig is growing fat. Kendrick tells me to "lick my asshole, bitch" loud enough so that both José and Morris can hear, and I take away his L'il Pig feeding rotation. I am relieved not to leave L'il Pig in his care. I worry that Kendrick will make good on his threat to bite his head off or tear out his legs.

I call Kendrick's mother in for a meeting. She doesn't return my call. I send home a note with Kendrick, but I doubt it gets to her. I have told Ms. S vaguely about his language, but I am too embarrassed to share the particulars with her. Her smile is tight around the edges, like she thinks I am just another soft white woman who can't take the pressure of this difficult school. She gives me lectures on cross-cultural understanding and leaves diversity pamphlets in my mailbox.

On the second-to-last day before break, a shadow crosses the windows and another body hits the ground. This time I don't prevent the students from going to the windows to stare at the mess. Maybe because of the mud and the warmer temperatures, this body has exploded as though it has hit a land mine. The extremities are almost unrecognizable, thrown so far it seems as though they fell out of the plane at a different moment than the torso, which is a mess of red, like half-hardened Jell-O. I hope it's not a woman; it's impossible to tell. I am glad for this small mercy, that it doesn't look like a body at all to haunt them in their nightmares, but rather like the landscape of an undiscovered planet.

Jake and I go to his parents' house in Phoenix for Passover, and I read the Four Questions in Hebrew after Jake's eight-year-old niece reads them in English. I fight the urge to correct her pronunciation. Since becoming a teacher, I sometimes forget I don't have dominion over every erring thing.

I like Jake's family all right, and they like me, I think. We both know we could have done a lot worse than each other. There is a lot of talk about the wedding, which will be held at Jake's parents' country club in Phoenix. His mother wants to know who I'm inviting from my family, and I give her the small list. I'm not particularly close to my parents, but I'm inviting them both, with their respective spouses. My mother's sister won't come, but a few of my friends from college probably will. Since Jake's parents are paying for the wedding, I'm sure they appreciate the abbreviated list.

While Jake's nieces and nephews look for the Afikomen, I look closer at the ten plagues listed in the Hagaddah. A not-insignificant percentage of plagues fell from the sky. Jake is telling a long joke he heard at the gym, and when the laughter dies down, Jake's father asks me how my new school's going.

"Something weird's been happening," Jake answers for me, reaching for another macaroon. "Tell 'em, Lizzie."

"Well," I clear my throat. I don't want to talk about this. It will make me seem crazy. "Um, we've been having a spate of bodies falling onto the playground."

"What do you mean?" Jake's mother leans in. A lock of blond hair falls out of her coif into her eyes.

"Apparently, illegal immigrants climb into the landing gears of planes heading toward the U.S., and when the landing gear goes down, the frozen bodies fall out."

"Onto the playground?" Jake's sister asks.

"You're making this up," Jake's brother-in-law says.

"Oh yeah, I read about that." Jake's father is retired and, like his son, reads the newspapers religiously. "That's your school?"

I nod.

Jake's father looks at me closely, through squinted eyes. Jake has his father's chin, and in his look of scrutiny I can see the traces of Jake's empathetic façade. When they look like that at me, I can't know anything about what they are really thinking or feeling, no matter how well or how long I've known them.

"Jakey, is this appropriate holiday dinner conversation?" Jake's mother stands up and gathers the dessert plates. "Really, Jakey."

On the plane on the way home I feel a bump on takeoff and become convinced that there is a body in the landing gear, though intellectually I understand there is no earthly reason that someone would need to stow away in the landing gear to escape political oppression in Arizona. As we climb higher and the golf courses and haciendas fade to blurs and then to white as we reach the clouds, I grow chilled. I can imagine her in there, the alien immigrant, with her thin jacket and her worn-out shoes. She grows cold, freezing, frigid; then she falls unconscious, slumped against the retracted wheels. I grip Jake's hand tightly and he rubs it mechanically as he flips through business magazines.

"The next time we'll be on a plane is to go to our wedding," Jake whispers in my ear and kisses my neck.

I look anxiously out the window when I hear the landing gear release. Below, I can see my school, eerily quiet because of the break. Tomorrow it will be overrun with children, loud and aggressive. Kendrick will have learned new words from his uncle and will be trying them out on me. I steel myself for a barrage of abuse.

But now there is only a smooth expanse of dirt. I sigh, relieved. This trip has harbored no fugitives. A small respite.

I am exhausted. I barely sleep the night we arrive home. There is a cold snap here, a resurgence of winter, which seems even colder compared to sunny Phoenix. I can't get warm, though I sit in a bath and curl up next to Jake, drink hot tea until my bladder aches. At school, I assign the most asinine free writing exercise I have ever given: "Who is Your Hero?" I sit down at my desk and rub my eyes.

"Ms. Gold?" Da'nelle raises her hand in the first row. I walk over to her. "Is that your real name?"

"It's my husband's," I say, fibbing just a bit; we'll be married in under two months. "What do you mean?"

"How come girls take boys' names?"

I pause. "That's just how we do it. In other cultures they do it differently."

Da'nelle looks unconvinced. Behind her, Morris sings, "Da'nelle Gutierrez," José's last name.

Da'nelle spins around. "Shut up," she says.

"Hey, I don't like those words," I say, but Da'nelle has turned back to me.

"Can I say that you're my hero?" she asks.

"If you really want to," I answer. "But you have to mean it. I won't give you a good grade just because you're buttering me up."

Da'nelle looks confused. "Because you're flattering me," I translate.

She shrugs.

When I look at the papers in the teachers' cafeteria, Da'nelle and her cluster have predictably picked Jennifer Lopez as their hero. The boys have uniformly chosen a baseball player, with a couple of Colin Powells thrown in for extra sucking up.

I use L'il Pig for that afternoon's Math Block. The kids have forgotten everything over the week-long break. "So if L'il Pig has four legs, and we decide to cut the nails on one of them, what fraction of his legs have cut nails?"

My question is met with universal silence. I see Da'nelle rooting around in her purse for her lip gloss.

Suddenly, I don't think I can take the too-sweet odor. "Don't, Da'nelle," I say.

She pouts.

"How many?" I demand.

"Do guerny pigs whatever even got nails?" Morris asks.

Outside, there is a thump, like someone beating the dirt out of a rug.

We all spin toward the window, but it is not a body. A backhoe has spilled its raised load onto the dirt. Apparently, the powers that be have decided we should have grass—there is an enormous block made up of layers of sod. Illogically, they have delivered it before the ground has thawed.

I let the students watch the men lay the sod down in rows perpendicular to the school. I try to explain "perpendicular" but give up when I realize that no one is paying attention.

Exhausted, I tell my students that they can talk quietly at their desks, but that if I have to tell one kid to be quiet, they'll sit in silence. Amazingly, they sense I'm serious and giggle softly to one another until the dismissal bell rings.

"Jake," I say. "I'm too tired to go to Hebrew class."

He is laying the socks out on the bed. Per our agreement, I do the laundry, he folds.

"Too tired?" he says. "Too tired for some Mazel Tov?" He leans in and kisses my neck. He smoothes my hair off my forehead. "Want me to pick you up something on my way home from the gym?"

I must feel guilty about skipping Hebrew class because that night I dream that L'il Pig has escaped from his cage, and I have to get to him before Mr. Lipshitz and John the Protestant from Hebrew find him and kill him. I know the dream is stupid, even as I'm dreaming it; still I wake up breathless and disoriented.

I pull Jake close to me; I ask him to talk dirty.

"What should I say?" he pants.

I answer for him, "Honky bitch, white pussy, wart cunt."

Jake pulls away. "What's with you?" He goes into the bathroom and runs the shower.

As though my dream means something, after lunch the next day, L'il Pig disappears. We look all over the classroom for him: behind the library, in the coat closet, in the file cabinet. I am half hoping we will find him and half hoping we won't. Maybe he's gone to a better place, though I can't imagine what a lone guinea pig would do out there in the world. And then, right before the dismissal bell has rung, when the students are sitting at their desks dressed to go home, Morris makes fun of Kendrick's jacket.

Kendrick is up in a flash and the two are wrestling each other before I can even tell them to cut it out. They pull at each other's jackets, each reaching for the face of his opponent. José starts the class in a chant. "Fight, fight, fight, fight."

Morris is a year older, and he quickly gets the upper hand. He pushes Kendrick over, and as Kendrick hits the floor, L'il Pig pops out of his pocket. The animal lies there on the ground, so still, and I hold my breath, afraid that he is dead.

"Kendrick," Da'nelle gasps.

Then L'il Pig regains his wits and takes off running across the classroom, his feet making tiny scratching noises against the linoleum. I scoop him up and hold him close.

"It wasn't me," Kendrick defends himself illogically.

The bell rings.

"It wasn't me," Kendrick says again.

"Just go," I tell him.

I sit in the empty classroom and cradle L'il Pig until Jake will start to wonder where I am.

The next morning, I arrive at school to discover the boiler has burst and the building was without heat for the night. L'il Pig is buried under most of the cage's wood shavings. I poke him. His body is stiff to the touch. He doesn't pull away. I can't feel his nervous heart. He can't have frozen to death, I think. Not so quickly. But maybe yesterday's scare did him in. Before I can do anything, the bell rings and the students file in.

They rush to the cage before I can prevent them, dozens of little hands reaching into the wood shavings. "Wait, stop!" I say, but it is Callie's turn to feed L'il Pig, and she screams when she uncovers him.

"He's dead," Callie says in a stage whisper. She stretches the word into two syllables: day-uhd.

She looks at me, her face skewered with terror.

"It ain't my fault! I didn't do nothin'."

"Of course you didn't," I say. The class stares at me. Da'nelle puts her hands up as though worried I will strike her. The kids are so defensive, exculpating themselves before anyone has even pointed a finger.

"Sometimes things just die," I say, sounding like Ms. S.

Kendrick snorts. He has gone to sit down at his desk near the window.

There is a silence.

"Ms. Gold?" Alandra raises her hand. "My grandmother died."

"I'm sorry to hear that."

"Ms. Gold?" Manny's hand goes up as his mouth opens. He leaves it in the air while he speaks. "I had a twin brother, but he died when we were borned."

"Ms. Gold?" Da'nelle squeezes out a few tears. "I had a dog and we had to put it to sleep. It was a mercy."

"Ms. Gold?" Deirdre doesn't bother to raise her hand. "Where do things go when they die?"

I freeze. "Well," I say. How can I answer this? *The Bible says that . . . The Talmud teaches . . .* "I guess no one knows for sure, because everyone who has been dead is still dead. But I guess everyone can believe what they want to."

The students fall silent. I know I need to answer them more definitively. "I choose to believe that when you die there's just nothing. Like being asleep with no dreams."

"Forever?" Kendrick asks. Everyone looks toward his desk next to the window. Kendrick sits tall as the cold sun barrels in around him.

"Can we bury L'il Pig?" Da'nelle asks.

"Yeah, can we?" her posse echoes.

I construct a little coffin out of an emptied Kleenex box, and then I take the students out to the playground. The sodded area where the bodies usually impact has been roped off by yellow caution tape, but I hold it up and the children walk inside, bouncing on the springy new grass. I don't bother to reprimand them; it won't grow anyway in the frost. I look up to see two planes cross each other, the arriving one lowering its landing gear without incident.

I mumble a Kaddish while the children watch me, silenced. It's easy to lift a row of sod and stick the Kleenex box underneath. I ask if anyone wants to say anything. Da'nelle's coterie elbows her.

"Fine," she says. She clears her throat. "If God wants L'il Pig back with him, then, Lord, take him from us to your bosom. Amen."

"That was lovely," I say, putting my arm around her back. I can feel her shivering. I should have insisted the students wear coats. The boys snicker at the use of "bosom."

Inside the building I can see Ms. S at the window, frantically waving me in. She must be concerned that we are in the line of fire, or that we are trampling her new grass. I ignore her.

"Fuck God," says a small voice.

I spin.

"Fuck God." It is Kendrick, standing with his hands on his hips. He spits toward the coffin. "Fuck Him."

I let my arm fall from Da'nelle's back and grab Kendrick by the wrist hard enough that he moans. "What?" he asks. "I didn't do nothin'. You ain't allowed to touch me like this, Teacher. Leggo me, cracker bitch."

Leaving my students dumb behind me, muted by the roar of the passing planes, I drag Kendrick by the wrist toward Ms. S, who has come out of the building, trotting forward on high heels, motioning like an air traffic controller guiding in a plane.

CARRY THE WATER, HUSTLE THE HOLE

I

April 20, 1997

No matter what the commercials say, I'm no Tiger Woods. I'm an all-white Wisconsinite lesbian biology Ph.D. student with Thursday afternoons free.

About the only thing Tiger and I have in common is the Stanford golf course. I remember him from before he was a mega-star, a Jackie Robinson, a Michael Jordan-esque commercial endorser. I remember him when he was just the star of the team, when I used to watch matches from the cart path, before he could get stuck in the rough twice and still manage to birdie holes. I remember this.

Memory is important to me. It is the subject of my research experiments on stereotaxically altered lab mice, to test their memory capabilities. In the early mornings, I send them swimming through the maze in search of a submerged platform. I'm still in the beginning stages of the project, but if and when I get them to find the platform (*If, oh if,* the scientist's refrain) I will systematically destroy parts of their limbic systems until they forget their way again.

I haven't gotten very far. Mice are smart, and sensitive. Put them in warm water and they splash around contentedly like geriatrics in a Florida retirement community, completely uninterested in some scientist's platform. Put them in water that's too cold and they float helplessly, waiting for me to pluck them out. If I don't, they panic, give up, drown. At least, I think they would. I've always rescued them. Maybe they're just being dramatic to get my attention.

When I finally provide the right water temperature, triangulate the appropriate visual cues to orient them, and get them to predictably find the platform, they get a reward: I pick them up and put them back in their cage. I "rescue" them. I can understand their reluctance to participate in the experiment. I'm not much of a knight in shining armor.

Some reach the platform and make a leap, not into my arms, but toward freedom, or toward oblivion as if they know what surgery awaits them. It's as though they're imbued with a sense of hopelessness, as though some primitive rodent instinct, counter to all laws of species preservation, is calling to them to end it all.

Most mornings I've come in to find a number of jumpers splayed on the floor. I should mention here that I'm storing the mice on the shelves in my office, which is attached to the lab. I understand this is illegal, but I just can't trust that the storage facility won't feed them something that would alter their maze-negotiating abilities. What I can't figure out, though, is how they get out, or why they're so attracted to the tile floor. Granted, leaving the top of their habitat open was probably not the greatest idea—I lost half a dozen that night—but now with a plank and a heavy *Principles of Neural Science* on top, wouldn't you think they'd stay inside? I wonder if the janitors are sabotaging my experiment, removing the board and coaxing the mice to jump at night. God, I sound paranoid.

II

April 30, 1997

If I were a poet I'd write an ode to the Stanford golf course. I swear it's what keeps me sane. I mean, if I didn't spend my free afternoons out there with emeritus professors and whacked business school students swinging away at dimpled little white balls, what the hell would I do with my time?

"There's always someone crazier than you." That's a direct quote from my undergraduate O-Chem professor. He was trying to make the point that genius is a little cuckoo. I fit right in here.

III

Shall I compare thee to a summer's day?
    Thou art more fun and more complicate;
    Rough rains may flood the course in May,
    But summer's lease in Cali hath a long date:
    Often too hot the eye of heaven shines,
    Be sure to hydrate, wear a hat, play by wits
    And by rules, for fair from fair sometimes declines,
    By chance or nature's changing course permits
    But the USPGA watches without fade.
    And keeps ocular possession of the ball thou ow'st;
    Nor shall death absolve you of your conscience's shade,
    As time shall pass the sport of golf grow'st
    So long as Stanford men [and women] can breathe, or eyes can see,
    So long lives this and gives life to thee,
        O Stanford Golf Course!

IV

May 9, 1997

The mice and I are running maze permutations. I have a stopwatch in my right hand. Kestral here has had his hippocampus damaged by a sharp rod I inserted during stereotaxy. He is, in my lab's parlance, hippocampally impaired. He could find the platform in under a minute before.

I lower him into the water, back end first. He stares at me for a second, hoping that I'm kidding, that it's just a joke and I'll take him out right now; then he starts to paddle.

There's a knock on my office door, and before I can say "Come in"—which is not what I would probably say, because I know it's Diane (scientists don't knock) and I know she's come to TALK, which in Diane-speak means LECTURE—Diane hangs her long frame in my doorway.

"Jetta," she says, "I want to talk to you."

She's a tall woman with long hands. I have a sudden memory of meeting her, at a support group in Redwood City, and of her long hands, which are what attracted me to her in the first place. I'm attracted to hands that look like golf clubs, that have the capacity to stroke or chip or thwack. She's been crying.

"I'm timing mice," I say. "Hippocampally impaired mice."

"They can wait," Diane says.

"I don't think they can," I say, looking down at Kestral, who is swimming laps around the outside of the pool, ignoring the visual cues. "They're prone to auto-termination."

"Look, I don't give a shit about your mentally retarded—"

"Altered—" I interrupt.

"Mice. Whatever. Look . . . " She switches tactics, looking with disdain at the disheveled cot next to my desk. "You're sleeping *here?*"

"To keep the mice alive," I say. I look at the smooth tiled floor. Between the tiles is yellow grout the color of

Cheez Whiz. I run the toe of my shoe back and forth across the tiles and wonder if this is why the mice keep jumping.

"Were you going to tell me you were leaving me, or just wait until I noticed my bed was empty?"

"Leaving you?" I say. I haven't realized that's what I have done. I haven't thought about it. Or maybe I have. "I honestly don't remember," I say. I know this will hurt her, but right now I truly can't recall my life before the mice. When I think about it, suddenly, like this, there is a dark blank space, like a dream I just woke up from and yet can't recollect. I have to think about my past sideways, like a downhill lie, and hit down on it.

"Are you off the haloperidol?" she asks.

Diane has always considered the remedy of my "peculiarities" as her own personal crusade, as though she can cure my "impaired" mental health with loving gestures and patience. Now she has nothing to say to me, no tender moments left, no wick of time to burn slow. I can hear her steadied breathing, almost see the practiced calm and restraint. A pair of students trickles into the lab behind her.

"Let's go out into the lounge," I say.

I pull Kestral out of the water and stick him back in the plastic transport cage. I feel bad for him. I've made him attempt a task that I know he can't complete, so I leave him a dollop of Cheez Whiz. I shouldn't do this—I shouldn't feel sorry for the mice and I shouldn't change the protocols for rewards. Diane and I walk to the faculty lounge where I pour myself a cup of coffee. Diane doesn't drink coffee.

"The mice and I are involved in a mutually co-dependent symbiotic relationship," I say.

"If you don't love me," she says, "I wish you'd just say it." Diane has a flair for the dramatic. She puts her head in her hands, expecting me to contradict her.

"It's not that," I say. And it's not.

"Then what is it? Tell me." Diane raises her head from her hands long enough to fix her brown eyes on me, not with their usual pity or compassion, but with an accusatory glare; I know she suspects infidelity. A sudden memory: I've been sleeping with Jed from the pro shop.

"No," I say. "No one else."

Diane looks at me, blinking rapidly, disbelieving. I realize I've answered a question she hasn't asked. I can hear a small breath escape her lips.

There is a long pause while I look down at my coffee. Clumps of Coffee-mate drown in the liquid. I can't remember if I stirred or not. "I want out," I say. "I don't know if I love you. I can't remember."

"That's great," Diane says. This is not what she has expected, I know. She wants a large, dramatic fight, raised lesbian voices to be heard in the hallway, a fabulous recon-ciliation with violin music and distant fireworks. She doesn't expect me to want to be with mice.

"You can't remember. You know what? I've been dealing with you and your mice and your psycho-babble intro-spection and your Big Fucking Problem that you haven't told me, whatever the hell it is, for too long. Take more pills, slit your wrists, I don't care anymore."

She replaces her head in her hands and starts to sob loudly. She turns and pauses, waiting for me to call her back, to take her in my arms, but she should know me well enough by now to know that if I ever knew how to comfort, if I ever knew what was good for me, I've forgotten it now.

When I get back to the lab Kestral is on the tiled floor, neck broken, Cheez Whiz uneaten.

V

The Limbic System—A Brief Overview

My transcription of a taped recording of a "Biological Psychology for Non-Majors" undergraduate lecture by my advisor, Professor Ian Hari, fall quarter, 1997.

The limbic system is a set of subcortical structures that form a border (or limbus) around the brain stem. It constitutes part of the forebrain, the most anterior and prominent portion of the mammalian brain, the outermost part of which is the cerebral cortex. You can see here—slide please—the diagram, which illustrates the other forebrain structures, including the thalamus—the source of information to the cerebral cortex. Next slide please.

So the limbic system has often been described as the "emotional core" of the brain. It seems to be responsible for motivated and emotional behaviors as simple as eating and drinking and as basic as sex drive and aggression.

This slide shows the major structures of the limbic system. This is a coronal view of the system. Here you can see the hypothalamus, located near the base of the brain just ventral to the thalamus. The distinct nuclei are responsible for feeding, temperature regulation, fighting, sexual drive, and activity level.

Next slide. Here is a sagittal section of the same thing. Damage to these areas alters these behaviors. I've seen some individuals with temporal lobe epilepsy undergo wild personality or emotional changes. It does not seem to affect their sex drives, but they do choose their partners indiscriminately and seem emotionally detached from them.

Um. Um. Oh, OK, so the hypothalamus also regulates the secretion of hormones through its effects on the pituitary gland.

The hippocampus—next slide, thank you—is this large green structure wedged in between the thalamus and the cerebral cortex in the posterior region of the forebrain. Its two major axon tracts are the fornix and—oh, this is interesting: we get the word fornix from the Roman arch where prostitutes gathered, hence the word fornication. The other tract is the fibria. And as long as we're on etymology, the hippocampus is the Latin word for sea horse, which, as you can see—OK, well, not in this slide, but trust me—is the shape of the hippocampus.

The amygdala, please note pronunciation, nestles between the hippocampus and the hypothalamus. It seems to be responsible for aggression and emotion in that damage to it causes subjects to become lethargic, tame, and emotionally unresponsive. Cerebral science, as usual, is a series of linked hypotheses. Most of what we know about the brain is by what it is lacking. That is to say, in individuals with damage to certain parts of their brain, what behaviors seem aberrant, abnormal? How has the individual changed? Where is the dearth?

VI

May 5, 1997

This is a deceptive hole, the sixth one on my dad's golf course. He was head pro at the Prairie Lakes Golf and Country Club in Glatoscua, Wisconsin, population 2,350, weekend population over 10,000. Dad gave lessons, managed the grounds crew, staffed the pro shop and sometimes even served as ranger when Mom couldn't handle the drunks.

"Jetta," he used to say, about this hole in particular, "I'm glad they don't teach you sewing anymore in school, because sewing won't help you. You can't hustle sewing, Jetta, but I'll teach you how to hustle this hole. If you learn nothing else, learn how to make a buck off a long par five, won't ya?"

Stanford's tenth hole is a long par five. It runs right next to Junipero Serra, a back entrance into Stanford's inner sanctum. I look down its curved fairway now, a scene I've contemplated many times, and I remember my father and me, out on Prairie Lakes, a cold day in March, too early in the season to really play. The memory sneaks up on me, sideways, like the last dog-leg on a winding hole, like a flag you can't see until you're right on top of it, and every swing after that is blind, over the edge of a cliff with the pin straight down below. Choke up on that wedge, won't you, send that sucker straight up in the air so it'll stay put when it lands?

My father sets up my shot and I swing hard to carry the pond, but I splash anyway and we try the shot again. Am I trying to hit the water? he wants to know. We try some more, each shot arching long to the far lip of the reservoir, then plopping back down into the murk as though it had a will of its own.

He gives up eventually and says that when I'm older he won't give up so easily, that we'll stand out here all day if that's what it takes to get me to carry the water. We play on until my punishment: the twelfth hole.

If you don't carry the water, you don't hustle the hole. It's my mantra.

VII

May 5, 1997

There are only mice in my life; it's true. Jed is as mousy as it gets.

He's curious, behind the desk, writing my name in the 1:15 slot in pencil, making sure to get all the complicated letters of Graciescu to fit in the small white box. He sniffs me out, preens, rubbing his mouth-rimming beard/mustache combo. He decides what he wants to say to me, reconsiders, says nothing.

His eyes are brown like Diane's, dull, and he has long arms, which (sorry, Diane) have long hands beat by a mile. He is training to be a golf pro, he says.

I appear unimpressed. When he moves from around the desk I see he is thick around the bottom. He absently fingers a half-eaten cheese sandwich which is weighing down the starter's book. He carries my clubs to the tee, a chivalrous gesture that angers Diane, watching from her convertible in the parking lot.

She walks over to wish me a good game and kisses me hard on the lips, which draws a "dykes on spikes" joke from the twosome I'm playing with, some old queens from

Stanford's in-house legal department. Jed backs off for a minute, but I can tell by the way he tries to scrape the mud off the bottom of his shoes at the mat that this sororal display of affection turns him on.

I shoot a 47 on the front nine, which would have been lower had I not bogeyed the par three or freaked out on the sixth hole. By the time I reach the tenth my partners have gone ahead to play their own game, and I'm left to mutter to myself.

I tee up low, leaving just a finger's worth of space between sod and ball, lining up with the pin far across the water. It's at least 250 to the water, 300 over and I haven't hit my driver that far in a long while, if ever. After all, I'm no Tiger Woods. Even on the range with the wind behind me. But I scope it out anyway as though I were actually going to attempt to hit it over the water. You don't carry the water, you can't hustle the hole.

Just then, I hear the whir of a golf cart; it's Jed driving the refreshment-mobile. It coasts to a stop, and he doesn't realize I am not even remotely planning to swing.

I nod in his general direction, close one eye and peer across the water again. The light is getting low and glints off the water, fracturing the beams the way the fluorescents bounce off the tiles in the lab. I put my hand to my forehead as a visor. I step back from the ball and turn to my bag, which is lying behind me.

"Like a drink?" Jed asks. "My treat, just don't tell the guys at the shop."

"No thanks," I say. I am never sure why liquid is always involved in seduction. "I'm not really thirsty."

"No? You're looking at the water as though you're getting ready to drink it."

"Really?" I laugh. "Just looking to carry it. You don't carry the water, you don't hustle the hole."

"Right," he says, as though he understands what I'm talking about. He's very convincing. I almost believe him. "I'd lay up here. Even Tiger can't carry that. Not with this wind in your face."

"I know," I say. "I'm getting out a three-wood."

"Hmmm." Jed settles back in the driver's seat to watch me swing. I bend over from the waist to reach my bag, letting my shorts move up my thighs to an un-regulation length.

I return to the ball, address it, and visualize the trees on the right. I play a pretty nasty hook, and I try to compensate by aiming right. It usually works. Plus, if I aim for the trees the likelihood I'll actually hit them is cut in half—Murphy's Law.

I draw the club back, keeping my left elbow straight, remembering not to turn my right foot, keeping the motion smooth, so smooth, swinging easily down. The ball flies off the tee with the smack of a true hit and I watch it soar down the fairway, near the water but not in—that I'm sure of—not in. Definitely not in the water.

VIII

From *Today's Golfer* magazine in my advisor's office. January 1984 issue. Headline: "Women on Spikes: Competition or Comedy?"

Dear Mr. Swing,

My wife and I were playing our local course the other day when she rolled into a construction site. Her ball was in the direct path of some sort of tractor-type thing. I screamed and waved a club, but the driver of the machinery merely waved back, scooping up my wife's ball in his bucket and rolling forward with it.

To make a long story short, he was finally persuaded to discharge his load next to the course, at which point my wife's ball rolled onto the fairway, a good hundred yards ahead of where she had last left fairway boundaries.

She insisted that this was beyond her control and should be counted as a natural part of the course. She didn't take a penalty stroke, merely played the ball as it lay and later submitted her score to adjust her handicap. She asked me to sign the scorecard as her witness and I did, and now I'm afraid that I am in violation of USPGA rules. If the tractor driver tells someone, am I in danger of being discredited by the rules police?

Yours in Fear of Retribution,
Reluctant Witness

Dear Mr. Witness,

Usually we deal with golf rules in Ask Mr. Swing, but your letter brings up a good point. Golf has always been a model of decorum, manners, and rules. Since golf is an individual sport, care must be taken to self-regulate, and as the saying goes, "To thine own self be true."

That said, the USPGA rules do not stipulate what should happen when construction work interferes with an out-of-bounds ball. However, with the sport's increasing growth rate as well as the frantic development that seems to be occurring near and around golf courses, this is a problem that will only increase and needs addressing.

I believe that your wife should have removed her ball to the approximate place of departure from legal playing area and taken her one-stroke penalty. Fifty lashes with a wet noodle to her for her dishonesty and attempt to take advantage of an otherwise inconvenient coincidence. And shame on you for allowing and abetting her to do so. There are no rules cops except those that exist in your head, Mr. Witness, and by signing her scorecard you have condemned yourself to a number of sleepless nights. Guilt is as an albatross around your neck. Long may you live with the remorse you surely feel, and do mend your ways before you hit the course again.

Yours,
Mr. Swing

IX

May 2, 1997

Jonah has attacked his third mouse of the night. I can hear the squeals and fear what I will see when I get up off the cot and turn on the light. Sure enough, he has clawed through the barrier between habitats and taken a large chunk out of Eugenia's backside. I turn my back to prepare a syringe, a lethal dose of insulin to put Eugie out of her misery, and when I turn back around, Jonah has climbed out of the cage and is scrambling up the bookshelves.

"Come back here," I say. "This instant, down now!" I'm feeling desperate: my voice rises; I beg the furry rodent. Jonah stops and stares at me. He blinks, licks his genitals. I can see he's aroused.

I take a step closer. I put the syringe down on the desk, on top of the computer monitor. The screen saver draws concentric geometric shapes, then changes to form complex compounds. I recognize 5-HIAA, a five-hydroxy indoleacetic acid which is a serotonin metabolite indicating low serotonin turnover.

Jonah has backed away from me, drawing dangerously close to the edge of the shelf. "Jonah," I say, coaxingly. "Come here, little one. Cheez Whiz? You want some Cheez Whiz? You like Cheez Whiz?"

I extend my arm for the Cheez Whiz, just out of reach on the table against the wall. I take a small step toward it, which is enough to make Jonah flinch.

I hear the thud before I see his body hit the tiled floor. I know it is impossible, but there it is. His neck is broken, I can tell, but he writhes around, like a tipped beetle trying to right itself. Only his forelegs move, parodying bicycle pedals.

I sigh and, as the tears fall, inject him with the syringe. Then I make another one for Eugenia. I want to say something, to pray, but I can only remember "Hail Mary full of grace." Mary, I remember suddenly, was a mouse that didn't survive her psychosurgery. She was having problems with the platform anyway.

X

May 4, 1997

Today I wake up and can't remember what I look like. I go into the bathroom in the hallway and stare at myself in the mirror. I look fuzzy. Then I remember I wear glasses and wander back into my office to find them. They are next to the computer, resting on the Cheez Whiz. I put them on and return to the bathroom.

I run my hands through my hair and pull it above my head in a bun. My features are familiar, at least. I have brown eyes beneath the glasses, with flecks of gray and green. My nose is long and turned a little to the right and I have a slight scar on my left cheek from a fall. My eyelashes are long and my eyebrows are thick. I have a pronounced chin.

Now at least I know what I look like, but every time I blink I forget again. Every time, a little flicker of memory gone, then replaced by the most current version of my face, like a strobe light souvenir.

XI

May 5, 1997

My ball rockets down the fairway, hovering over the grass like a helicopter. It sails right, a surprise, and travels far for its lack of height. I can hear Jed say "Whoa!"

And then it stops. My ball stops and I hear the thud. I've hit something. Something that is moving, spinning in low circles, a fuzzy caramel dot on the horizon.

"Jesus, what'd you hit?" asks Jed, and he motions for me to get into the refreshment-mobile, which I do, leaving my clubs on the tee. We race over to the edge of the fairway, or as fast as the liquid-laden cart will go, and I can tell before we even get there that it's a squirrel.

Jed stops. The brakes lock and we slide toward the suffering squirrel. I step calmly out of the cart and stand over him so that my shadow forms a blanket over his struggling form. He is on his back now, squirming. I can see the large indentation on his cranium. I almost expect it to be dimpled, like the ball.

"I'll radio Grounds, or Pest Control or someone," Jed says from the cart.

"No, don't bother," I say, and I lean over and pet the squirrel once before taking his head in one hand and his body in the other. I twist them opposite, breaking his neck cleanly. I carry the body over to the trees and lay him under a eucalyptus. "Hail Mary," I say.

"Wow," Jed says. "You OK?"

"I'm not sure," I say.

"I don't know what to do about that." He rubs his beard/mustache. "I think I see your ball, but I'm not sure the rule book says anything about that. Do you think it counts as an unmarked obstacle? Or is it like hitting a rock? Interference?"

"Leave it, I don't really care," I say. "I wasn't keeping score anyway. I can never remember what I'm laying."

There is a long pause. I climb back into the refreshment-mobile next to him. I can hear him consider his words. "Want to go have a drink? There's beer in the cart and I know this place off the twelfth . . ."

I don't say anything, and Jed takes this as a yes. The cart bounces over the uneven ground as we enter the woods, and I turn to watch the body of the squirrel until it's out of sight.

XII

May 5, 1997

Lying even with the twelfth hole is a clearing. The forest floor is littered with used condoms and empty beer cans, old tournament balls here and there along with a collared pink shirt.

"You want a beer?" Jed asks.

I nod, and he twists the cap off a brown bottle, handing it to me before opening one for himself.

"You want to talk about it?" He puts his right arm over my shoulders.

I can't help it. I start to cry and Jed leans forward to put his beer in the cup holder, taking my head in his arms. "It's OK," he says, "it's just a squirrel."

"I should have tried to carry the water."

"Don't be silly," he says. "You did the right thing."

And then we're kissing, and his hands are inside my blouse, and my shorts are unbuttoned. He puts one finger inside me, then pulls it out to stick in two.

"This is OK, right?" He breathes into my hair, and then he is inside me, moving, and my neck is pushed into the metal hand-rest on the edge of the cart. It digs into the base of my skull and stings, like an incision.

I have a memory flash, like blinking, of the twelfth hole of Prairie Lakes, of a golf cart punishment like this one. Jed shudders, mentions God, and I say, out loud or not I can't remember, "I should have tried to carry the water."

XIII

From my Lab Book, April 20, 1997:

Mice like Cheez Whiz.

XIV

May 6, 1997

My advisor, Professor Hari, comes to see me. He is a large man, with many chins. I've never seen him outside his office. Not at the Faculty Club, not at the shopping mall, never at the movies at Shoreline, and certainly never at his house. Other Ph.D. candidates get invited to dinner; Diane visits her dissertation director's house, but she's in the Communications department.

My office and bedroom is looking a little unkempt. Another mouse escaped last night, and discarded insulin syringes are scattered about the worktable. The Cheez Whiz has been attacked by the other mice who must have worked their ways out when I nodded off for a moment, or maybe I set them free. I can't recall. Greta's body is shrouded on the keyboard for burial. The screen saver draws Parachlorophenylalanine, a serotonin synthesis blocker.

I am on my knees under the cot looking for the escaped patients when I hear footsteps. Before I can attempt to hide the mice, Dr. Hari enters, looks for a place to sit, finds none and decides to stand.

"Jetta," he says. "Ms. Graciescu." He crosses his arms across his large belly. He is wearing a white coat which does not close; the left lapel falls back against his chest where pocket pens weigh it down.

"Ms. Graciescu," he repeats, as though he's trying to identify me, as though this is my biological classification. "I've had some rather disturbing reports about you. Your students say you haven't showed up for lab in a week."

I shrug. "The mice..." I say. I let the word trail off. I see a tail between the desk and the computer stand. It's just a blur of brown.

"And," he takes a look around the room, "are you storing mice here? That's incredibly illegal. If someone found out.... what the hell are you doing?"

I'm not sure if he means right this second, sitting on the dirty floor or what am I doing scientifically. "You know what I'm doing, you read my proposal." I stand up.

"And I approved it, much to my current disappointment. How do you expect to collect reliable data? I don't know what to do with you."

I look at the floor, rub the toe of my shoe in the gooey grout. "I think I need to change emphasis…"

"You need to change more than that, Jetta. This cannot continue. There's inspection next week." He takes a step toward the door and I can hear the squish even before I see Milo dart out from under the desk and run under Dr. Hari's foot.

"What the—repulsive." Dr. Hari closes the door behind him and I can hear his alternating footsteps, squish-squeak, squish-squeak fading down the hallway. I scoop what's left of Milo into a Petri dish.

XV

May 6, 1997

And then I go play golf. Jed pencils me in again and is waiting for me in the refreshment-mobile near the twelfth hole. This time he is slow and I almost enjoy it because I keep my eyes open the whole time, looking at the sky through the maze formed by the tops of the trees. I keep my eyes open so that I don't blink, not even once. The sky is a deep blue, and the fir trees cast a green shadow on its surface so that it's like I'm over the water, a ball well hit, strong, with the wind behind me. A ball that will carry the water.

XVI

May 8, 1997

The last batch of mice come out of stereotaxy lethargic, tame and unresponsive. One develops temporal lobe epilepsy, which manifests itself in a burst of hourly energy followed by a narcoleptic episode. I grind up my own tablets of sertraline hydrochloride, stockpiled since I haven't taken them all month, and mix them with saline, injecting the solution into the large vein that runs along the bottom of their bellies.

Ashley and Io, the females, perk up a bit, but Randall and Taj start to attack each other. I separate them; Taj bites me, then begins to gnaw at his feet until I sedate him.

I go out to play golf, and when I return Taj has somehow sliced his stomach open on the water bottle, eviscerating himself. The girls are sulking in the corner, watching Randall's lifeless body swing from the exercise wheel.

XVII

Hickory Dickory Dock
The mice run up the Clock
The Clock's funding's denied
The Mice commit suicide
Hickory Dickory Dock.

XVIII.a

From my Lab Book, May 10, 1997:

Hardly any satisfying conclusions can be drawn from the completed research. Systematic destruction of the limbic system in mice produced little, if any, coherent evidence. Due to the small size of the structures modified during surgery, it is possible that the destruction of multiple areas failed to completely ablate the intended structure.

Also problematic were the post-surgical responses. Of the sixty who survived surgery, fifty-three died of causes unrelated to the surgical incision. The mice were extremely accident prone. Thirty-two plunged to their deaths, despite efforts to contain them; one was eviscerated by his own actions; eighteen were fatally attacked by their cage-mates, another's neck was broken while climbing the exercise wheel, and one threw himself under an oncoming foot.

An attempt to improve survival and navigation rates through ingestion of sertraline hydrochloride resulted in observed mood elevations, but could not be linked to any marked improvement in maze navigation. Other resulting symptoms experienced by the subjects included sexual dysfunction, lethargy, extreme aggression and cannibalistic tendencies.

No mice successfully completed the maze post-surgery. Even with appropriate visual cues, the mice showed no interest in completing the maze, nor gave any sign that they had any memory at all of having seen it before.

Results remain inconclusive.

XVIII.b

May 10, 1997

I take Ashley and Io to the golf course. Jed watches me as I remove them from my pocket on the tenth hole. I am surprised to find them squirming in my shorts; I don't recall placing them there at all, or even that I work with mice. If you ask me what I do, I'll say I golf, though I'm no Tiger Woods.

I put the mice down on the tee and give them a little pat. They look out at the water in front of them and sit. Io curls up under Ashley's stomach. "Go!" I shout. "Shoo!"

They don't move. They barely breathe. "Come on," I say. "Get a move on it!"

I stamp my foot behind them, hoping the vibration will dislodge them. "Goddamn it!" I say. "Move your lazy asses!" They blink rapidly in the sun. Tears begin to fall from my eyes.

"Hey, take it easy, Jetta," Jed says.

"Mind your own business," I say. I stride over to the cart and remove the driver. "Mind your own goddamn business."

"Jetta, wait. What're you doing?" Jed asks, leaning forward. He has the good sense to stay in the cart.

I walk up to the nesting mice and line up the shot. I can see the pin across the water.

"Christ, you're crazy," Jed says, but he stays put. I'm sobbing now and I can't see as I take the club face back, my eyes closed. I can only hear the un-ball-like sound as I make contact, watch the blood, the lymph, the dendrites, the glia, and the axons fly as if winged toward the hole, shining in the late-afternoon sun.

"Carry the water, hustle the hole," I say out loud. I wonder where I've heard that before.

THE WORLD TASTES GOOD

"Eccentric" was the word Father used. He was a doctor, and he said it was a detached, clinical diagnosis, even though he was close to the patient, our mother. He said eccentricity was a degenerative disease for which there was no cure, only a steady decline. He told us this (my twin brother and me) on a walk one day, and repeated it frequently, under his breath, as if to himself. We had to believe him—we were only ten—even though we suspected Father was unqualified to diagnose a disease that didn't have to do with physical deterioration. He was a radiologist and spent his days in a darkened room looking at black and white pictures of the most elemental parts of humans. He never met patients, never saw flesh on the bones, never imagined that inside all those cranial images there was a live brain firing its synapses and re-uptaking neurochemicals; smiling, crying, living.

If Mother was eccentric, Basir and I could hardly be classified as "normal." We had that tangible but indescribable aura of strangeness that children recognize and pounce on. We were teased mercilessly at school. "Homeschooled, homeschooled," they taunted, which was ridiculous, really, because we were all on the playground at recess and it was obvious that we were enrolled at Tubman Elementary same as the rest of them. But it still hurt, and even though Basir was the boy and a full three minutes older, he cried, and I had to fight them all one at a time until the recess lady blew her whistle and I got sent, dirty and a few times bloodied, to the principal's office. This was one of the reasons we moved. As much as we hated that school, both Basir and I were sad when we left for the country and the children's taunt became a prophesy—homeschool, by Father, who was demanding, and Mother, who was eccentric.

Summers Mother worked at the bus station, selling tickets. The regular lady had a house in the Ozarks she liked to visit and so each morning Mother and Father drove off together in the old Woodie to the city, a forty-five minute jaunt. Basir and I were left to complete our dry correspondence courses. Mother liked the country because there was room for her strays. That was the other reason we moved. At first, it was merely animals—cats and dogs and rabbits who didn't particularly want to belong to anyone, let alone a crazy woman, her radiologist husband and a pair of mismatched twins. But then she branched out and began to bring people home from the bus station, give them a good home cooked meal, something exotic like Indian dal, or tête de veau, and lead them to one of the rooms upstairs. Occasionally, frequently even, they stole from us until we had nothing left in the house of any value. They took the cassette player, the television, Mother's crystal vase, even the everyday silverware, so we ate with chopsticks for a year or two until Father brought home six place settings from the hospital cafeteria. When there was nothing left to steal, our guests seemed angry at the suckers they had fallen in with, the poor sods sent to them by God, or the Great Spirit, or the Candy Man (as I had taken to calling the Supreme Being in our atheistic house).

Sebastian had a large suitcase when he arrived, which he hauled out of the back of the Woodie and dragged up the stairs. Pretty soon we heard music emanating from his room, and like the Pied Piper's susceptible victims we found ourselves outside his door, listening quietly as Sebastian sang along.

Sebastian traveled with a record player and hundreds of vinyls. He had all the greats: Chopin, Joplin (both Scott and Janis), Mozart, the Stones, Mingus, the Temptations, Edith Piaf, Sesame Street's Greatest Hits, Concert for Bangladesh, Bach, Strauss . . . Of our three favorites I liked Wagner's complete *Ring* cycle the best for its dark orchestrations, creating drama in our otherwise uneventful lives. Basir liked Tommy, which was the only musical Sebastian owned besides *Carousel*, a boring, long-winded, un-hummable operetta. We often begged for Sarah Vaughn. Over and over again, the way children will, we listened to the records.

But Sebastian rationed them. Our favorites we could play as often as we liked, but only one other record every day, and those in alphabetical order, so that it seemed we were never going to get to hear the Zoo People, even though it had the best cover—animals in cages with human faces. And then one day toward the end of the summer, he played it. It was experimental, a little too world-rhythm for our taste (we really liked lyrics, especially those filled with desire and hope), with a long xylophone solo somewhere in the middle that took up an interminable half hour while Basir squirmed and tried to annoy me by pulling my hair. When it was finished, Sebastian took the record off the player solemnly. He left our house the next day, driving off with Mother and Father in the morning.

I remember he would tuck his long hair behind his ears and play an album by a folk singer called Rusty Trimes, a soft-voiced tenor. Sebastian said Rusty was his uncle, and that he was there when Rusty recorded his favorite song, "Tie Him to a Tree that He May Grow Tall." That song was about him. The little towheaded boy was Sebastian himself, and every time we reached the part of the song where the tree gets chopped down after being attacked by beetles,

Sebastian would let a tear or two roll down his cheeks. This used to scare us, the idea that an adult could be so vulnerable as to cry; Basir would sob too. Rusty Trimes had that effect on people.

There was Jenny, a woman remarkable for her piercings. She had nearly thirty small rings all over her body, through any slightly overhanging piece of skin. Ears, navel, tongue, eyebrow, nose, nipples, even the small fold of skin over the joint of her pinkie finger was pierced with a tiny hoop. She also had a clitoris ring, which she showed Basir and me one evening when Mother was busy in the kitchen. She pulled the lips apart and Basir said it looked like when we had to pry the dog's mouth open to find something he shouldn't be eating. There the ring sat, gripping the small button. It was the first time I had seen a vagina, darkly pink like raw meat. I remember the complication of it, the folds of skin falling over each other like unkneaded dough or a pile of blankets, the mystery of what lay underneath a tight, wet secret.

Jenny encouraged Basir and me to kiss one day, and we did, sitting on the throw rug in her room. I took Basir's face in my hands and asked him to open his mouth. I put my mouth on his. We kissed for what seemed like forever, his tongue rough and strong, and then he pulled away, and I wiped my mouth with the back of my hand. Saliva made it feel cool. "Did we do it right?" Basir asked. Jenny just laughed.

There was a man whose name I can no longer recall, a lapsed seminarian, kicked out for a certain penchant for practical jokes. He covered his superior's door with duct tape so that when the good monk left his chambers for elevenses, he became entangled and had to shave the rest of his head. Even then, this story sounded untrue, implausible really, but it made him seem as though he'd come to terms with being something other than what he had intended. He stroked his goatee and clucked his tongue at me. "Bertina, Bertina," he sighed, as I showed him my knees, freckled with scabs. We were in the kitchen; I was trying to gross him out. "What are we to do with a tomboy like you?"

"Oh how do you solve a problem like Maria?" I sang, a song from *The Sound of Music.*

"Yes, how do you hold a moonbeam in your hand?" he quoted back to me. I was shocked he knew the words. I kicked my shoes against each other. Dried mud fell in cascades of dust and gathered on the linoleum floor under my chair.

"Who can take a rainbow," I challenged, "sprinkle it with dew, chocolate cover coat it with a miracle or two?"

"The Candy Man can," the ex-monk answered, seriously, speaking, not singing. I could see the red marks around his mouth where shaving had irritated his skin. "Because he mixes it with love and makes the world taste good."

We stared at each other for a moment. I had never met an adult who knew all the words to my favorite cassette tapes. I had found a collection of children's musicals at a rummage sale, and Mother gave me fifty cents to purchase them: *Willy Wonka and the Chocolate Factory* and *Sound of Music: London Cast. Annie. Grease.* I played them over and over, when we still had a cassette player. Later, the player was lifted from our house, like everything else. But by then I knew the words by heart and could hold the small, plastic cassettes in my hand as mnemonic devices and sing softly to myself.

The staring continued. Finally he said, "Right. I think we understand each other here. Go back to your math."

Zacchai, a tall, bushy man, brought a canvas painted with a bull's-eye which he stuffed with straw in the backyard. In a leather box like a violin case he carried a shiny wood bow, polished to perfection and stretched into a quarter moon with synthetic gut. He spent the better part of a summer teaching me and Basir how to shoot arrows, the quiver hanging heavy on our backs, producing papoose-shaped sweat marks on our T-shirts.

Basir and I were hopeless shots—more often than not the arrow would miss the target completely. "Here's your problem," Zacchai said. He often started sentences this way. "Here's your problem," he said to Father, fixing the creaking third stair by fashioning shimmies out of firewood and jamming them in under the stair itself, then sanding them flush with the step. Father's technique had been less technical but more intuitive. Armed with a bottle of vegetable oil, he was swearing and drizzling the staircase into silence. "Here's your problem," he said to Mother, coming up behind her and reaching around to take the apple from her hands, peeling it expertly so that the peel stood, the empty shell of an apple, scored all the way around and all in one piece, perfect, standing by itself on the counter. The skinless, naked apple rested dully in his hand.

"Your problem," he repeated, standing over me and leaning to put his head on top of mine, like a living totem pole, "is in your aim. See the circles? See how they're concentric?"

"Yeah . . ." I nodded. His head bobbed up and down with mine.

"Well, don't aim for the bull's-eye. It's much too specific, too central, too small. Aim around it, aim generally, for the larger circles on the outside; work your way in; eventually you'll hit it. In fact, just close your eyes."

"Close my eyes?" I raised an eyebrow. Basir moved behind me quickly.

Zacchai pursed his lips and nodded.

I closed my eyes and drew back the bow. Quivering with tension, I held it for a second and aimed in what I thought was the general direction of the target. I released— the string would leave a red mark on my forearm as it scraped its way back to the bow. I opened my eyes in time to see a duck, in a flurry of wings and squawks, dive into the pond, just barely dodging the arrow as it landed on the bank.

"Oh well," Zacchai sighed. "It might have worked."

Then there was a stream of insignificant houseguests who merge in memory into one intricate person, a laundry list of names and peculiarities. Patricia and Meade, Miguel, Lorraine, Zanthe, Tupper and Bobby and Dolly. They were all part of our education, Mother said, part of what we couldn't learn in a farmhouse in the middle of nowhere with no television. She made them tell their stories, let them smoke at the dinner table for support as they related their chronologies with varying degrees of confidence and locution. Some recited them as though asked their social security number, others broke down in tears when they got to the part where their stepbrothers raped them, or Ma got fired, or Curtis didn't come home from Vietnam. But it all sounded like an overloaded country-western song to me, too many sad events for one eight-bar melody.

These were all little lessons, like chapters from our correspondence courses. From Sebastian I learned that adults cry, from Jenny about the mysteries of womanhood, from Roberta that nothing hurts worse than knowing you hurt somebody's feelings, and that a woman will only take so much before she walks away, and only then will the man miss her, miss her so much he'll hold his head in his hands and squeeze until the headache hurts worse than the heartache, and that this is what drugs do to you, and why people take them. And I learned that the world is a big place, and that people fade away like documents written in pencil left out in the sun, and that you have to let them go, have to have your heart broken wide open so that they can escape. I heard about full-moon raves in Thailand, and voodoo ceremonies in South America, about corn festivals in Wisconsin and logging competitions in Washington, about historical protests and domestic ones, and it was all secondhand. And secondhand knowledge is like secondhand smoke—all it does is make you recognize the smell when you light up yourself for the first time. But it was Gregor and Ignatz who completed my education, who taught me the only real lesson I learned that actually helped me in life—that the only benefit of collecting peoples' experiences is that when it happens to you, you know you're neither alone nor original.

Gregor and Ignatz had been sleeping in the bus station for several days when Mother found them, curled up together like brothers in the smoking lounge. She poked Ignatz on the shoulder—he seemed the milder of the two—and handed them two cups of coffee, milk, and sugar. They sat up and gulped them. Then, as Mother told it, she looked into their eyes, the way she did with all of our guests, and decided if they were good people or not. Mother never told us what it was about eyes that made people good or bad. Father used to say that she could have found something more original than eyes; the very notion of the eyes revealing something important about the soul within was banal and clichéd and had no scientific basis. That eyes were all about genetics and that perceived depth in the retina came from either the placement of the rods and cones of pigmentation, or the amount of emotion in the viewer.

Mother always grew indignant at this, storming out of rooms. Once she threw a coffee cup and it hit Father on his right shoulder before it fell to the ground. Picking up the pieces, Father said sadly, "Ten years ago I could have caught it."

That summer was one on the cusp. Basir and I were twelve, children flirting with adulthood, or at least I was. Basir continued to be small, smaller than a normal child, and certainly smaller than I, his twin. We could not have been more dissimilar, like licorice twists and Lemonheads: sweet and pliant versus sour and hard.

Basir's hair grew dark and curly as though he came from Turkey like his name, while mine was strawberry blond. He tanned easily; I burned like a hog on a spit, as Father used to say. Basir was quick, but I was wittier; I made everybody laugh. And although Basir was older, like I said, he still came to me to pick up the dead mice by the tail and throw them out into the pond, or reach my hand into the small cistern where he had dropped the one pen that still managed to leak ink in a functional way, or untangle the knotted mess of the barn rope swing.

It was the beginning of the summer so we supported several cats and an insulted mutt sulking around the barn, as well as a wounded crow who was waiting for her wing to heal, and who would wait a long time for the feathers to grow back (forever, I assumed, but we never knew because she took off walking down the road one day after witnessing a particularly gruesome family fight, squawking loudly, and shaking her head like a shocked parishioner).

Our first human strays of the season came home soon after, a pair of gay Latvian porn stars named Gregor and Ignatz. "Are they actors in the gay porn industry or are they gay actors who do porn?" Father asked, a little too loudly, since the men were just outside at the pump, laughing and splashing water on their exposed torsos.

"I didn't think to ask," Mother said. "They don't really speak English." She was standing at the sink, slicing okra. She liked to use the stems too, making us individual casseroles like little pot pies. "They mumbled something about a Latvian community in the city, about a lost letter of introduction." She was over-explaining. It was getting dark and I could tell dinner wouldn't be ready for hours so I got an apple out of the basket and started to munch.

"Don't spoil your appetite, Bertina," Mother said, and we all ignored her, sitting at the kitchen table.

"I'm not really a doctor," Father said suddenly, pretending to rip off a mask. "I really am a traveling sword swallower leaping through time eating okra." This was a game Father invented after seeing something similar on a cartoon show back when we had a television.

"I'm not really a juniper berry," Basir returned, ripping off his mask. "I am an itinerant farm worker whose only skill is weaving corn silk into gold for deserving maidens."

Father nodded brightly. "I'm not really Basir," I said, reaching my arm over my head to grab at the bottom of the mask and pull it off. Underneath, I imagined, my skin was clear, my nose straight and my eyes at the proper distance from the center of my face. If I could just pull off this mask, I would have straight teeth and plump lips. "I'm a deserving maiden."

"Well, of course you are, dear," Mother said. "Now go feed the cats and the birds."

"There are feathers all over the yard again," Father said. "We should either move the bird feeder or quit feeding one species."

"No!" Mother protested. "I like it like that. It's like *National Geographic* out there. When you're all gone I stare out the window and watch Mother Nature's creatures duke it out."

"We're never all gone," Basir said. "We're home-schooled."

"I spend all day repairing life and you wantonly destroy it," Father said.

"Like Kali and Shiva," Mother said, throwing the okra into the frying pan.

"Like fire and water," Basir said.

"But Shiva destroys too," my father said.

"Precisely," said Mother without looking up. The frying pan hissed okra. "Now you're getting it."

There was a pause. "Like Mona and Lisa," I said, and although it was not my finest effort, everyone laughed anyway, because they were used to me saying witty things. Then the gay Latvian porn stars came in the house and the adults started drinking Russian vodka and the evening progressed from there.

Gregor and Ignatz kept the door to their room closed, and we never heard noises at night. Father speculated, still, under his breath about their nocturnal proclivities, their past vocation. Father said he needed to know, as the resident physician.

"Maybe I need to know, as resident kid," Basir said.

"What about them?" I asked. They both looked at me. "Maybe they, as resident gay porn stars, don't need to tell you."

Since arriving in our house Gregor had eaten nothing but Lucky Charms cereal for breakfast. He jogged to the small crossroads that passed for a town five miles down the road and bought a box daily, as well as a carton of whole milk, though there was plenty in the refrigerator. By the time he got home, the milk was practically butter, but he liked it that way, thick and clumpy.

"You can't eat that for breakfast," Father would say. "It's candy, not sustenance." But Gregor's English was poor. He poured a large bowl of Lucky Charms, singing the jingle in Latvian. We used to have a television, and I knew the tune by heart. I would sing along with him, teaching him the English words. I had taught him "red hearts" but "orange stars" was proving hard for him to pronounce in English. Basir said I should let it drop and move on to "yellow moons" since orange was kind of a specialized word anyway.

Despite my father's warnings, Gregor was strong on this diet, the picture of health and life. He couldn't have contrasted more with his partner, Ignatz, a scrawny runt, skinny and elongated like taffy. He had bags under his eyes, long dark sacs of infinite weariness, an aura of existential moodiness and mellowed angst. And yet he seemed happy here, or at least content. He'd been showing Basir how to roll cigarettes, smoking them on the back porch, looking off into the fields intensely, as though waiting for a husband to come back from war, frightened that a telegram announcing his death would precede him.

He and Gregor had intense conversations in Latvian. Sometimes they appeared to be fighting, and Gregor would take Ignatz's head and press it to his chest so that Ignatz's cheeks would pucker out from the pressure. It was either a hug or a wrestling hold; we couldn't be sure which.

After Mother and Father left for work, Basir and I did our homework for a few hours, waiting for Gregor to get back from the store and for Ignatz to wander down the stairs with his bedroom hair and entertain us. Usually, though, we ended up entertaining them. We played hide and seek around the barn, we had Gregor push us on the rope swing, we let him dunk us in the pond, we all ganged up on Ignatz and tickled him until he cried or wet his pants, which we all found hilariously funny. Basir would make us lunch, the most disgusting things he could think of: tomato and syrup sandwiches, garlic jelly on lemon yogurt, turkey graham-cracker casserole. But I would eat anything, no matter how bad it tasted, just to prove a point, and Ignatz never ate anything anyway, just pushed it around his plate, even when Mother made meatloaf, which, despite her eccentricities, everyone agreed was especially good. And Gregor, of course, only ate Lucky Charms.

Afternoons, we napped on the sunporch. Basir read comics and I read the novels Mother brought home for me and hid from Father—the ones with half-clothed women and men with long hair on the front. I was learning about desire, its sublimation and its indulgence, and Basir was learning about violence and vengeance, and sometimes we switched reading material, because we were curious and auto-didactic, and the lessons were basically the same, in different packaging.

Then Mother and Father would come home and ask what we did that day. I'd show Father my math, and Basir would read out loud the essay he'd written on the Louisiana Purchase or the Bay of Pigs, and they would nod and tell us it was good, but that we should try harder, and Father would ask Ignatz if he was comfortable. "Are you comfortable, son?" he'd say. And Ignatz always answered the same way, every night. "Happy as a clam, Sergeant," although it sounded like "hoppy isn't planned, resurgent." It took us a couple of weeks to understand what he was saying. We thought maybe he got it from watching *M*A*S*H* on a TV in the bus station.

After dinner Mother and Gregor would go for what Mother termed a "private nature walk." She was teaching Gregor the names of plants and animals, and though she never expressly forbade it, we were not allowed to join them. These walks seemed to make Father antsy. He sat with his hands clasped and pretended to read medical journals but never turned the pages, sipping occasionally from his glass of brandy.

Summer was almost over. Father was reading yesterday's paper. Basir was reading a history textbook. I looked down at the math on the page. It was calculus. I was supposed to graph points, draw the rectangle they were delineating, and then rotate it around its left axis and measure the volume. I liked math; I liked the objective, confirmable nature of the problems' solutions. Sometimes I worked ahead in my correspondence book.

Pretty soon, Gregor traipsed down the stairs. He was sweaty from his morning push-up routine, and the dust in the air illuminated by the light settled softly on his shoulders. I had imagined, last night, lying in my bed upstairs with the rose-patterned sheets, what it would feel like to touch those shoulders. Though I knew about the facts of life, and even had a copy of *Our Bodies, Ourselves* on the shelf upstairs (a used version, annotated by some horny kid so that it included all the slang I could ever want to know), I had a very nebulous idea of what exactly the sex act was like. I had the vague notion that it would feel good; I'd read enough to know that human beings do little by choice that doesn't make them feel good. And I'd started sliding my hand down into my pajama shorts, which produced a feeling not unlike having to go to the bathroom.

I'd once tried to use one of my mother's tampons, just to see what it felt like, and the resulting pain was surprising and disappointing. The pictures in *Our Bodies* clearly showed a male organ that was at least twice the size of the cotton stick I'd only inserted partway because my muscles clenched in protest. My father and brother walked around naked occasionally, too, and the thought of wanting anything the size and shape of my father's penis—a gigantic newborn squirrel—inside of me was unfathomable. Still, Gregor's shoulders instigated in me a flutter, like the nervous ineffectual flapping of the wounded crow's wings, a sensation not all that unpleasant.

Basir stepped up behind me now. "Morning, Gregor," he said. "Do you want to eat raw manure today?"

Gregor's English was still inferior and he answered all queries with a head nod and a heavily accented, "Yes, sure."

"Basir," Father cautioned. He turned the page of the newspaper, disappearing behind it.

"What?" Basir asked. "I just wondered what he wanted to do today. We've done everything else possible around here."

"Are you saying you're bored?" Father let the paper fall down into his lap. We were allowed to say anything, anything at all, except that we were bored. That was the cardinal sin in our house. You were supposed to be able to entertain yourself at all times, or to help out around the house if you had nothing else to do.

"No sir," Basir answered quickly.

"He just desires some outside stimulation, I think," I said quickly. My graph looked like a connect-the-dots version of an elephant, one point out of place in the lower right quadrant. "Fuck me," I said.

"What?" said my father.

"What?" said Basir.

"I can't make this graph work," I complained.

"Don't say things you don't mean," my father said. "Don't throw out idle invitations."

Gregor watched us from the bottom of the stairs. He cleared his throat. "Lucky Charms," he said. It sounded like "Rookery Chimes."

"I asked you if you were bored, Basir," Father repeated.

"It's just that nothing ever happens here," he said. "We read about it all, but we never see anything. It's like being blind."

"You think it's like being blind?" Father asked. He leaned forward and clasped his hands together, like he did when he was mad. Mother was out on the sunporch weaving cornstalk wreaths. This was her latest artistic endeavor after no one bought her pottery, her paintings, or her tatting. She was looking for her "true medium," the one through which she could most "honestly express" herself. She was singing the words in Spanish to the Beatles' "I Get By With a Little Help from My Friends": *Sobrevivo con un poco de ayuda de mis amigos* . . . The words didn't quite fit the tune, and she had to alternately hurry to stuff them all in the measures or hold them inordinately long, usually on the consonant, which I remembered from the school choir as something not to do.

"Get dressed, young man," Father said, although Basir was already dressed. It was another rule in our household: you must dress in the morning, even if you were planning on sunbathing nude first thing. Mother often painted in the nude, and Father did Tai Chi in his birthday suit on the side porch as the sun went down. Basir used to like to chase me around the house holding his little penis out in front of him like a sword. But we were all always dressed around the breakfast table. It was as though our family tried for a thin semblance of normalcy that wore off by mid-morning, shrugged off in exhaustion with our blue jeans and T-shirts.

"You're coming with me to the hospital today," Father said. Basir's eyes lit up. We'd been begging to be allowed to Father's hospital, but he'd always answered our entreaties with a stoic "That's not a place for children. You'd only be in the way." I once had the obstinate audacity to ask him if he really worked in a hospital, if he really were a doctor, and his face turned red and he clasped his hands and his body shook so that I thought he was going to have a seizure, but apparently, he was only trying to keep himself from striking me in anger. That night he brought home an X-ray of a male pelvis. Inside the heart-shaped bones I could see the smaller vertebrae, the extremities and claws of a tiny animal. "Do you see?" he asked. "Do you see what people will do to try to hurt themselves? This is the kind of thing I don't want you to see."

And now today, suddenly, we were going to get to go. I stood up, excited, and turned to go up the stairs to my room. "What should we wear, Papa?" I asked.

"No, not you, Bertina," Father returned to his paper.

"Not me?" I asked.

"Just Basir," he said. "He's the one who's bored. You're working on math."

"But I'm bored too. I'm bored silly, I'm bored stiff, I'm bored to distraction," I pleaded.

"Sorry," Father said. "You're twins, but you're not Siamese." He buried his head in the *Times*. Basir shot me a gloating look before running up the stairs—one at a time, not two like I could—for his shoes. I stood incredulous in the living room.

"No, you can't," I said. "You can't do this. You can't do this to me." I tried not to cry, but the tears began to slide down my cheeks anyway.

Mother must have heard me; she stopped her singing and walked into the room carrying a nearly complete wreath. "What's going on?" she asked.

"Basir's going to the hospital and Father won't let me go too," I whined through sobs.

"So you'll go next time," Mother said.

"Next time?" I asked. "Next time? When was there a last time for there to be a next time? I know about random numbers and chaos theory. You can't say 'next time' when there might not be one."

Mother sighed heavily and walked out onto the front porch, letting the screen door slam loudly behind her. She wound up and tossed the wreath Frisbee-style into the front yard. In its wake, corn tassels scattered like seeds in the wind.

Gregor immediately sprang to fetch it. He moved so quickly it looked as though he were flying. We all stayed silent. He trotted back with the diminished wreath and handed it to Mother like a dog gifting a bird he'd caught. She looked down and took it from him.

Gregor came into the house and patted my shoulder. I could smell his sweat. "Bertina," he said. Then, "Lucky Charms." Looking over at the sunporch, he wandered into the kitchen.

I ran out the back and went to sit in the cornfield
There was an inexplicable small circle of grass in the middle
of the field, and I liked to sit there, surrounded by the corn,
and stare up at the sky. It was there I fled to now. Pretty soon
I heard the Woodie's cough as it turned over, and I could
imagine its trail of dust as my brother, mother, and father
sped down the road to start their day elsewhere, Gregor
running in their wake.

I sat there for a while, thinking about how unfair
life was, wondering if it would ever change, lamenting my
solitary fate on the farm, all the while digging a hole for my
tears in the grass next to me with a stick. I contemplated the
idea that I was adopted, which would explain why Basir and
I looked so dissimilar, and why I was so developed while he
remained a child, and why my parents hated me so much.
Finally, I got tired of crying, and lay down to look at the sky
while I still could before the sun rose too high. I watched
the clouds organize themselves into shapes, and softly sang
a tune from "You're a Good Man, Charlie Brown" in which
the Peanuts gang identifies different cloud formations. I
found a submarine in the air, and a diamond ring, and a
dragon. And my hands moved from their folded position
on my chest down to feel my hipbones. And pretty soon the
right one found its way into my shorts, and then beneath
the cotton panties I wore and started rubbing there.

I imagined Gregor standing in the kitchen. He took
the corn-tassel wreath and placed it around my bare shoulders, running his hands up and down my arms to match
the rhythm of my hand between my legs. I imagined he
bent over to kiss me, and I felt the textured hardness of
his tongue, like Basir's. I moved my hand faster and faster
and it was like waiting for a sneeze which finally came—a
lightening-blip in consciousness—and I realized I had been
holding my breath and closing my eyes. When I opened
them there was a shadow across my chest: Ignatz.

I sat up on my elbows, embarrassed. I wanted to
disappear, wanted to be swallowed up by the corn, or

abducted by aliens on the spot, but Ignatz squatted beside me. I realized there was no way he could tell anyone in my family anyway, but the thought that he would share this with Gregor, that Gregor would know this about me, was almost too much to bear. I closed my eyes, as I used to do as a child, hoping this would make me invisible.

Ignatz laughed. He threw his stubbed-out cigarette into the corn and leaned closer, stretching out his hand to push my bangs back off my face. He smelled like smoke. I opened my eyes. "Bertina," he smiled. "Good." He showed his teeth when he smiled—small crooked yellow ears of corn.

I felt a strange sense of resignation, as though this were a calculus problem I had to complete to be able to progress to the next math chapter. I was anxious more because I didn't know what would happen, or rather the order in which it would occur, than because I didn't want it to, or was afraid. I closed my eyes again; the cloud dragon disappeared.

Ignatz sat down and unbuttoned my blouse. I was wearing a training bra underneath that clasped in front: two interlocking hands. Ignatz placed his fingers around the clasp. "Bertina," he said, and then something that sounded like "Comme t'est belle," which was a line from an Edith Piaf song, but couldn't really have been what he said, since Sebastian had taken his record player with him, and Ignatz didn't know French.

"I am?" I said.

"I am?" he repeated. "I am? Hoppy isn't planned, resurgent." He undid my bra and let the elastic snap back the cups to my armpits. I held my arms stiffly at my sides. Ignatz drew a slow circle around each small breast, then ran a finger down my stomach to my belly button. He gave my stomach a small kiss. Then he placed his hand over my left nipple and let it lie there, just resting. I could feel the roughness of his palm and its smooth center and feel the pressing of my nipple against it—a miniature gumdrop.

When he removed his hand, I felt cold. It's not a violation, I thought, if you let it happen.

Then I felt him move away, heard him stand up and rustle back into the cornfield. I kept my eyes closed until I was sure he was gone. I stood up and rehooked my bra, rebuttoned my blouse, then started out of the cornfield. I knocked the husks out of my way as I walked, and listened to them hit each other, rebounding dully behind me. When I reached the field, Gregor was back from his run. He was yelling at Ignatz, but I couldn't understand them. I wondered if they were fighting about me. I saw Gregor's mouth moving angrily, little beads of spittle flying from between his teeth. Ignatz looked at his feet. He was so small compared to Gregor, almost as though they weren't of the same species. And then I saw Gregor pause. Ignatz looked up and Gregor swung his fist at him, hitting him squarely on the jaw. Ignatz's head reeled right with the blow and he took one, two steps sideways before falling onto his hands in the grass. Something turned over inside my stomach, a little stone of gladness.

Gregor looked out a moment, saw me standing there, and immediately ran to Ignatz, taking his face in his hands, examining, then holding the wounded head to his chest. Ignatz's legs splayed, and Gregor held him still, his eyes closed. From where I stood they looked like a pietà from my art book.

I went inside to the kitchen. I got a striped towel from the drawer and spread it on the table. A half-eaten bowl of Lucky Charms was sitting there, the milk forming swirls of melted, multicolored sugar in the bowl. I dumped some ice from the plastic mold onto the towel and knotted it.

When I got back outside, they were lying together in the yard, hugging each other in the warm sunlight like fetal twins. I walked closer. They appeared to be sleeping, and I left the ice in the towel next to Ignatz's head and walked back into the house where I rotated elephant shapes around Y axes by myself until everyone got home.

Gregor and Ignatz left the house a couple of days afterward. Mother and Father drove them into town in the morning. Basir and I swam in the pond. It was a hot day, and we treated the pond like it was a bathtub, lounging around and barely moving. It was too hot to get out and do anything else.

Basir made half-hearted attempts at conversation. He said the hospital was boring. Father sat all day in a windowless room and looked at X-rays. In between, he slept, feet up on the console. Basir splashed me a little. He ripped off an imaginary mask, and though it hurt me to see his face fall when I didn't follow him in the ritual, I didn't feel like playing. He gave up finally and dove repeatedly for rocks at the bottom of the pond, throwing them at the distant treeline.

Mother brought home a new stray soon after—Jimmy, a short, blond man from Montana who had no luggage. Jimmy didn't talk much, didn't play an instrument, told tales, tedious even in their brevity, of his life as a drifter. He didn't smoke, ate little, and slept a lot. He had to be talked into playing with us, and proved to be an un-imaginative playmate.

One day Jimmy went with Mother and Father into the city and only Father came back.

"She's eccentric," he said, by way of explanation. He spoke softly, looking out the window like Mother used to do. "It's her eccentricity," he diagnosed.

I made macaroni and cheese for dinner. "I suppose we won't be feeding the birds anymore," Basir said.

"Or we can quit feeding the cats," I offered.

"Birds can fend for themselves," Father answered, spooning more mac and cheese onto his already full plate. "It's the cats you have to take care of."

"Birds can just fly away," Basir said. He pretended to rip off a mask. "Look, I'm Icarus."

Father and I didn't pay any attention. He was not the first man to be abandoned. We were not the first children left half-orphaned. We were neither alone nor original.

That fall Father enrolled us in seventh grade at the public school in the city, and the three of us drove back and forth every day. The classes were way too simple, and Basir and I began to spend less time together as I found a group of girls to befriend and gave up my tapes of musicals for rock and roll. He started drawing comic books with some of the smaller boys. That fall I got my period—little red dots in the crotch of my underwear like strip candy. Under the sink I found Mother's tampons. I read the instructions and sat on the toilet, forcing myself to think about sailboats bobbing tranquilly on a lake while I attempted to insert one. In the spring we moved back into the city, and while I was on top of a stepladder, cleaning out the highest kitchen cabinets, I found an old box of Lucky Charms, the marshmallows clumped together like a distorted rainbow. I passed the box to Basir and he got out two bowls and we each ate a silent bowl of stale cereal.

A PERSONAL MATTER

The boy was bundled beyond recognition. Not that Franklin could have recognized him—he had never met the boy before. The mother had changed very little since he'd last seen her in the courtroom, although with her hair down she had a sort of feral look that startled him. They were standing outside on the stoop, watching as Franklin approached from his car. Seeing her in her prim flowered dress (a little tight around her hips) whose lace collar suggested that she had either been to church or was planning on attending, Franklin felt a gulp of lust in his abdomen.

He bent down, not without difficulty, his knees creaking out a plaintive sound like a docked boat, and peered into the boy's face. The boy's eyes were dark and oval, like Greek olives, but beyond that his features were obscured by some sort of knit face-surrounding accessory, covered in turn by the hood of his parka, curls of white fleece around his face. His arms like a body builder's stuck stiffly out from his sides. The parka itself was multicolored and patched as though assembled from many different jackets. The right lapel had a decal of a freckled baby; RUGRATS said the embroidery below it.

The boy had on jeans and miniature Timberland boots. The left one was untied.

"His shoe's untied," Franklin said, putting his hands on his knees to help himself stand up.

The boy's mother sighed and turned the boy around roughly, refusing to meet Franklin's gaze. The boy complied—a child used to being handled by adults. She bent down to tie his shoe, exposing a knee. She wasn't wearing pantyhose, and Franklin could see the weak outline of a scar.

"Pay attention to what he says, Ty."

"He's gonna buy me a pumpkin," the boy said solemnly, as if repeating.

"That's right, honey, a Halloween pumpkin."

"A Halloween pumpkin," the boy repeated. The words were slurred: *Ha-ween pup-kin.*

Franklin sighed. This visitation had not been his idea. His lawyer told him that in a judge's eyes an interest in the child, some effort, might ease the inevitable blow of child support. It was a small thing really, a morning with a three-year-old, pumpkin shopping. Of course, the afternoon would be spent consoling Evelyn, who had refused to descend the stairs that morning, crying instead into her body pillow, the wound freshly reopened.

Franklin stretched out his hand. "Come on, Tyrone," he said.

"Tyrell," his mother corrected.

"Come on, Ty," Franklin repeated, cajoling. "Let's go buy the best pumpkin we can find."

"Go on," said his mother. "Have fun."

"I'll have him back by one," Franklin said.

"Uh huh," Tyrell's mother said. It sounded like a warning.

Franklin and Tyrell walked toward the car. It was a beautiful fall day, the clouds muting the brightness of the sun, but still warm and crisp. Franklin unlocked the passenger door to his car and opened it, as though he were on a date. Tyrell climbed in with difficulty, throwing his bundled torso at the seat and swinging his tiny legs in behind him, then raising himself onto the seat with his mittened hands.

Franklin walked around to the other side of the car. He got in and buckled up, then remembered to reach across Tyrell and do the same for him. The boy watched him do it—the same dark, inexpressive eyes as his mother. Then Franklin started the car and they drove off. He could see Tyrell's mother retreat into the house and close the door. The boy took a deep breath. Franklin wondered if he were trying not to cry. A thin stream of snot ran out of his nose.

Franklin was too old for this, too old to start raising kids again now. His three were grown and married. One even had two kids of her own. And he didn't like children, had agreed to have them because that's what people did, and it kept Evelyn busy. But this was back thirty years ago, when fathers didn't have to raise children, just provide food and shelter and bark discipline occasionally, and then take them to the ballpark once they were old enough to understand the game. Not that he didn't love, or that he regretted his children, but they were by-products of Franklin's life, proof of normalcy in a way that this child wasn't.

Franklin's secretary, Rose, had downloaded a list of all the pumpkin patches in the area, and Franklin took it out of his sport coat pocket and studied it now. There was one on Fourth and Townsend; they'd try there first. He thought he should try to make conversation with the boy. He cleared his throat. "So who's that on your jacket?" he asked brightly.

"My parka," he answered. He was still looking at Franklin. His voice was muffled in all the clothing.

"Who's on your parka?" Franklin repeated.

"Where?" asked Tyrell.

"There." Franklin took a hand off the steering wheel to point at the boy's lapel where the decal was attached.

"That's Angelica," the boy said simply, as though Franklin should know who Angelica was.

"Oh," said Franklin. He waited. "Do you go to school?"

"I go to preschool," Tyrell answered. "At Saint Steven. My teacher is Mrs. Birdthistle."

"That's a unique name," said Franklin. Up ahead he saw a Burger King on the corner of Townsend and Seventeenth. He made a mental note to take the boy there for lunch.

"I like art and recess the best," the boy continued, "because I take my saber and bang I shoot Orson and Jerome and they all go dead." Tyrell made dual pistols of his hands, shooting at the windshield. He was getting excited, his little torso bouncing up and down.

"Oh," said Franklin. He didn't approve of violence. He looked at the clock over the radio. 11:07. Two hours.

Tyrell rolled down his window, letting in cool air, then rolled it back up. He rolled it down, then up again. Down, up, a few more times until Franklin said, "Hey, please don't do that." It was just an Accord. It probably couldn't stand the abuse. He searched back in his memory for other car trips. "Want to play a game?"

There was no answer from the passenger seat.

"It's called *I Spy*. You have to ask me questions until you guess what I am spying. It's something in the car. Ready?" Franklin looked over at Tyrell. He was staring blankly out the front, his mittened hands in his lap.

"I spy with my little eye something green. It's in the car, OK?"

Tyrell remained silent. Franklin tried again. "It's green, so ask me what it is. Say, 'Is it in the front seat?'"

Tyrell continued to be enthralled by something outside the car. "Come on," Franklin said. "'Is it in the front seat?' Say it."

"Is it your shoes?" Tyrell asked finally.

"No," said Franklin, relieved. "My shoes are brown."

"Is it your shoes?" Tyrell asked again, after a moment.

"No. Something green," Franklin said.

"My shoes?" Tyrell asked.

"Your shoes are brown too. Ask about something else."

Tyrell fell silent, looking down at his shoes. Now the right one was untied.

"Ask about the dashboard." There was silence. Franklin could faintly hear the football announcer. He had turned down the radio while looking for the address to pick Tyrell up. "Come on, do you know what a dashboard is? It's this front part here, with all the buttons. Come on, what's green on the dashboard?"

But Tyrell wasn't playing. Franklin waited, then turned up the radio. The announcers were making small talk between plays. Franklin felt awkward and panicky—trapped. "It's the clock," he said. "I was spying the green clock."

This couldn't have been worth it, he thought. Watching Evelyn cry as he told her, in public, no less. That had been a stupid instinct. Watching her dab at her eyes with a napkin, then escape to the bathroom to cry in a stall. And how would he have felt, if the positions were reversed? Probably no worse than he felt at that moment, so embarrassed he could cry—a secretary from the floater pool, not even someone that he loved, or had an emotional connection with.

He couldn't even really remember how it happened. It seemed like somewhat of a trap, in retrospect. Rose was on vacation, and Franklin had been out with a client for lunch: a couple of martinis on the expense account, some good fish stories about convention girls. And then later, back at the office, he'd called Maria in to take dictation.

She had one of those bodies they have up on the walls in mechanics' shops, all tits and round ass like something had made it swell up in an allergic reaction. Compared to Evelyn, who regulated her intake of food as though stranded on a desert island, Maria was voluptuousness incarnate. She wore her hair in a tight ponytail which made her eyes slant, as though she were Asian. She had what Franklin would describe as a murky look about her—a mixed race, coffee-with-cream complexion. She was Afro-Caribbean, or Cuban-Puerto

Rican, or something like that. And she fucked like Franklin had heard those girls were supposed to, half-clothed and moaning softly. Franklin had been fascinated by the large cross that hung between her breasts, watched it disappear in her cleavage as he kneaded them. She came almost as soon as he entered her, which produced the same immediate reaction in him, startling him—he usually liked to "take his time," a kind euphemism that his wife favored.

It hadn't happened more than a few times over that week that Rose was gone, certainly nothing ever went beyond that week, and he never lost his head and promised that he'd leave his wife for her, or anything like that. He never thought to question what she saw in him, a vice president, still trim. He did buy her a gift, but that was standard. A diamond pendant, which she never wore to the office, he noticed. A discreet girl.

And then she had disappeared from the office, was transferred downtown or fired; Franklin hadn't bothered to ask. Everything was as normal. It was as though Franklin's "indiscretion" had never happened.

About two years later a letter arrived. In a manila envelope marked PERSONAL in magic marker. Rose brought it in, holding it by the edge as though it were Franklin's dirty underwear. Franklin had no idea what it could be, but he opened it behind a closed door anyway, the "personal" scaring him as much as a pistol in his face. Enclosed was a letter from Maria and a picture of Tyrell, the two of them at the boardwalk amusement park in the summer. Tyrell held her hand and squinted at something out of the frame of the picture, as if distracted. Franklin read the letter; the dates did seem to match the vague memory he had of the encounter. Then he scoured the boy's small image for vestiges of himself: the telltale Dumbo ears, or the bulbous nose, his father's high cheekbones. But the photo was too small to make out accurately, and Maria's tall body cast a shadow over the boy's features, effectively obscuring them.

Franklin spent a panicked moment, his heart racing, his mind spinning with improbable scenarios that seemed to take on more possibility with each passing second. The inevitable blackmail, Evelyn's leaving him, his ousting from his job. He forced himself to calm down, took a sip of the water on his desk, wiped his forehead with a handkerchief and called his lawyer.

"Better meet in person," Franklin said. "It's a personal matter. Do you have some time this afternoon?"

At the lawyer's office, Franklin broke down in a desperate manner he had never let himself experience before—not even at the funerals of his parents. The tears flowed freely and the lawyer seemed to take it in stride, offering him tissues calmly as though grown men came to his office every day and cried their eyes out over their infidelities; as though the lawyer didn't specialize in tax matters and investment strategies.

The lawyer looked at the letter while Franklin dried his eyes and cleared his throat, embarrassed. "Well," he said, when he had finished reading and sent his secretary out to make a copy. In the Xerox, the picture grew even more fuzzy, just two blurry figures—the Ferris wheel a giant gaping mouth behind them. "Well. Nothing to do but sit back and wait. See if she makes the next move."

"Just wait?" Franklin said. "Just do nothing?"

"Well, we don't know what she wants, exactly. We don't even know if it is your child."

"Right," said Franklin. The lawyer leaned back in his chair and clasped his fingers. Above his head the diplomas' gilded letters sparkled.

"See what she wants. It's pointless to speculate, to worry at this juncture."

"Pointless," Franklin repeated.

"So." The lawyer stood up. His blue suit straightened itself, hanging loosely from his shoulders. "Buy Evelyn some jewelry and don't say anything and maybe this will all blow over."

But of course it didn't. After the papers arrived, suing Franklin for child support, after the positive paternity test and the first couple of court appearances, where Franklin had to feign interest in this child he didn't even feel responsible for, Franklin was awarded monthly visitation rights, a dubious victory at best. And worse—worse even than Evelyn's crying fit at the restaurant—was Mia's accusatory telephone call. Franklin could hear his youngest grandchild screaming in the background. Mia made little more coherent sense, ranting and raving hysterically about hurt and trust and how could he do this to her mother? And Franklin took it all stoically, interjecting "I'm sorry" whenever there was a break in the child's sobbing and Mia's accusations. Afterward, the phone safely back in its cradle, the incredible cacophony it produced finally silenced, Franklin placed his head in his hands and wondered if the punishment were more severe than the crime deserved.

Looking at the boy next to him in the car, Franklin again searched his face for familiar features. From what he could tell, the boy's mother's ethnicity had obscured any of Franklin's features. The boy sat with his hands in his lap and kicked at the glove compartment. There were faint smudges of mud where his shoes left a mark. The announcers quietly feted a touchdown.

Franklin spotted the pumpkin patch up ahead on the right. It was a vacant lot, nestled next to a shoe repair shop. They had fenced it off, decorated it with multicolored corn and hay bales, and gathered the orange pumpkins in the center.

Franklin pulled the car into the lot and put it in Park. "Well, I guess we're here," he said. There was no response so he got out of the car and walked around to the passenger door, opening it slowly. Tyrell tumbled out as though he had been packed in too tightly, got to his feet, and looked around, turning his entire body to panorama since his neck wouldn't move in its scarf.

"It look OK?" Franklin asked.

"I'm hot," said Tyrell.

"You look pretty bundled," Franklin agreed, with false cheer. "Take something off and we'll leave it in the car."

Tyrell just stood there and it dawned on Franklin that he was expected to both decide what needed removing and to remove it himself. He unzipped the boy's jacket.

"Not the parka!" Tyrell cried, taking a step back. "Keep it on."

"I'm just going to take off the sweater underneath," Franklin sighed. The boy reminded him a little of Arthur, his oldest, so stubborn. The boy made Evelyn and Franklin call him "Green Lantern" for three years, wouldn't answer to "Arthur" at all, not even at school. Until finally everyone started calling him Lanny and it stuck. Even now, all his college buddies and work associates called the house asking for Lanny Overmeister, and it always took Franklin a minute to remember that to the rest of the world, Arthur was Lanny.

Arthur ran away once. It involved not eating his broccoli at the table one night. Franklin had had a long day at the office. The property he had been in the process of acquiring—a long and involved battle with residents requiring much legal wrestling and wrenching—had finally been bought out by a different firm and Franklin's four months of hard work had come to naught. Big fat fucking donut hole. Right before review time. He walked in the door, late because he had stopped for a couple of martinis, and sat down to a dinner already in progress that more closely resembled the floor of the New York Stock Exchange in its loud volleys of unintelligible code.

"You will eat it because I tell you to and I made it for you," Evelyn was saying. She looked tired. She must have been pregnant at the time with Loden, and the initial joy at the discovery had dissipated, eclipsed by Franklin's anxieties about work, his worrying about money and how to afford three children. Her eyes had dark circles and her face was blotchy with red patches. Pregnancy, contrary to the popular myth, did not make Evelyn more attractive, but rather irritable and lumpy and discolored, her face pinched as though any extra flesh had been abducted by her stomach.

"I'm not gonna!" Arthur must have been about five. "How are you going to make me?" he taunted.

"I'm not eating mine either," Mia announced. She pushed it to the side of her plate with her baby fork. "Me too neither also," she said. They always had this solidarity, these two, a common cause against their parents.

"You will," Evelyn warned. "You will or you'll be so sorry."

"Look, Arthur—" Franklin started.

"Green Lantern!!!" Arthur screamed.

"You will eat your broccoli because your mother says you have to. Don't make me get involved."

"Fat chance of that," Evelyn muttered under her breath. She reached over and began to cut Mia's meat.

"Mommy, don't! I can do it, I want to do it!" Mia whined then burst into loud wails of tears.

Franklin put his hands over his ears. The small kitchen seemed as though it were going to burst with all the noise. The entire family was taunting him, making fun of his failure, purposely killing the martini buzz he had so carefully cultivated.

"Do something," he pleaded with Evelyn.

"You do something," she answered. She brushed a loose piece of hair off her forehead.

"Can't you control them?" he asked.

"Obviously not," she answered. "I've been controlling them all day, and we've had enough of each other at this point. Why don't you do something?"

"All right," he said. "You know what? I will."

"It's about time," Evelyn said quietly. This infuriated Franklin. Hadn't he been doing something, working to put food on this table? He stood up. His family looked at him expectantly, a smaller version of the board members he would have to face first thing tomorrow. There was a long silence.

"You," he pointed at Mia, close to the breaking point, "shut up." There was a gravity to his voice. Mia's sobs immediately turned to whimpers. "And you," Franklin directed his finger across the table at Arthur, whose face flushed red with indignation. "You will eat your broccoli all at once, right now, this instant, or you will go to your room and I will come in and spank you later."

Franklin had only spanked Arthur once before, and that was for talking back to his mother. He had called her a Bean-Brain—an insult he had heard in nursery school, and Evelyn had been sufficiently pregnant with Mia to take it to heart and cry her eyes out. Franklin found her bawling on the couch, the phone receiver to her ear, talking to her mother. And he marched right into Arthur's room and spanked the boy until he cried. This did little to ingratiate Franklin to Evelyn, though. The boy's tears dried her own and she cradled Arthur in her arms, looking at Franklin accusingly.

At the table Arthur let a few tears escape. Mia immediately ceased her sobbing and put a small cube of meat in her mouth and began chewing loudly. Franklin looked at Arthur. The boy's eyes were his mother's green, sparkling and defiant, and finally he broke the gaze and ran out of the room. They didn't discover he was not in his bedroom until after dinner, after Franklin had had a couple more gin and tonics to relax and went in search of his firstborn to mete out the punishment.

Franklin would always remember the moment he opened Arthur's door, dreading the spanking he had cornered himself into delivering, and saw that the room was empty. He had expected to find Arthur's quivering shape on the bed, under the covers, and he planned to spank him lightly, then hug the boy the way he had seen Evelyn do. He was even looking forward to the comforting rhythm of the boy's small heart, beating faster than his own, and the decrescendo of his sobs as he consoled him. But Arthur was nowhere to be found.

Franklin looked under the bed. Evelyn was a good housekeeper; there was nothing, not even lint. Franklin walked back into the kitchen. Mia was drawing at the kitchen table; Evelyn had started on the dishes.

"He's not there," Franklin said.

"What?" Evelyn turned. Her hands were gloved, the yellow rubber covered with white suds.

"He's run away, or he's hiding." Franklin sat down at the stool near the counter.

"He's run away?" Evelyn looked shocked.

"Don't worry," Franklin said. "I used to do it all the time as a kid. He'll come back."

"We're going out to look." Evelyn said.

"He'll come back, don't make a fuss," Franklin said. The word "fuss" sounded funny in his mouth, too long, like "fuzz." "That'll just reinforce his behavior. My father always used to wait and eventually I started to wonder if they were missing me and I came back to see."

"That was not this piece-of-shit neighborhood," Evelyn said, throwing the gloves in the sink. "That was not the 1970s. Mia, honey, put on your shoes, we're going out to look for your brother."

Evelyn and Mia left the house: silence. Franklin poured himself another drink and took the papers out of his briefcase. He went over in his mind what he would say the next day, decided to go in early to make a flowchart or two. Rose could come in and help him. He called her at home now. A man answered—her husband? Boyfriend?

Rose got on the line. "Mr. Overmeister?"

"Sorry to bother you at home, Rose, but I think we'll have to go in early tomorrow."

"About the Lear Project?" One of the vice presidents had christened it the Lear Project after the original owner died and three real estate investment firms had started bidding on the property.

"Yes," Franklin said. "Say around six o'clock?"

"Are you drunk?" Rose asked.

"No, my son ran away." Franklin was surprised to hear himself say this, as though it explained the slurred words, the phone call to Rose at home.

"Oh dear," Rose said. "Are you looking for him?"

"My wife is."

"And you're waiting at home to see if he comes back?"

"Something like that." Franklin rattled the ice around in his glass. Some condensation fell on the papers he held in his lap.

"He will. They always do." Rose was childless, yet she had a certain authoritative comfort that Franklin had grown to trust.

"That's what I'm counting on," Franklin said.

"Seven o'clock, then," said Rose.

As Franklin hung up, the front door opened.

"We found him," Mia sang out, bounding into the living room. "I called his name out loud like this: Green Laaaaaaaantern!" Mia screamed.

"He was in Mrs. Bell's yard, swinging on her playset," Evelyn said wearily from the front hall. Mrs. Bell was Arthur's violin teacher. From where he was seated, Franklin couldn't see his wife and son, but he imagined she had her arm around his shoulder.

"Oh," said Franklin. He wasn't sure if they heard him. "Oh," he said, louder.

"I'm giving them a bath and putting them to bed," Evelyn announced. She was livid, he could tell, but by the time she finished with the children, there would be the dishes, and Franklin would be snoring loudly on the couch, the ice cubes melting dissolutely inside the glass beside him.

Franklin heard them start up the stairs, their individual steps merging into one thumping knock, rhythmic and portentous in its regularity, the silence echoing coldly between each step.

Now, Franklin removed the hood of the parka and the scarf beneath that wound around the boy's head. He had long, tight, curly hair that was—what was that word? Nappy. Or was that a racial slur? Franklin wasn't sure, but the curls sprang tautly against the boy's head, dry and stubborn.

The boy let out a long sigh and allowed Franklin to undress him as though he were a doll. Finally, Franklin had a pile of winter clothing mounted on the passenger seat and a much smaller Tyrell was zipped back into the patchwork jacket.

"Better?" Franklin asked.

Tyrell nodded.

Franklin pointed at the pumpkins and started walking. Tyrell jogged a few steps to catch up. "Have you ever bought a pumpkin before?" Franklin asked.

"No," Tyrell said.

"Well, there are a few guidelines." Franklin knew the child wouldn't understand him, but he was attempting to fill the silence. This was familiar, a ritual he used to complete with his other children: the fall pumpkin-hunting session, the kids overdressed by their mother. "You want a round pumpkin, and it should stand up well by itself. You don't want it falling over and rolling off the porch." Franklin remembered that the boy didn't have a porch. But he didn't look as though he was following Franklin's instructions anyway. He looked like he was watching something enthralling across the street.

"And you want a smooth one. If there are too many ridges, you know, bumps, it's tough to carve. You can carve a face in it at home later, you and your mother."

"OK," Tyrell said.

"And, of course, a fresh one," Franklin continued. "So that it won't start to rot before Halloween."

They reached the first barrier of hay, and Tyrell stopped beside it obediently, waiting to be lifted over. Franklin picked him up, surprised at how light the boy was. He set him down gently, giving him a quick rub on his arms.

There were a few other people. A yuppie couple picking out several pumpkins, probably for party decorations. Another father in a red and black flannel jacket, and his kids. He was smoking detachedly, watching the children run around stealing pumpkins from each other. Another family or two, cheeks rosy, squinting in the sunlight. Franklin felt as though they were all watching and wondering about him, this older man with a small child of a different race. Did they think that this was his adopted grandson? Did they think that he was simply taking the neighbors' kid out for the day? Or could they guess that this was the midlife crisis child of an unfaithful husband? Regardless, the two made a strange pair, Franklin could tell: a stiff and nervous white man, tall and preppy, and this mystery-race child, calm and observant.

"I want this one," Tyrell said suddenly, pointing to a green and white striped squash. "This one right here."

"That's not a pumpkin," Franklin said. "Pumpkins are orange."

"But I want this one," Tyrell whined.

"Look," Franklin said. "This one isn't even round. It's shaped like a hot dog, not like a face. Let's find a pumpkin."

Tyrell sighed again. He let out his breath like an old man, like it was a tremendous effort to breathe and the resulting exhalation was a relief.

They poked around the patch for a while. The pumpkins were set in concentric circles like a bull's-eye, so every time Franklin and Tyrell found a good one, Franklin set it outside the target next to the other favorites. They got into a rhythm, Tyrell pointing at one and Franklin removing it from the ring. They turned it around, made sure the stem was secure and that the ridges were not too pronounced, and finally Franklin set it next to the others. There was a row of about eight promising specimens.

"You know, you have to pick one," Franklin said. "So start thinking about which one is your favorite."

"I want all the pumpkins." Tyrell said *pup-kins*.

"Pumpkins are expensive," Franklin said. "You'll pick one." Tyrell's face fell. He looked as though he might cry, but it might just have been a look of concentration. They had almost reached the final ring of six pumpkins, the largest ones, the kind of paradigms that would garner ribbons in state fairs, the ones that were compared in size to dogs and small ponies as opposed to different kinds of game balls, when Franklin felt a tug on his sleeve.

"Excuse me, mister?" Tyrell asked.

"Mister?" Franklin repeated. He stopped. The word hit him like a slap. He did not expect to be called "mister." "Dad" would have upset him, but "mister" seemed so impersonal. He wondered how Maria had referred to him, if he had an epithet attached to his name like "asshole" or "prick," or if she had told Tyrell anything about him at all. He hadn't thought to tell Tyrell what to call him. *Franklin*, he supposed. The boy should call him Franklin. He had no intention of being a father in any sense but the biological. Mister.

"Call me Franklin," he said.

"Mister," the boy said, "I have to go potty."

Franklin's heart sank. There was not going to be a bathroom nearby, that was for sure. He looked down at Tyrell. The boy had his legs crossed and was bobbing up and down.

"Number one or number two?" he asked. For years he didn't take Mia anywhere, not until she was old enough to go to the bathroom by herself, because he wouldn't know what to do with her. Once, stuck at the zoo, he asked a blue-haired lady to take Mia into the toilet and the woman looked at him as though he'd just asked her to do a fan dance on stage for him. Still, she took Mia's hand and disappeared inside the ladies' lounge.

"Number one," the boy answered, and Franklin breathed a sigh of relief.

Franklin took Tyrell's hand and walked over to the trailer where a high-school-aged boy sat drinking coffee from a thermos. "Excuse me," Franklin said. "May we use your bathroom?"

"Sorry," the kid said. "It's all backed up and not connected, so we're not allowed to use it."

"So there's no bathroom?"

"Sorry." The kid had pimples on his forehead, angry red dots in a row. He didn't sound sorry; he sounded indifferent.

"And where do you go?" Franklin asked raising his voice.

"Well, during the week, I use the shoe repair store there, but it's Sunday today, so, I dunno, the alley?"

"Right," Franklin said. He could hear the frustration in his voice. He was not going to let Tyrell pee in an alley.

"Mister?" Tyrell asked again. Franklin looked down at his face, the boy's brow furrowed in concentration.

"You can't hold it?" Franklin asked. The boy shook his head.

Franklin looked around. The shoe repair was indeed closed, and across the street the bank was locked tight. There was a public park down the street, but no facilities, and on the other corner the bar's gate was closed.

Franklin picked Tyrell up and jogged with him over to the blue dumpster in the alley between the lot and the store. He set Tyrell down.

"Hurry," the boy said, and Franklin saw he was going to have to undress him. He fumbled with the snap to his jeans, then pulled down the small white briefs. Tyrell's tiny penis, uncircumcised and dark, hung small and wrinkled. Tyrell kept his hands at his sides. A stream of urine started, wetting the underwear at Tyrell's feet, and Franklin saw he was going to have to hold his penis. Franklin took it in his hand like someone else's cigarette and aimed it at the wall. He felt an overwhelming sense of disgust and fundamental unfairness at the inappropriate intimacy, as though he had been singled out for suffering for no particular reason. They must have looked ridiculous to anyone watching. Tyrell sighed again and watched the urine gather in a dark pool next to the wall. The stream stopped and Tyrell waited for Franklin to pull up his pants. Franklin said nothing, but when he was done he walked in front of the boy back to the pumpkin patch, letting him negotiate his own way over the hay bales.

When they returned to their row of favorites, the man in the flannel jacket was picking up a small round one on the end.

"Excuse me, that one's mine," Franklin said.

"There was nobody here," the man said. "My son wanted it." He dropped his cigarette to pick up the pumpkin, stomping the butt out with his heel. He was wearing old tennis shoes.

"Yeah, well, we were just over there." Franklin pointed vaguely back over his shoulder. He could feel Tyrell leaning against his leg. "And these were the ones we were choosing from."

The man put the pumpkin down. "Then I'll take this one." He picked up the pale orange oval pumpkin next in line.

"No, we're choosing *between* these," Franklin said. He felt a strange sense of possessiveness about the line of pumpkins for potential purchase. The flannel-jacketed man's children stood in a similar row off to the right. They all carried a pumpkin except for one.

"Look, man . . . ," the father began. "You don't own these pumpkins. Come here, Jimmy," the man called, and the boy without a pumpkin came out of the line. "You pick the one you want. These are all good ones."

Jimmy came forward and pointed to the one the man was originally handling. It was a particularly good example, smooth and round, honest-stemmed and upright. The man picked it up.

"OK then, let's go."

Franklin looked around for a higher authority. He sensed the teenager was not going to be of use. He didn't know who he wanted to suddenly appear—a judge, or a policeman, or some sort of ombudsperson who could settle this for him. There was no one in the empty lot, and the streets nearby were empty. The man started to walk toward the trailer.

"Give me back that pumpkin!" Franklin said. The loudness of his voice, its threatening vehemence, startled him.

The man turned and looked at him.

"We're buying it. We're buying all of them. The whole row," Franklin said.

He waved to the teenager who loped over to them as if in slow motion. "I'm buying them all," he said, taking out his wallet. "Including the one that man is holding."

"All eight?" said the boy. Franklin nodded, pulling out a couple of twenties. "I can let you have them for fifty, I guess, then, eight of them," the boy counted under his breath as he pointed to the row.

The man in the flannel jacket let the pumpkin drop to the ground where it thudded dully against the hay. "I guess we don't have much choice but to find you a new one, Jimmy," he said, scowling at Franklin.

"I guess you don't." Franklin handed the teenager the money. It was more than he had planned on spending. He would have just barely enough money for lunch. He looked down at his side. Tyrell was smiling widely, his teeth in a straight row. None of Franklin's kids had ever needed braces. "OK?" he asked.

"Uh huh," Tyrell said. "Pup-kins."

Franklin and the teenager loaded the pumpkins into the trunk of the Accord. Then he and Tyrell climbed in and Franklin backed carefully onto Townsend, headed toward the Burger King. If Maria didn't want all the pumpkins, he would take them home and maybe Evelyn would want to roast the seeds like she used to. They could invite Mia and the grandkids over, and Loden could come take pictures—a pumpkin-carving ceremony was the kind of thing he liked to document. Franklin let himself imagine that it could be a real event. The familial images coalesced in his imagination; for the moment he repressed the knowledge that Mia was no longer speaking to him and Loden hadn't picked up a camera since high school.

"And after you hollow it out, your mother can roast the seeds," Franklin said. "Does she know how to do that?"

Tyrell sat silently again, a grin fixed on his face.

"Can she roast the pumpkin seeds, do you think?"

Tyrell turned to him. "The clock is green."

"Right," said Franklin, remembering the game. "It's the clock."

They fell back into a silence punctuated only by cheers from the football crowd on the radio. They would drive to the Burger King and Franklin would order a Whopper, and Tyrell would order a kid's meal. They would share the french fries in silence, and Franklin would put the plastic toy together and discover exactly what a Rugrat was. Right now, though, at each stoplight Franklin could hear the pumpkins roll toward the front of the car and then roll back again as he accelerated, their combined bump as they hit the backseat a pulsating, if erratic, rhythm.

BLUEGRASS BANJO

It may just be a trick of memory, but when we think about that night it seems as though it was Elsie's name the band was singing. Something twangy and bluegrass about the distress Elsie Rojan caused the town, about the brief search and the trial and the tree swing that still hangs in her parents' front yard. "Elsie, Elsie!"

We were sitting on blankets and lawn chairs in front of the summer stage by the lake. We remember it as a moonless night, windy, finally—during that summer it seemed we couldn't buy a breeze—and the trees behind the stage swayed as though dancing to the music. It was a Labor Day concert, the end of a long summer of time spent on front porches drinking beers and looking into a sky that we remember as starless almost every night. The band wasn't local: a touring bluegrass quartet. Mandolin, bass, guitar, and banjo. They lacked a fiddler, someone said, and we all agreed.

We should have known something was wrong. A dark night and windy, darker and windier the more we look back on it. We were all trying too hard to have fun; it was a whole-town outing. The mayor welcomed the band, spoke encouragingly about community, the reopening of the plant, the warm summer nights we all had enjoyed. We stared at the skinny guitarist, his red beard sparse near the ears, and at the banjo picker, a cowboy with a large round belly. The mandolin player had a high voice and sang the soprano parts in a falsetto. The bassist was from a town nearby; he was almost a hometown boy, and a crowd favorite. He tried to keep the music low, like the doo-wops from those old songs, but occasionally he'd break out and slap the strings against the instrument's barrel, creating a staccato rhythm like the screech of background violins in horror movies.

The older children had scattered after dark to play in the field next to the bandstand. We could hear their shouts in the breaks between songs, when the banjo player tuned his strings and tried to sell his album. He had a wide, white smile and attempted to downplay the serious subjects of the songs—prison time, loneliness, foreclosures—with witless humor. His bolo tie grazed the top of his stomach; one string lay on either side, each with a metal tip like a long fang.

We were all there, the town fixtures and representatives: Mr. and Mrs. Millard, large in their custom lawn chairs and well into their six-pack, whooped and howled in time to the beat, clapping their hands and swinging their sausage legs. The Johansons brought Jimmy in a red wagon and encouraged him to stand and sway as best he could on his baby feet. The Peterson twins, dressed in identical red jumpers, pulled each other's hair until one began to cry and Mrs. Peterson separated them.

The Wolfsons sat on the blanket in front of us. They'd brought white wine and grapes, and Mrs. Wolfson wore tight black pants and stylish sandals. She had her husband's cardigan over her shoulders. Mr. Wolfson was tan and had a full head of hair. They were too old, we said. Too old to have a twelve-year-old son. Too old to kiss like that in front of everybody. Too different from the rest of us—so different that we couldn't understand how they could be so happy when they had a "difficult son," adopted, no less, from some forest in Ecuador.

We heard Mrs. Porter behind us, clucking her tongue at the Wolfsons, expressing her disapproval, and ours. Frowning at their dark son, Gabriel, who was always in trouble in her sixth grade class—feeding the lab mice rat poison, stealing from the teachers' purses, bringing in centerfolds and charging the other boys for a thirty-second peep. A big bully, a leering child too mean for his age, brow knit in anger, too full of rage to belong to our town.

The Rojans had brought lawn chairs and sat on the left side of the stage. In the small circle of bushes near the playground, their older daughter sat braiding her friend's hair. In the streetlight's gelled glow, insects circled warily. Elsie had gone to play with the other seven-year-olds, running around in an elaborate game of tag just past the tire swing, out of the light.

Couldn't we have predicted it? We remember little Elsie as sweet, trusting, and blond, two braids like a doll's down her back, running off with her friends in perfect confidence. And Gabriel, resisting his mother's embrace as the music started, elbowing her in the eye as if by accident, loafing off into the woods to smoke, we thought, or to encourage the other boys to make fires and pull the legs off insects.

It must have happened during the final song. The song whose words could have been a warning to us about Elsie. "Elsie, Elsie!" Though those couldn't have been the real words, the true lyrics are fuzzy in memory. It was a fast tune, and the Peterson twins got up and danced a modified Irish jig in front of the stage. Once they got things going the Millards put down their beers to move around too. We all stood up, wiped leaves and crumbs from our laps and held hands, bouncing up and down to the song.

The wind picked up. The sky seemed to get a little darker and the music quickened slightly. The bassist slapped the instrument hard, as if trying to get the rest of the band to follow him to a slower rhythm, but the song pulsed, the lyrics warped with longing. The song picked up, faster and faster. We danced and spun until the stage and our neighbors were all a blur, losing ourselves in the music as the guitarist sang about the girl who'd taken the train to meet the devil. And we remember that her name seemed to sound like Elsie's. The rhymes were clever and the solos fine and the banjo soon took his turn. It was a long-necked banjo, white paint chipping with age. The fat musician picked wildly, one hand flying nimbly over the frets, the other hand, with its artificial nails like claws ripping at the strings, made each one wail out after the other. He wore a pained expression, as though the music were getting away from him, and gradually he looked up from the instrument and into the audience with a wide-eyed helplessness. His hands seemed to pick the music at a pace too furious to be human. We stopped dancing to watch this banjo-picker obsessed by music. We, were possessed, mesmerized, our small town's picnic blankets arranged like a patchwork quilt beneath him.

And then he stopped. There was a moment of silence and then the Millards started clapping and hollering and we all joined in, hooting and stomping our feet, and the band had to bow.

The evening ended, and as we were all packing up our things, putting fried chicken back in baskets and dumping leftover colas onto the lawn, the strains of Mrs. Rojan's voice could be heard, like an echo of the music: "Elsie, Elsie!" And Mrs. Wolfson like the bassist thumping out "Gabriel!" And we were all still too flushed from dancing, from the wild romp of the music that had taken hold of us, had held our attention in the moonless night and twirled us around like leaves in the wind, and too preoccupied with our packing and that of our neighbors to be worried. In a town like ours, Elsie would come home and Gabriel would lumber back to his parents' car, shrug off his father's friendly pat.

The banjo player put his instrument back in its case. "Elsie, Elsie!" And until he shut it firmly, it wouldn't have to be that Elsie wouldn't come home, that they'd find her in the tall trees just behind the stage at first light. And until the musician latched his case closed, we wouldn't have to see her with her dress pulled up over her head, the two braids wrapped around her neck as though suffocating her of their own accord. We wouldn't have to remember—for who could forget?—the boys' tearful confession that Gabriel had told them about it, bragged about the crime in the woods just behind the stage we were all watching, distracted by the savage tune of the bluegrass banjo, its player singing "Elsie, Elsie!" into the night.

THE CULT OF ME

After the war I settled in Santa Rosa, which is not where
I'm from, but which is warm, with a good VA hospital.
I did a little freelance tech writing for a while, and
then I opened the research firm, funded it with grants, and
computerized it. After Waco, the government came knocking.
Probably to check up on me. Then, when they realized it
was on the up and up, contracted me. Now I collect statistics
on millennial cults. All kinds: Christian Doomsday, UFO
Deliverance, Avenging Planet, Angry Separatist, New Age,
Christ's Coming, Asteroid, and Y2K chaos cults. The data-
base is cross-referenced by members' names, ages and races,
leaders and ideologies, geography and possessions. It is this
last piece of data the government wants; Uncle Sam's just
got to know who's stockpiling ammo and who's building
fallout shelters underground.

Nothing surprises me anymore. People will believe
anything, if they want to strongly enough. And that's why
I'm the one who does the research, because there's a part of
me that wants to believe, too. Wants to be so sure that if I
dress in black and wear Nike shoes that the aliens will come
take me to a better place. I wish I could be that sure. Instead

all I'm sure about is that if there is a God, he cares very little about man, or about me.

On Saturday, June 5, 1999, I was at a garage sale. I'd been going to all the sales near Santa Rosa, investigating the Morningland cult, which likes to recruit members by cornering them in driveways under the California sun. It's harder to think clearly with someone else's junk in your grip. I couldn't be sure if this was a Morningland sale or just a simple, innocuous method some neighbors were employing to get rid of the stuff piling up in their attached garages. I milled around, waiting for that certain vibe, that palpitation of instinct that would clue me in. I was thumbing through linens when I felt someone's hand on mine.

"Are you going to buy this?" she asked. "Because if not, I will."

"I don't know," I said. "I'm just looking."

"Oh." The woman looked confused. She knit her brow as if making a serious decision. "Do you think I could use this as a drop cloth, you know, for painting?"

"I don't know if it would be thick enough," I said. "What kind of paint are you using?"

She didn't look like the type who would be painting her own apartment. She was kind of what they call mousy: brown hair, old formless housedress with fake hippie designs at the waist and repeated around her hemline, long straight nose. Nothing wrong with her, just nothing remarkable.

"Oh, house paint," she said. "The walls are yellow, and I heard somewhere that yellow encourages mental disassociation. I'm trying to associate these days. I just spent the last few years disassociating."

"Ahh," I said. I was trying not to draw too much attention to myself. Cult members are notoriously antisocial, and they expect prospective members to be as well. If you speak to them they look so startled that you want to apologize, only you don't because you worry that that will startle them further.

"I'm Naomi," she said. I nodded. I didn't want to say my name.

"Maybe if I buy a lot of them," she continued. "Maybe then the paint won't seep through." She looked concerned as she surveyed the meager pile of tablecloths.

"They usually toss them in for free, when you buy the paint," I said. "At least, at Home Depot they do."

"Oh." Her face fell and she let the hand that was fingering the tablecloth drop. "I just sort of wanted these to get one last use."

I felt the need to cheer her up. "That makes sense. Don't let me discourage you, then." And she drifted away, the way people do at garage sales.

I sifted through a table of carpentry items, contemplated a broken level. A third of it was missing so that there were only two bubbles of liquid instead of three. The table must have been unbalanced, because the liquid rested to the right of the balance line in both. I decided not to purchase it; I hardly ever attempt to fix anything. Instead I bought a lamp: two intertwined snakes whose heads supported a lime green shade. And at the last second I threw in a baby bib with a stained Big Bird on the front. I took it up to the woman who was running the garage sale. She kept the cash in a shoebox.

"Three fifty," she said. I didn't know if this was a Morningland sale or not, and nobody had approached me, nor had I seen anyone approach anybody else. But cultists are paranoid by definition, and if they'd seen me talking to that girl they probably would have hidden their activities, and my chances at infiltration would have diminished significantly. I decided not to stick around and walked slowly to my car.

As I was putting the lamp in the backseat I caught a glimpse of the mousy woman again, talking to someone in the driveway. I made a note of it and pretended, even at the time, that it was just my detective instincts taking over; pretended that I didn't see something solid about her, something in her eccentric normalcy that indicated balance and symmetry.

There are some mornings when it hurts so bad that I can't even think about getting out of bed. I wonder sometimes if I had a wife, if that would help me when it feels like there's a fire in my stomach, like someone put a big rock on top of my abdomen, like little elves in crampons are trekking in my intestines. And if you haven't experienced pain like this—chronic daily agony—then maybe you won't understand this story, because the instinct to grab someone's hand and squeeze tightly, so tight like you're transferring the pain to them, won't make sense to you. And the urge to reach up and take hold of something that will pull you out of your misery, your abject suffering, won't be one you can relate to. But maybe you will get it; maybe a small part of you might understand how those of us who are in pain have the energy to search for something, and in this quest find a palliative, if not a cure.

I keep all the crap I accumulate during my investigations in the gazebo in back of my house. I have a ceramic dog, several sets of various religious texts, a tractor engine, the complete works of Buddy Holly on LP (including some fairly valuable German and Japanese editions), lots of large rocks with markings that could be runes but are most probably just erosion's striations, cancellation stamps from a post office in San Bernardino, a twelve-foot cross with all the stations in inlaid lacquer on the sides, a staff and cloak, a large sign with an alphabet of black letters that can be stuck on with a special stick (lost) which reads "I WILL UTTERLY SWEEP AWAY EVERYTHING FROM THE FAZE OF THE EARTH," SAYS THE LORD—ZEPHANIAH 1:2 (the z in place of the c because the c was long gone, it was explained to me when I bought it), and a collection of butterflies mounted on pins beneath glass, which is not an artifact but rather an inheritance from a deceased uncle. To this pile, I added my new lamp.

I wasn't attracted to Naomi necessarily. I cut off that part of my life when I came back from the war. That physical part of me doesn't work, and I have convinced my mind not to work that way either. Who could love a man who is no longer a man? Who could love a man who pees in a plastic bag, and who thrashes in his sleep and cries from the pain? Only someone who loved him before, I suppose. Only someone who loved sacrifice. I know about loving sacrifice, and how narcissistic and exalted a love it is, and how its object is never a person, but rather an ideal. I couldn't compete with that. I wouldn't want to, even if someone wanted to love me as a sacrifice. Even if.

I ran into Naomi again the next weekend at a garage sale on Buena Vista Court. I came pretty much near the end of the sale. I'd been at another sale over in Granada Estates, which was actually a large flea market, a complete waste of my professional time, although I did come away with a working, if slightly battered, juicer, which is what my doctor recommended I do with all the fruit I'm supposed to ingest every day. I was driving home when I saw the sign for Buena Vista, a hand-lettered box top with a tomato plant stake, a red arrow pointing me right. I followed it, then followed a second sign left; a third wound me around a roundabout. I made a final left down a street marked CUL DE SAC, which is a fancy California term for "no outlet," and at the end of Buena Vista Court was a small garage sale. I stopped the car and noted the location in my stenographer's book. Then I tucked the book back into the glove compartment and got out of the car.

Naomi was standing by the linens again, fingering them as if by rubbing them enough she could make a genie appear. As I approached, she held one to her face and ran it against her chin. This time she had on linen overalls.

I remember that I was unsurprised to see her. I don't know what that means except that it seemed normal that she would be at yet another garage sale. After all, I was.

"Oh hello," she said. "You again." I looked up, startled. I hadn't expected her to recognize me, or to address me if she did.

"Hello," I said. "More tablecloths."

"You were right," she said. "About the paint. About it seeping through."

"But you're buying more?" I asked. "A glutton for punishment?"

"No." She looked over my head at the street. The sun was particularly bright. It glinted off the cars blindingly. "I just finally admitted to myself that I like to collect old tablecloths."

"Admitting you have a problem is the first step toward recovery," I said. In my head, it sounded like something that would be funny. Out loud, it fell like a ton of bricks.

"Maybe," she said. "Do you like this blue one, even though it has a chocolate stain?"

"I like it *because* it has a chocolate stain," I replied. She smiled. I hadn't made anyone smile in a long time. Suddenly, I remembered that I was working, or should have been, and I smiled again, sternly this time, and walked away.

I was looking through the record collection—no Buddy Holly but some nice 70s classics—when I felt a shadow on my back. When I turned, a large bearded man held out an early Elvis vinyl.

"Looking for some oldies, guy?"

"Beatles," I said. "I'm looking for *The White Album*."

"Can't look here." The man pointed at the table where the records were fanned like cards. "Gotta look here." He pointed at his heart. "Or here." He pointed toward the sky.

The man was sweating heavily. Under his blue shirt, I could see the strained lines of a high-cut sleeveless undershirt.

"What do you mean?" I asked.

"'Thus says the Lord: Learn not the way of the nations, nor be dismayed at the signs of the heavens, because the nations are dismayed at them, for the customs of the peoples are false.' That's Jeremiah 10:1."

"'You shall indeed hear," I returned, "but never understand, and you shall indeed see but never perceive. For this people's heart has grown dull, and their ears are heavy of hearing, and their eyes they have closed; lest they should perceive with their eyes, and hear with their ears, and understand with their heart.' Acts 28:26." One thing I'll say for me: I know my Apostolic Scripture.

The man nodded at me. His face grew suddenly serious, and he held his Elvis record like a shield. "Are your eyes open, guy?" he asked me.

"I'm trying, but the sun's so bright I have to squint."

"Come into the shade," he said. "The Maplewood City Community Center on Wednesday night."

"Yes," I said. "I'm interested." The man walked away quickly and whispered to another man turning plastic plates over carefully to read their undersides.

I took a Bee Gees record and went over to the table where a woman was presiding over a cookie tin. "Seventy-five cents," she said. "That's a good choice. 'How Deep is Your Love,' and all."

I paid her silently, triumphantly. I had gotten what I wanted, an invitation to a meeting. A fortuitous detour of my day.

"I'm Naomi," a voice said behind me. I turned.

"I remember."

"Do you know anything about plumbing? Because, well, this may sound forward, but I need someone to help me move my couch away from the wall so I can get in to paint behind it."

"What does that have to do with plumbing?" I asked. Talking with this woman was threatening the groundwork I'd laid. I worried now that they would be suspicious, or wary.

"Nothing. My faucet is leaking. They were two unrelated thoughts."

And so to hurry away I agreed to follow her back to her house.

This won't be a story where I tell you about the war. You've already heard too many of those. They saturate the consciousness, until they're so commonplace as to be banal. I'm not going to describe the heat, or the fear, or tell you horror stories of the villages we burned, or what we made the women do. I don't even remember most of that stuff anyway. I couldn't even tell you how I got injured, probably, if it weren't in my file. In all those academic medical terms, along with lists of numbers, records of my fluid levels, my medication frequency, numerical archives of my health.

Never thought I'd be a man who works with numbers. I don't believe in numbers necessarily. I remember in math class when I was fourteen and we learned imaginary numbers. I went to see the teacher about that, after school. I wasn't the kind of student who would normally do that, go see the teacher, and I asked him about it. "Imaginary? Like it's made up?" I asked. "All numbers are made up," he said. "Every one of them. Someone made them all up, arbitrarily." I think I must have stormed out of his office. I felt betrayed. They were all made up, huh? Then what could you count on, pardon the pun? Since then I've not trusted numbers, because I've been one, a statistic. One of 35 surviving members of my squadron, one of the 303,704 who returned from the war imperfect, unwhole.

So I know they're all bullshit, but I compile them anyway, because it makes the government feel better. For example, there are 1,243 self-proclaimed prophets in modern America. There are 123 cults in northern California alone, which has the highest cult-per-capita ratio in the fifty states. There are no cults in North Dakota, although some would argue that those lodges like the Elks are cults, or that the air bases are the government's version of cults. I'm not a suspicious person; I think that the quickest way between two points is a straight line and that the simplest explanation is the truest. I don't care if our atmosphere is being eaten away by toxic gas. I know that my computer system won't crash on midnight December 31—and I won't care if it does. If this is the age where any idiot can broadcast his opinion on the internet, then no one's voice is any louder than anyone else's. So this tale is just a hit on my website, just a little something that happened to me once.

I should have said no. She was already starting to need me. It may be selfish, or self-pitying, but I can't be helping people. They can't grow to need me because I might not be around. The flip side of needing nothing is that I have nothing to offer. Nothing I'm willing to offer.

I moved Naomi's couch, and then I tightened the washer on her bathroom faucet with a little elbow grease. She made me a cup of coffee and we chatted, and she told me she was getting divorced, that this was a sublet from a friend who was hiking the Appalachian Trail for a year or so. It was like being in a trance, listening to her speak. As though it were all happening to somebody else, hearing her say that she didn't just bring men home from garage sales, but she needed the help because she didn't know anyone else in Santa Rosa, and that there was something restrained about me, and she knew that I wouldn't hurt her.

She took my cup to the sink and then patted my hand twice, friendly, which made me cringe. I stood up to leave. "Thanks for the coffee," I said. "I need a cigarette." She didn't try to stop me as I opened the door. The ache in my belly had begun, a tight clenching of my muscles around a central pain, dull but intense, that would gather strength over the next several hours and incapacitate me for a couple of days.

I stood in the recessed door of her building and lit a cigarette out of the wind and sun. There was another man smoking there. He nodded. I put my lighter back in my pocket and walked to my car.

When I got home the pain was already bad. I emptied the catheter bag into the toilet. The drain let the urine out slowly, so that it sounded almost as though I was taking a piss for real. I took twice the recommended dosage of painkillers and tranquilizers and got into bed, clutching my stomach with both hands, curled up into a ball.

I thought about Naomi, and how someone like that could never understand something like this, although it did seem as though she just wanted her couch moved and someone to talk to. Another wave of pain hit, like a car revving into a higher gear and, pulling my knees closer to my chest, I began to cry.

That night I dreamed that I was in Vietnam. We were in the jungle, a routine sweep and scan, fanning out in a secure zone to search for civilians or discarded weapons when someone shouted, "Sergeant!"

I was only ever a lieutenant, but in my dream I knew that I was the one being called. I ran to the voice, entering the deepest jungle.

And then, below my feet, the ground turned into junk. Piles and piles of the same sort of crap I see at garage sales: headless dolls and mismatched china, rusted saws and baseball cards. I tried not to step on anything, but it was useless; the ground was carpeted.

When I reached the soldier, I saw that he was bent over a woman. I knelt beside them. It was Naomi, her brown hair darker now, the curve of her chin familiar. She was wearing the same dress as the day I first met her, flowered and shapeless. I held her head in my arms as her breathing became labored. She had a large wound in her stomach. I could see her intestines straining to get through, and I knew that she must have been in a lot of pain.

"Naomi," I said. She wouldn't live much longer.

"Why?" She looked up at me, her brown eyes growing dim already. I had to strain to hear her. "Why would you do this to me?"

On Wednesday, June 16, 1999, I went to the Maplewood Community Center. Contrary to my previous belief, the meeting was not of the amateurish Morningland cult, but rather the more sophisticated Abbadonian Dawning. High Priestess Veronica Ohm (Asian female, late fifties, 5'1", shoulder-length brown hair) presided over the meeting, at which there were approximately fifty people in attendance. A deli tray from Safeway was served, as well as lemonade, too sweet. Veronica said a blessing over the congregation, and read minutes. A longer incantation, in praise of the sun, was invoked by the entire assembly. There seemed to be three or four people besides me who didn't know the words either. She then spoke for twenty minutes regarding the environment, our misuse of land, and her vision of the utopia that would be revealed when God ended the world and took away the chosen in UFOs. Then the assembly stood up and held hands, with Veronica in the middle. She spun several times, then stopped, faced east, and screamed. She fell to the floor in a swoon.

The man who had approached me at the garage sale then motioned me over. Along with three women, I was led to a smaller room and given literature to peruse. The bearded man stepped in and cleared his throat. Without preamble, he began to describe the cult. He was a convincing speaker, quoting Scripture liberally. From Job 26: "Sheol is naked before God and Abaddon has no covering . . . He has described a circle upon the face of the waters, at the boundary between light and darkness. The pillars of heaven tremble, and are astounded at his rebuke." Only the chosen would be saved from the rebuke, Indians and parents of young children among them. I felt almost hypnotized, drugged. His words swirled in my head, an eddy of hazy suggestion.

He took me aside. "We need her too," he said. "The woman from Sunday. That is why I approached you. Because you could bring her to us."

I hesitated only a moment before I agreed.

If I were a different man, I might have walked away from the cult, away from my work, and lived the rest of my life with a mostly clear conscience. I consider myself a good person; I can't explain why I did what I did, not even to my own satisfaction. Maybe I did, just this once, let others' belief cloud my judgment. Maybe I was swayed by the historical precedent of the superstitious' faith in the ritual of chance.

When I thought about seeing Naomi again I felt like I did in my dream. How could I do that to her, saddle her with my loneliness, my disability? Burden her with the expanse of my need, just because I liked the way she needed me. Introducing her to the man with the beard seemed more natural, inevitable. I had made her no promises. That's the way it was meant to be.

"Oh," she said, opening her front door. "It's you." She looked surprised.

"Yeah, hi, I . . ."

"Come on in." Naomi opened the door wider. Her living room was utterly changed. She had painted it a seaweed green and added a pale blue trim at the baseboards, waist-high, and about an inch from the ceiling. She had draped sheets over the existing tables and set candles on them. All of the paintings were hung at different angles and at different heights throughout the room. There was a Chinese painting of the Wheel of Life at chin height, while a mirror was raised above my head and reflected the top of the open door. A Venetian mask hovered just above a chair and a child's abstract drawing hung next to the window, which looked across the street to a low-rise apartment complex. The windows were open, and I could hear the shouts of children playing in a pool, the splashes punctuated by the lifeguard's whistle and the stern voice of a disapproving parent.

"Sit down?" Naomi asked.

There are things you learn in my line of work about the manipulation of people. That, like numbers, if you twist them around enough, set them across from equal signs, perch them on top of common denominators, you can get them to do what you want. But here's the irony: they'll never do what you want. Never exactly what you want. The emotion will be there, but the actions won't follow. Or else, the actions seem promising, but the emotion is lacking. Never that perfect symbiosis of volition and execution, never that marriage of benevolence and desire. Because desire is selfish, first and foremost.

Manipulation is about tapping into the selfish core of the desirous individual. Naomi wanted to want. She wanted to be a member. And once she was a member, I could follow her into the Abbadonian darkness, infiltrate and inform on them. I let her want, and this is something I'll never forgive myself for—something that keeps me up nights when all the faces of those demoralized women, those shattered children, never makes me lose a second of sleep: I let her lead and then did not follow. She became the only other member of the cult of me.

You may wonder why I'm still alive. Or at least I hope you wonder that. Why I haven't done myself in, joined one of these doomsday cults and slit my wrists on some equinox or other, or sacrificed my corporeal being to the fire and brimstone or the coming of the mothership. Why I've never used the cults as an excuse to end it all.

Frankly, I simply don't have the energy. Sometimes my body aches too much for me even to move to swallow all those pills. Sometimes I think I deserve this, and I suffer through the pain because I've done something that merits it. And sometimes life feels unfinished, the way Job needed to march on to the end. That for the pain and the suffering to have meaning it must have trajectory. But mostly it's because I identify with the cult members. We survive on God's most meager rations. It's embarrassing and contradictory, because I know I've had my chance and squandered it, and in spite of that I dare to believe. It's because, I'm ashamed to say, I have hope.

I sat down again on her couch and she made me sweet chamomile tea and we ate vanilla wafers. And she told me

how she wanted to be a massage therapist, or maybe study
holistic medicine. She told me my chakras were unbalanced,
and that she could sense a sharpness coming from my abdomen,
like a sword or ray of piercing light. I talk to a lot of people
about new age spiritual matters, and it's a series of passwords
like volleys exchanged outside a speakeasy. Do we understand
each other? Does our speech contain the same subtext?

Naomi spoke softly and she took my hand. I could
feel her loneliness, see the artwork hanging at odd angles,
hear the soft gamelan music in the background, the warped
sitar and the tabla tapping out tum-tiki-tiki-tiki. And I
could still pretend it was about getting her to want to be
with me, and then transferring that newly awakened need to
my work.

And to that end I told her. I hadn't told anyone in
years, and I can't say it didn't feel good. I told her about the
women, and the naked, burned children, the discarded limbs
like poppy plants in the wet fields. I told her about the catheter,
and how it had been twenty-five years since I'd made love to
a woman, and the last one was named Lily and her skin was
so pale you could see the blue veins beneath the needle's pock
marks, and I couldn't even pretend that we were in love or
that she was anything but a ten-dollar whore.

I think I cried. I don't know whether I was acting
or not, designing my face to draw Naomi in. Regardless,
the desire was there. I cried because I was devoured by an
immeasurable sense of sadness and loss. And selfishness. I
cried because I knew that I would give her up, and that I
didn't want to.

She cried too, then, slow controlled tears of nostalgia.
I laid my head in her lap, and she stroked my hairline with
manicured nails until the sun started to rise. And I'll leave
it at that, at those actions.

But I'll say this about the emotions: I felt, in that
instant, in the warm touch of her fingers on my forehead,
the promise and the compromise of caring. And I saw in
the thin rays of morning light that filtered in through her

curtains some sort of hope. That's what was different about this time, about her. And I began to shake, and she took her fingers away.

She got up to go to the bathroom and right then both parts of me, the acting one and the real one, knew that it was time to leave. I stood up and Naomi came into the living room. I took her face in my hands and kissed her forehead, pressing my lips against its expanse. When I pulled away she kissed me quickly, on the lips but with her mouth closed. She had brushed her teeth and the toothpaste left a cool mint tingle on my mouth, like the lingering sting of a scrape. I felt my face flush red from embarrassment.

When I reached the downstairs door I paused to light a cigarette. The same man was standing there in the dawn. He was wearing a T-shirt and pajama pants and had his arms crossed to fight the morning chill, which was drawing goose pimples on his arms.

"She make you smoke outside too, huh?" he said, pointing with his nose at my cigarette.

"Go to hell," I said.

I read this over and I can tell you won't understand what I saw in Naomi, how I knew that she would do what I wanted her to. Or rather, how I knew that she only wanted to be told what she wanted. I slid a piece of paper under her door the next day, and I'm told she went to the meeting. I didn't go back to the cult. I know my government contact was disappointed by my report that I was unable to locate or make contact with this cult. I had never failed him before. Nor had I ever lied.

A few months later the police responded to a complaint about a barking dog and traced the source of its annoyance to a Lawndale garage where they discovered the bodies of fifty-three women, twenty of whom were pregnant. Among them was Naomi Perdan, thirty-five, Caucasian, sixteen weeks along with a male fetus.

I know what the policemen saw walking into that garage. The women's faces, ashen and pale, their open eyes and mouths the only source of color in those emotionless faces. I do not envy that first patrolman's finder's guilt— as strong as if he'd murdered them himself—that will tie him up at night with the memory of unexpected death. The women on mats on the floor and their hands touching, maybe. These women who joined the cult because they were abandoned by fathers or husbands, or overmedicated, or not medicated enough, or just searching. Women for whom life outside Abbadonian Dawning, or Rise Up America, or Chin Fan Tsi, or Outer Dimensional Awareness, was impossible, for whom hope was too intangible, too nebulous, for whom living without divine purpose was merely existing. When they abdicated responsibility for their lives, it shifted onto the policeman who found them. I can empathize with his devastating realization of that burden, for I feel it too. When I close my eyes I see her in their midst, dark Naomi, who stroked my hair until dawn. Naomi among the rows of dead women, facing west, waiting for the sun to set, waiting for the Rapture, wanting to wait, or just waiting to want.

GOOD SHABBOS

Fifty years later, in a town in France—the seat of the Resistance—a woman is invited to dinner. She can't decide what to wear or bring. Her confusion is understandable; in French, *carry* and *wear* are the same verb. Pants and wine? A skirt and flowers?

The family lives in the old part of town, the Jewish part, where the cobblestone streets still make walking an unbalanced, unnatural action, and the woman bobs and weaves, lifting her skirt and clutching her flowers. The stones are shiny with the omnipresent winter rain but the umbrella catches the drops. In English, the word *umbrella* comes from the Latin for shade, but the French use it to ward off the rain: *parapluie*, "for rain." There are more rainy days in Paris than in London.

She reaches the square St. Antoine and crosses around the small statue of the saint to the opposite side, number three. She rings the bell beneath the name, an Arabic stew of Ms and Js and vowels. It does not sound Jewish to her, has no -gold or -stein or -burg to clue her in. She had thought the boy was Muslim until he invited her over.

The interior is dark, though she hears scurrying footsteps within. The son opens the door and greets her with two silent kisses on either cheek. "Good Shabbos," he says. "Good Shabbos," she returns. "Are the lights broken?"

"It's Shabbos," he says, and it takes her a moment to realize that lights, as electricity, are taboo.

She follows him up the ancient staircase. They wind around the central elevator cage and their deep breaths echo, preceding them upward as they climb. The stairs have troughs from where footsteps have worn the centers smooth.

The interior of the large apartment is lit with candles. There is a single lamp burning over the table. She has made the right decision, it appears, regarding the skirt. The three women present all are wearing modest, ankle-length dresses. They rise to greet her—kisses all—the mother, the aunt, the little sister. The boy presents his father, who shakes her hand.

They are less curious about her than most. They have been to America and seen many like her. They are doing her a favor, not vice versa. They lapse into Hebrew, frequently, assuming that she follows.

But she is not a Jew like they are. She is an American Jew, a lapsed Jew, an ethnic Jew. She is of the neurotic, nose job, bagel-eating kind.

They perform the ritual washing of the hands, light more candles, and bless the bread and wine. This much she knows how to do, but does not sing along with the family. The tunes are unlike the ones she learned growing up. They bear more than a faint resemblance to the melodies heard in taxis all over the town, oriental and strident.

Dinner is sauerkraut, dished up with lots of mustard. The cabbage is spicy, the meat cured but undercooked. They tell her about their time in America. They rented an RV and toured the West: Bryce Canyon, Moab, the Grand Canyon, does she know these places? Yes, she lies.

She was a bas mitzvah, no? Yes, she was, and she can read Hebrew, but slowly, and only if the vowels are inscribed below.

Then the father begins to speak. He leans forward to tell her how they have owned this apartment for generations, how his father was a doctor and his grandfather a banker and his great-grandfather a member of the town council. How his grandmother hid him and his older brothers in a secret closet behind the cupboard for three years during the War, how no one knew where his father had disappeared to.

The War. How many times is the War mentioned during this dinner, fifty years later? It forms a long shadow, dancing around the plates as flickering candlelight. The father tells her about the closet absently, as though relating a story he heard secondhand. Is it because he will never need this secret again? Or because he trusts her; she is one of them.

They liked America, they say. It abounded in kosher food. They had brought their own food to America, just in case, but they discovered sliced turkey, and peanut butter. In Los Angeles, they ate out, a dairy restaurant on Fairfax.

She was right, the woman thinks, not to have brought wine. But were flowers the right gesture? They rest on the counter in the kitchen. They would not be right with the elaborate candelabra that serves as centerpiece.

The little girl yawns; the woman asks if she is keeping her up. No, the girl responds, but she had to get up early this morning for school. She must walk to school now, in a group of no more than four. Their uniforms give them away otherwise, and the city is wary of metro cars transporting groups of Jews in navy jumpers, moving targets.

Last year, she explains, they bombed the Jewish school. Men posing as city gas technicians dug a trench to work on pipes in front of the door. They attached a bomb to a timing device set to explode at 4:05, just after the final bell rang. The children would be milling on the sidewalk, like they always did, talking and laughing and sharing candy before making their ways home.

But they cut the power by accident while installing the explosives and whoever reset the school clocks set them slow, three minutes slow so that the children were safe in class when the bomb exploded. Only the classroom nearest the street had injuries. Two children lost limbs; a couple went deaf, and several complained of tinnitus. They did not tally the nightmares.

Is she not worried, now, to go to that school?

No, she smiles. Where else is there to go that has no class on Shabbos? She wants to be with her friends.

Lightning never strikes the same place twice, her father says. The word, *éclair*, sounds like a dessert to the woman, like something good.

They offer the woman sweet kosher wine but she thinks she'd better go; it's too late for the metro and it's a long walk home. They offer to accompany her, on foot of course. The father will; the mother has already started on the dishes in the darkened kitchen, but the woman declines the offer. She'll be fine, she says, she's sure. The word sure in French means both *positive* and *safe*. But she wonders if that's true, this visitor from America, fifty years later, who has no hidden cupboards, and whose watch is set with Japanese precision. Whose umbrella is for shade, not rain.

THE PEOPLE YOU KNOW BEST

The Doctors Without Borders, Marca's rowdiest book club, straggled in on the second Thursday of each month, except for August and December. The name was a pun on their boycott of the popular bookstore that didn't work because it was spelled the same as the international medical organization. They had the tendency to repeat their office protocols at book club too, making everyone wait and then demanding a full hour, even if book club started forty-five minutes late. Their phones and beepers constantly erupted with electronic chirps, and the doctors spoke swiftly, regardless of whether someone else happened to be expressing his opinion at the time. The group was all male and mostly married; originally, it had boasted two female members, but they had dropped out due to "family considerations." It was the book club's uniquely masculine makeup that had catapulted Marca to book club facilitator "eminence"—after the long article in the City section of the Sunday *Times*, her website hits went up by a factor of 100. Now she had a waiting list.

Despite the doctors' habitual tardiness, the doorbell rang tonight at precisely 7:00 PM. When she opened the door, she didn't recognize the man standing there.

"Hello," he said. "Am I early?"

"For book club?"

"Yes. Don said it would be OK if I joined. Am I early?" He rubbed his hands as though cold; Marca looked at them: meticulously groomed, nails polished.

"No," Marca said. "You're right on time. I'm just— I'm not used to the doctors being on time."

"Radiologist," he explained. "We're a different breed."

"Make yourself at home." Marca stood back from the door. The man entered. He was on the short side, about Marca's height, and his hair was beginning to thin at the top. He had a pleasant face, the kind that sold breakfast cereal or garden tools: high, round cheeks and an impossibly straight nose.

The man surveyed the living room, as though deciding where to sit was tantamount to diagnosing a fracture; then his gaze settled on the settee near the window. This was Marca's favorite piece of furniture. Her grandmother had always insisted they sit on it when they had their tea parties. It was the first piece of furniture Marca's grandparents had bought together, after he graduated from journeyman tailor to sole proprietor of a shop that was now part of a Chinese community center. The man sat down, moving pillows to support his back. Giorgio, her Lab/shepherd mix, plodded over to him and poked his face in the man's crotch.

"Giorgio, stop," Marca said, but the man merely smiled and lifted Giorgio's face to his own, letting the dog cover him in slobbery licks. And then came the cooing noises that only animals elicit from men: high-pitched rhetorical questions and ear-scratching sound effects.

"His name is Giorgio?" the man asked. "Hello, Giorgio, I'm Peter. Yes, who's a good dog?" Marca was unsurprised by the attention he paid to Gio. Everyone loved her dog. People stopped her on the street to ask his name and pet him. Little children turned circles with excitement. And, despite the strict no-dog rules at many establishments, Giorgio was welcome nearly everywhere Marca went around the Lower East Side: the dry cleaners, the pharmacy, the bakery.

Marca loved him too; he was the world's best dog, her baby. He'd been with her since puppyhood, over eight years, comforting her as men came and went, called or didn't, poured wine, cooked dinner, made love. One ex-boyfriend still came by to visit him. He was a good dog, always coming when she called, never chewing important documents or peeing on the floor. He was undemanding, low-maintenance. Marca was proud of him and his popularity in the human world, and maybe, in a secret place, just a little envious.

"Hi, Peter. Marca." She extended her hand and Peter shook it weakly, still nuzzling the dog.

"I'm going to get the food ready," she said. She hoped that he would offer to help her in the kitchen. It had been her experience that book clubs were the best way to meet men, and Marca had been single for several months now after the Children's Place book club (made up of executives at the children's clothing store headquarters) broke up in the wake of a series of cataclysmic (by book club standards) events: Marca and Dave had stopped seeing each other, Julianne got transferred to Atlanta, and Janice had a baby. But Peter seemed as though he had no intention of getting up from the settee, so Marca went into the kitchen alone.

Her groups paid her more to act as disapproving teacher than book club facilitator and discussion leader. Yes, Marca did supply them with podcasts of interviews with authors, pertinent facts, a list of provocative questions (and her grandmother's rent-controlled, huge-for-New-York apartment for them to congregate in), but most of her groups wanted to be told to shut up, sit down, and participate. They wanted her to censor the louder members, draw out the shy mice . . . Marca sometimes felt she should purchase a riding crop. A writing crop.

Though it had been nearly three years since Marca had quit cobbling together a mediocre existence as an adjunct English lecturer at local community colleges to pursue the more lucrative career of cyberotica writer (and, now, book club facilitator), it was not until recently that everything she did reminded her of sex. And not sexy sex either, just the mechanics of it. Spoons, traffic lights, vibrating cell phones, iPod holders, clipboards . . . She felt dirty, all the time, as though she had bedbugs or some unmentionable disease that required a colostomy bag. To distance herself from the task, at the beginning of each writing session she typed at the top of the page: IN THE LAND OF CYBEROTICA . . . to differentiate it from her normal realm. Pornography was supposed to be a day job.

Her fiction could be read at a website at the rate of $29.95 a month, all major credit cards accepted. In the Land of Cyberotica, thin businesswomen tied up burly computer programmers with power cords. College basketball players fucked perky cheerleaders at halftime as the bleachers swayed above them with the crowd's excitement.

Cyberotica paid exceptionally well, especially for such an easy task. Marca had never had writerly aspirations, and yet she had taken to it the way some people are able to get up on water skis their first try, or take apart and put back together car engines. Marca read a couple of stories and she got it. Just like that. Cyberotica opened for her like a repressed virgin after a glass of wine, to use the parlance of the genre.

Marca knew what attracted, what sold. Public places, for one: the threat and danger of discovery. Also, no one wanted to read about single people, but about those to whom sex was forbidden: nuns, teenagers, married men. Cyberotica was like a Chinese menu of copulation, with assembly instructions. Pick kinky or straight, then pick penetration or not, then pick a prop, or not, then insert part A into slot B and presto: prose porn is born.

After the computer was turned off, though, Marca imagined herself cocooned within a womb of suburban security: married, a large house somewhere with lots of land, a foreseeable future. Was this the paradox of the new millennium, that being tied up was socially acceptable, but wanting to be tied down was somehow deviant? How ironic, to have a common marital fantasy she could admit to no one but herself, while her uncommon sexual fantasies were all over the web, spreading like something spilled.

In the Land of Cyberotica . . .
Elizabeth Farmwell, federal prosecutor, sat at her desk, her Blahnik high heels resting on the leather blotter. She was getting hungry. For lunch? Or for . . . ? Impulsively, she reached her hand into her silk blouse, where she liked to play with her gold chains while reading briefs. She wound them around her fingers, pulling tightly then releasing. She pulled and released again, and her stomach contracted in a way she knew wasn't hunger pangs.
She reached over and hit the intercom. "Dominic, can you come take a letter?"
Dominic stood in the doorway to her office. He was the best assistant she'd ever had—competent, enthusiastic, ambitious. She had hired him after hearing that he'd won the Mr. Universe pageant the previous year and was hoping to jumpstart a modeling career here in New York. Elizabeth had taken one look at his bulging biceps, his solid rear, and the mouthwatering bulge in his tight pants and hired him for personal as well as professional assistance. Young as he was, he did require some training, but he was a passionate learner.
"You needed me?" He held a steno pad in front of his chest.
"Oh yes," she responded. "I needed you." She spread her legs on her desk, revealing the hairless pink flesh beneath her skirt. She never wore underwear.
"Ah," Dominic breathed out. She noticed he lowered the notepad to hide his growing dick. "I think I see the problem."
"It needs a man's touch," Elizabeth purred.
Dominic put the notepad and pencil on the desk and walked behind it, spinning Elizabeth's chair. He knelt down in front of her and kissed his way up her inner thigh. He was not much of a teaser; he got right down to business, licking and sucking on her clit, his whiskers tickling her labia, until she cried out and snapped her legs around his head.

When she had calmed, he stood up and began to unzip his pants.

"No," she said. "I have too much work to do."

"But," Dominic protested. "You can't leave me like this. Will you at least watch me while . . ." His voice trailed off as he rubbed his thick dick. It was wider than any Elizabeth had ever seen, stubby and dark. It took him only a few pumps until he shot into the garbage can, on top of opposing counsel's threatening letter.

Today's Doctors Without Borders book club, once it finally got started, was particularly verbally violent. Healers played rough after hours, attacking each other's opinions with vehemence usually reserved for cable television. Marca found herself entering the fray only when fully armed with rhetoric. Normally she bolstered herself with Giorgio's tacit encouragement beneath her chair, his chronic detachment reminding her that really, it was just a book discussion group and not a fight to the death. But tonight he had switched camps, remaining not just near newbie Peter but next to him on the settee, where he knew he wasn't allowed. He looked at her with defiance, his ears pinned back on his head, his haunches quivering beneath Peter's stroking.

"To me, Hassan represented a certain purity that the narrator would have liked to achieve," said Artie. He was Marca's favorite in the club; literary, self-censoring, and smart.

Everyone began to talk at once. Marca held up her hand, a conductor instructing the wind section to pause while the violins turned their pages. "Sam?"

"I just wanted to say it's cheap, in my opinion, for an author to use a physical deformity like that just to make the poor schmuck sympathetic."

Marca sighed. She felt the same way, to tell the truth. She had hated *The Kite Runner*. But all the book clubs wanted to read it: the Homos Hot for Hemingway, the Syracuse University grads, the Jews, the New Mommies, the Architects, et cetera. Marca had discussed the book with nine of her ten clubs.

Really, no modern book deserved to be dissected like this. It crumbled under the scrutiny. The blatant metaphors, the faux suspense, the cheesy, cheesy ending . . . It was like a magic show seen twice—the misdirect no longer works.

Peter the early bird spoke up. "Granted, I'm not in plastics, but isn't that a fairly simple operation?" His voice dripped with condescension for the plastic surgeons.

The room exploded into protests: medical care wasn't available in 1970s Afghanistan, the deformity was symbolic, you can't judge fiction by realist standards, in fact, cleft palate surgery was much more complicated and dangerous than it seemed . . .

To calm the outburst, Marca consulted her list of questions quickly to find one tangentially related. "In what ways do you think Hassan contributed to his own fate?"

As the fighting ground to a halt, the last man standing metaphorically rent and bloody, they began to leave to go back to their homes in Westchester or Cobble Hill, back to their waiting drivers or wives or girlfriends. Peter cornered her near the bookcase.

"Do you have any other book clubs?" he asked.

"Um, yes," Marca said. She tried to glean whether he was trying, incompetently, to ask her out, but his face was opaque, impassive, advertising soap or ice cream or tire sealant.

"Can I join them?" He seemed eager, little lines extending from his pursed mouth.

"We're discussing the same book," she said. "I don't think you'd want to . . ." Still, Marca felt a small thrill, tempered by a touch of annoyance at his awkward approach.

"Do you have one Thursday?" he insisted.

She nodded. "The Former Fatties. They're from—"

He didn't seem to care. "See you then." He waved to the dog before leaving.

Missive from the Land of Cyberotica:
Dear Mrs. Conanski: A few edits on this most recent installment. On page three, it's unclear which of the women is wearing the strap-on. Do you think you could write it so that both are getting penetrated? Perhaps one could straddle the other, and the one on top could insert the prosthetic manually?

Also, it has been our experience that readers dislike panty hose, even if they are ripped off quickly. Can she wear thigh-highs on page seven? Perhaps Dominic can roll them down? On page nine, where did she get the silk ties?

All best, Mr. Ramis

Her editor, Mr. Ramis, insisted on a last-name basis. He wrote overly formally (calling her "Mrs. Conanski," though Marca hadn't said she was married), as though she might one day wreck his home if he weren't careful. His attitude was understandable, even excusable; online everybody was dominatrix-thin with long hair, unquenchable libidos and late 1960s (post-pill, pre-AIDS) attitudes. It made sense that he would fear her. Online was nothing like reality, with its mores, codes, and standards; its cellulite and farts and inevitable disappointment.

On Thursday, Peter was again the first to arrive, which was awkward for Marca. She didn't know how to explain to the Former Fatties that he had invited himself to join their group. They were insular in a way that few groups were, having met in the semi-confessional setting of a Weight Watchers meeting. Marca was under strict orders to serve only vegetables and low-fat ranch dressing. Peter glanced at the food on his way in, grabbed a carrot stick, and forewent the dip to sit on the settee.

Marca was confused. If he were wooing her, he was doing a particularly inept job at it. She realized abruptly that she should probably never have allowed him to crash the book club. But she supposed he wasn't doing any harm; surely she could find a way to explain his presence to the

Fatties. She should find it flattering. After all, everyone knew how doctors could be completely terrible at human interaction. Obviously he liked her and didn't know how to tell her. It would make a good story, she imagined—how he stalked her various book clubs, and after, they became a couple.

Giorgio bounded up to him as though he were made of beef jerky. She hadn't seen her dog so animated in months. He licked and ran in circles and licked some more. He piddled a bit on the floor in his excitement, like a puppy, and Marca, embarrassed as though she were the one who had lost control, brought over a paper towel to clean it up. During the book club, Peter said nothing, but both he and Giorgio stared at her. Though she knew she must be imagining it, their simultaneous gaze looked suspiciously like the way a prisoner will stare at his captor.

On Wednesday mornings, Marca went for a walk with her friend Daye and their two dogs. Daye was an actress of a certain age to which she would never admit but Marca put at around fifty, if the permanent surprise (sure sign of Botox indulgence) and wrinkled hands were a sign. She had long brown hair she wore nearly to her waist, and she painted her eyes into wide circles. Daye's dog was a miniature spaniel named Buppy, whose hair was also too long, and a bit stringy from running through puddles.

Daye's most important role had been as Woody Allen's girlfriend in one of his early films. She had a dozen lines, which she delivered in a breathy, little-girl voice. She was surprisingly funny, Marca found, having Netflixed the film soon after meeting her. Surprising because she had very little sense of humor in person. Marca referred to her in private as "Humorless Daye." She thought that perhaps this failure was endemic in all actors. You have to take yourself seriously to be an artist; acting didn't admit introspection. It was all about out-trospection.

What Marca liked best about Daye was her dog. He was friendly but not pushy; he wasn't afraid to poke fun at himself, feigning fear at aggressive squirrels and pretending that garbage was eternally new. Marca supposed her feelings about Buppy weren't so different from the way people felt about spouses: if a mediocre person landed a fantastic partner, well, there must be something about that person that she had failed to see. A person could be elevated by the company who chooses her.

Today, Giorgio had greeted Daye and Buppy listlessly, going through the motions of sniffing the other dog's butt, but Marca could tell his heart wasn't in it. She was a little worried about him. He'd been depressed, leaving his food in the bowl as though forgetting about it, moping around from room to room. "Settle down," she'd told him. And, although he sat obediently, his tail thumped the ground in impatience.

They walked along the East River. It had suddenly turned cold after an Indian summer and Marca should have been wearing one more layer. Daye, a cold-blooded specimen, wore long sleeves even on the hottest day. Today she had on a long cardigan on top of a turtleneck. Over both she wore a large hand-knit scarf wrapped around her thin neck dozens of times.

"I think someone likes you," Daye sang, after Marca told her about Peter.

"He won't really talk to me. I don't understand it." Marca smiled, though. Men liked her infrequently enough that she still felt lucky when it happened, a grown-up version of being picked first for kickball.

"Men are strange," Daye said.

"True that," Marca echoed. Privately, Marca thought Daye fairly strange as well. And Peter was *definitely* strange, though on paper he seemed so normal. He held down a prestigious job, and the other doctors seemed to admire him. She wasn't particularly attracted to him . . . but she wasn't repulsed either. She should give him a chance. Who was she to judge what was normal, having just penned a scene for men who got off on dwarves?

Marca carried a leash when she walked Giorgio—
not because he needed one, but because the police liked to
earn a bit of extra revenue by handing out unleashed-dog
tickets to the tune of $75. When Giorgio saw a man in
blue, he always hustled right over to Marca, who clipped the
leash to his collar.

But today a pair of cops was approaching them and
Giorgio was not by her side. The male officer was lanky,
his female partner fleshy, as though they were caricatures
instead of actual law enforcement.

"That your dog?" the tall one said.

Marca looked at her leash, as though astonished that
Giorgio had run away. This had worked before.

The woman gave her a look that made Marca examine
her shoes like a child. "Yes," she admitted. "Giorgio, come!"

The dog was studying something on the ground
intently. He didn't look up. What was he staring at? Marca
wondered. He seemed almost stoned, intent upon decon-
structing the blade of glass, or more likely something
recently deceased.

"Giorgio!" she called again, sharper.

"Ma'am," the tall cop said, "I'm going to have to
issue you a citation." The words seemed so canned that they
triggered in Marca a standard-issue fantasy of fucking the
cop on a park bench looking out over the East River. She
tried to rid her mind of the image. She had to stop doing this.

"He's coming right now," Marca said. Finally, Giorgio
looked her way and began to walk leisurely toward her. He
loped a bit. She wondered if he were sick. A bird flew overhead and Giorgio stopped and looked up, wonder in his eyes
as if he'd never seen a bird before.

"What's wrong with him?" the tall cop asked.

"Acting like a lovesick teenager," the female cop chuckled.

"I'm going to take him to the vet," Marca said. "He's
not himself."

"I'm still going to have to issue you that citation.
Can I see some ID?"

"Come on, Gabe. The woman's going to have a vet bill too. Forget it."

"But—" the cop started. Then, ashamed of his lack of mercy, he stopped. They resembled nothing so much as an old married couple: Jack Sprat and his wife who between the two of them licked the platter clean.

"Keep him on a leash, lady," the female cop said. "You don't want to lose him." And they continued past Daye and Marca and their canines.

"What was that?" Daye asked. "What's up?" She had remained silent throughout the whole interaction.

Marca looked down at Giorgio. He was sitting at her feet, still, looking wistfully out over the gray river toward an equally gray Brooklyn skyline. He sighed.

In the Land of Cyberotica . . .

Elizabeth arrived at the Ritz in time to meet up with Officer O'Malley, who was surveying the scene. Elizabeth was no stranger to crime scenes; still, the sight of a corpse, fresh blood, and the disheveled suite made her draw a sharp breath.

Officer O'Malley took out his steno pad and read off the particulars. "The victim: female Caucasian, between 25 and 30 years of age, rap sheet typical, prostitution, solicitation, minor possession. Appears to have died of erotic asphyxiation."

"Poor lamb," Elizabeth sighed.

"You all right, miss?" Officer O'Malley asked.

"I—I think so," she said.

"Why don't I walk you downstairs?" As they left the hotel room Elizabeth noticed one important clue: if the killer had strangled the victim with the belt of a robe, where was the robe?

In the elevator, O'Malley's radio buzzed with unintelligible voices, and he turned the volume down. "Sorry," he said.

"That's OK," she said.

"A pretty woman like you shouldn't have to see something like that." His eyes sparkled with mischief. He was good looking, Elizabeth had not failed to notice, and, unlike some of the policemen she knew, this one skipped the donut shop for the

gym. He was tall, and less compact than Dominic, with graceful limbs and a wide grin.

"I may be pretty, but I'm used to crime." Elizabeth flirted back, taking a step toward him.

With one motion, he pinned her against the elevator wall, hitting the "emergency stop" button with his free hand. He nipped at her lips once, then planted his mouth on hers for a long kiss, his tongue dancing in her mouth. He ground his hips into hers to match the motion of his tongue, and she felt the hardness of his long, strong cock and knew her nipples must be betraying a similar attraction.

He unzipped his pants and she caught just the quickest glance at an uncut, eight-inch-long cock curving slightly outward, crimson with arousal. Then he pushed up inside her, hitting her cunt just where she needed him to. She came so quickly it must have seemed like she hadn't had sex in years. She came once more as he did, gasping and grabbing her ass.

A voice came over the elevator speaker: "Emergency response. Everything OK in the elevator?"

"Fine," O'Malley called, wiping his spent organ on the tail of his shirt and tucking it into his standard-issue blue pants. "Just hit the button by accident." He smiled at Elizabeth, wondering if she'd caught the double entendre.

From the Land of Fetish Cyberotica . . .

A secret so deep that not even Daye knew: Marca's secret identity had a secret identity—fetish cyberotica. This was the legacy of the internet's long tail, that even niche markets had niche markets had niche markets, fun-house mirrors of specificity. More lucrative than facilitating book clubs, more lucrative than porn, fetish paid up to four dollars a word. Of course, writing it taxed a part of Marca's brain she didn't want to believe existed. But she imagined, whether true or just to make herself feel better, that everyone had this secret part of his or her brain, the part that could imagine the repulsive, deviant, unsavory (not to mention unsanitary) proclivities her fictional characters indulged in.

Forget homosexuality. Gay porn was so banal it paid even less than straight porn. Forget waterworks and S and M and B and D and S and D. Forget Furries, Babies, Bears. There were worlds of sexual behavior that went unexplored by the mainstream population: beastiality, gerontophilia, abasiophilia, somnophilia, and the worst—cybersnuff. Marca got no sexual pleasure out of it, and the idea that it was inside her mortified and scared her. What kind of a person was she, who could imagine someone treating a dog that way? "It's just words," Daye had said once about her regular cyberotica gig. "It's not like you're filming X-rated movies." This had not comforted her. Words were worse than film, more powerful. Words were sacred.

She had to stop. But each time she tried, they sent her new assignments, upping the amount they'd pay her. So she'd write around the scenes, getting in as much adverbiage as possible until she could no longer postpone the graphic details, her wrists poised above the keyboard so as not to sully them. Marca wondered if by writing fetish porn she made herself one of them, the perverts; if she was complicit in their sexual deviance. Usually, though, as repulsive as she found it, she considered penning porn as a sort of charitable activity. She felt sorry for the poor freaks who had to resort to imagining paraplegics being sodomized to get their rocks off. *There but for the grace of God . . .* her grandmother used to say. She understood the shame of having what you want be utterly unavailable to you. She sympathized with her imagined audience, felt the solidarity of the marginalized. And it wasn't that bad, really. Typing the graphic scenes was like cleaning toilets. Not pleasant, but hold your nose and get to it and it will all be over soon.

Peter came to two more book clubs. He obviously hadn't read *The Red Tent* or *Dry Manhattan*, and he didn't pretend to participate in the conversation. Not that he could have gotten a word in edgewise in the Jewish Women's group, but had he been so inclined, he might have held forth during the silences that plagued the Merrill Lynch M&A group. Instead he sat with Giorgio, stroking his back and murmuring to him.

Peter treated Marca as he might a doorman, or a chaperone at the school dance. He was polite, but he placed her in some sort of category that didn't require him to get to know her in any way. Though Daye still insisted that he *must* be interested in her if he kept showing up at her apartment, Marca began to suspect that he viewed book clubs as a way to meet women, but that *she* was not the woman he wanted to meet.

Whenever Peter was over, Giorgio sat as straight as an aristocrat on the settee, tail curled underneath him as though waiting for his portrait to be painted. He didn't sigh impatiently or twitch dog tics. And when Peter left, Giorgio sat listlessly, hiding behind the piano for hours so silently that Marca wondered if he'd run away. His preference for Peter was devastating. How could he like a stranger more than her? More than the person who raised him? Unless he was trying to send her signals, tell her that Peter was the right man for her; that someday, eventually, they could all live together in mutual ownership. It was possible, she thought. He was a very smart dog.

The book clubs broke for the holiday season. Peter lingered after the last book club (he was coming over nearly every night, and still Marca knew almost nothing about him). Marca thought that perhaps at last he was gathering the courage to ask her out, but when she stood with her "available" look on her face—open, smiling, but not too widely—he merely wished her a happy holiday season and left. He was obviously pathologically shy, to the point of near absurdity. She considered calling after him, asking if he wanted to stay for a drink, but he disappeared down the steps so fast she didn't have time to make up her mind.

Marca went to Daye's ex-husband's apartment for Thanksgiving and had too much to drink. She was supposed to bring Giorgio, but he refused to leave the house, sitting down and scratching his nails on the wood floor as she tried to pull him by his collar. Eventually she decided that if he didn't want to go he didn't have to. But she would let Daye take the drumstick home for Buppy instead of keeping it for Gio. Two could play at that game, she thought, annoyed.

On the way over, she passed a mounted policeman whose horse was swinging its neck back and forth as though looking for something to entertain it, while the cop watched a football game through the window of a bar from his saddle perch. Marca remembered suddenly when Giorgio was a puppy. He'd been pulling on the leash, a toddler testing the boundaries of his independence, and was confidently sniffing everything, peeing on every pole and sign, his tail straight with bravado. And then a police horse snorted, and the dog practically leapt into her arms, trembling with fear and sticking his snout in her armpit. That's when she had really fallen in love with Giorgio, with his need for her. That's when his dependence seemed like a gift rather than a burden.

She told the assembled Thanksgiving guests about her strange radiologist boyfriend, who kept coming over to her house to pet her dog, in such a way that it garnered laughs.

Daye said, "Well, he's not really your boyfriend, Marca."

Marca blushed too suddenly to calm herself. "I know," she said. "It's just . . ."

"I mean, you haven't even kissed the guy, let alone been on a date with him."

"I know," Marca said, her voice betraying anger at Daye's willingness to embarrass her, when she was the one who kept insisting that Peter liked her. "I know he's not my boyfriend. It was just to make it funnier."

The room fell silent then in the way that parties can sometimes lull, and the words reverberated through the living room where they were eating. Daye's ex-husband's new girlfriend, embarrassed, played with her necklace, a large, flat, polished piece of marble with fool's gold veins encircled by pressed tin. It looked to Marca a little vaginal in design.

"OK," Daye said. "I just wasn't sure if you really did think you were going out with him."

"No," Marca whispered hoarsely, concentrating on her placemat.

The girlfriend cleared her throat. "Pumpkin pie," she announced. "From that bakery on 7th Street. Who's ready?"

Marca stood up to help her clear the plates. She felt the pressure of tears rise in her throat and realized that on some level Daye was right. She *had* been thinking about Peter as her boyfriend, her future boyfriend who just hadn't quite happened yet. In her mind, they were already arguing over who would walk Gio on cold nights. She realized it was precisely because she didn't know him that he had catapulted into her subconscious. As a character she'd invented, she could mold him into the boyfriend she wanted. If she were really dating him, he would most likely disappoint. She was becoming an adept liar—lying about her job, lying about sex, and now lying to herself.

The doorbell rang in early December. Marca had been going through her files, readying her receipts for tax preparation and the piles on the floor were designated by a system she kept confusing. She had thought it might be Daye; she kept calling to apologize to Marca's voicemail for the scene at Thanksgiving. But when Marca pulled the door open, she was not that shocked to find Peter standing there. He grinned grimly and looked over her shoulder. Was it possible that he had finally come to declare romantic interest?

"Hi," he said. "I was wondering, I mean, I know this is strange, but—There he is!"

Giorgio, having heard Peter's voice, came bounding out of the bedroom, tail wagging and body heaving with excitement. The reunion that ensued was almost pornographic in its intimacy. Marca had to avert her eyes, and felt a strange sense of jealousy, as though she had been confronted with the evidence of a lover's infidelity.

Face licked, Giorgio planted firmly against his left leg, Peter stood. "Can I take him out for a walk?"

Marca looked at the settee as though the answer might be written on it. The faded rose velvet revealed nothing. "Sure," she said. "Let me get my boots on."

Peter let out a small gasp. He recovered quickly, opening his eyes widely. "I mean, I thought maybe I could just take him out."

Marca paused. He wanted to take her dog out, without her? "It's not a big deal," she said, "my boots are right here."

Peter's face fell with disappointment. "I wouldn't want you to, I mean . . ."

Suddenly, Marca understood. He wanted to take her dog. Her *dog*, not her. Marca felt her face turn red in response. She couldn't possibly be this desperate that she had to resort to men who preferred her dog's company to her own. All of Peter's oddities that she had dismissed as timidity revealed themselves suddenly as mere preferences for Giorgio. How dare he?

"I don't think that's such a good—" she began, but stopped. If she refused, she would look hurt or disappointed; she would reveal to Peter that all along she had been waiting, expecting him to ask her out. It would be obvious that she was a chump; a sad, lonely dupe. And then Giorgio whined with an excitement so intense she felt it in her chest. Fine, let them go for a walk. It wasn't like she wanted to trudge through the melting slush to let him pee.

"OK," she said. "For how long?"

"I'd like to take him to meet my nephews. Is that OK?"

So Giorgio was going to meet the family. Marca felt suddenly like she wanted to cry. This felt so wrong. How come her relationships were so fucked up, so deviant from the romantic norm? She wanted to tell him that he should take *her* to meet the in-laws, that she would be the best girlfriend he ever had, if he had ever *had* a girlfriend. But it was too late. Instead, she said, "Don't let him eat any people food."

She held the curtain back and watched Giorgio and Peter climb into an Audi across the wet street. He rolled down the window a crack for the dog and buckled him in, the way a good suitor would. Then he leaned over to ruffle and kiss Giorgio's ears, started the car and drove carefully toward the west side.

Marca went back to her piles, but the organization, once nebulous, was now completely impenetrable. She felt her throat tighten. The tears fell onto a taxi receipt, smearing the cheap ink.

Marca sobbed on the floor for a few minutes until she felt more silly than comforted. She washed her face. She was hungry, she realized. In the refrigerator was a package of parmesan cheese and three Zimas, some olives and very old spinach. There was also a half-empty can of gourmet dog food. She put on her coat and went downstairs to the bar/restaurant on the corner.

Normally, Marca didn't spend time in bars by herself. She was not the kind of person who hung out sipping chardonnay, not caring if anyone was looking or not looking. She was more the kind of person who put on NPR and curled up with her dog and a good book. But she figured that around the holidays it was perfectly acceptable for a woman to go out alone to have a glass of wine and a burger and get out of her thoughts.

The bar was warm, even stuffy, after the cold outdoors, and Marca slumped onto a bar stool, taking out her magazine. On the jukebox, Patsy Cline sang Christmas songs, while the television broadcast silent basketball. Marca ordered wine and scanned the menu, then looked around the room. At the bar sat several singles, watching the game. The booths were filled with couples and couples of couples, but there was nothing particularly obnoxious about them, no guffawing or singing, no making out or goo-goo eyes.

Her chardonnay arrived and Marca toasted the air. It wasn't bad for a bar chardonnay, drinkable. Behind her she heard the bar door open, the whoosh of air sucked out onto the street and the quick brush of cold wind as the door closed. A man came over to a stool near Marca and took off his coat, putting his gloves and hat in his pocket.

His spindly profile looked familiar, and Marca recognized him as the cop from the park a couple of months ago. She felt her face grow hot, though she knew he couldn't have guessed her fantasy. Her subconscious was not nearly as opaque as she feared. He turned, feeling her gaze, and stared, narrowing his eyes as though trying to place her.

"East River Park, a couple of months ago, the unleashed dog."

He stared at her blankly. She continued, "Your partner said he acted like a lovesick teenager."

"Right," he said, his face relaxing now that he remembered. "Did you take him to the vet?"

"He couldn't find anything wrong."

"Oh," he said. "You mind?" He scooted down to the bar stool near her. He seemed nice enough, and she hadn't gotten dressed and gone out to sit alone. He ordered a Seven and Seven, her mother's old drink, which made her smile. When he got it he sipped, blocking the ice with his lips. She noticed the thin gold band around his finger.

"It's not like that," he said, following her eyes. "I come for one drink after my shift, calm down. You see some crazy shit, pardon the expression."

"Pardoned," Marca said.

"I mean, it's not all unleashed dogs. Today, for example, got a call to check out an apartment in Alphabet City. Old guy, and no one's seen him for a couple of days, mailman says the box is full of disability checks, so, you know something happened. Do you mind my telling you this?"

"No," Marca said. "It's kind of interesting." She was gathering the seeds of a new story. Cops were always sexy . . . Replace old guy in Alphabet City with hot chick in Grammercy and the scenario might be perfect.

"Good, because my wife hates it when I *bring it home*, as she says. She's just sick of it, after all these years. Four more till I got my twenty. We retire at twenty years."

Marca had her head in her glass of wine, so she said, "Hmmm" in acknowledgement.

"And Pattie's on maternity leave as of last week, so I don't got anyone to talk to." His partner had been pregnant, Marca realized, not "fleshy." She had to stop thinking of people in terms of their potential for cyberporn. "They stuck me with some guy who's like a mute or something. Can barely get his coffee order out. Anyway, I knock on this old guy's door, the crowd of neighbors like there always is. No one ever around when someone needs help, no one knows the guy's name, but when there's something kind of sinister it's, like, take a number."

"I don't know my neighbors' names, and I've lived in the same apartment practically my whole life," Marca admitted.

"Yeah, well," the policeman said. "You want me to go on?" He sounded a bit annoyed, as though she had interrupted him. "So I knock, there's no answer. I go around to the fire escape and try to look in the windows which haven't been cleaned in like fifty years, and I think I see, I dunno, shoes or feet or something, so I have the landlord let me in. And . . . are you sure you're ready for it?"

"I'm sure it's no worse than something I could imagine," Marca said, thinking of the necrophilia story from two weeks ago.

"Guy was in there all right, dead about a week, with that sick, sweet odor, but the thing was, the entire floor—it was a small apartment, but I mean the entire floor—was littered with gay porn mags. The really gross ones, with little boys and whips and assholes and there was like a carpet of these things. A foot, foot and a half deep. I couldn't fucking believe it. I'd never seen so many of those things."

"Yikes," Marca said. She worried that if someone looked at her hard drive after she'd died, it might look like two feet of porn.

"The only furniture was a folding chair and a milk crate and one of those TV/VCR combos and a stack of fifty tapes with names like "Up Your Butt Part III" or whatever. Poor asshole. Can you imagine him alone there, eighty years old, all that porn? I shudder."

"Yeah," Marca said. "Ughh." And by suggestion she shuddered involuntarily.

"Sorry," the cop said. "I didn't even get your name."

"Marca."

"That's a weird name." Marca knew that when people said that they wanted her to explain how she got it, but Marca didn't want to, so she just smiled and nodded as though she agreed that it was, indeed, a strange name.

"And what do you do, Marca?"

"I lead book clubs."

"Oh, a smart one," he said. She could see him lean back in his chair a bit. Men often did this when she admitted to reading and discussing books for a living, as though she would no longer be an interesting companion, or that she might judge them for their lack of literariness.

"Well, I'm having guy troubles," she volunteered, emboldened by the wine.

He nodded.

"He took my dog to meet his nephews. I didn't even know he had nephews." She was a little drunk. She should either drink more often or never drink; as it was, she was a cheap date. "It feels like I'm breaking up with someone. I mean, the dog likes him better than he likes me."

"Who, the guy?"

"No, I mean, the dog likes the guy—never mind."

"So what are you gonna do?" the cop finished his drink and motioned to the bartender to hit him with another. Marca envied people's ability to communicate so effortlessly. She felt that when she tried a gesture like that it was usually misunderstood, met with a quizzical glance that so embarrassed her she was then unable to articulate what she had meant. "What's that old saying? If you love something, set it free?"

"You know," Marca said. "For every one of those old sayings, there's another one that's completely the opposite."

"Well," the cop said. "Opposites attract."

In the Land of Cyberotica . . .

Elizabeth Farmwell, federal prosecutor, struggled futilely against the hard, scratchy ropes that bound her to the cane chair. "Ouch!" she cried. "Let me go!"

Her captor merely laughed.

"You'll pay for this, you hear?" she said. She was determined not to cry, though a lump of despair had gathered in her chest and was moving up her windpipe. It was matched by a similar fire moving in the opposite direction. How had her captor known she was so aroused by being tied up? She twisted and felt her swollen ankle ache.

Even if she did manage to escape her restraints, how would she make it back to civilization? She no longer had the car keys. In fact, she wasn't wearing much of anything—just a simple slip, she noticed, her nipples erect with cold and fear. He must have undressed her while she was unconscious.

Her captor moved near her. He had a musty smell she recognized, covered by a faint floral scent. He took her face roughly in his strong, gloved hand. "And to think I used to find you beautiful," he said. "Enough to try to let you live. I warned you off the case, Elizabeth."

"That's Ms. Farmwell, Esquire to you, mongrel."

"You used to let me call you Elizabeth." And with that, he moved back and tore off his mask.

"You . . . ," she stammered. "But, how? Why?"

"Wow," he said, as she stepped aside to let him into the apartment. "You have a really big place."

"It was my grandmother's," she said. "Thank you, rent control."

He walked around, taking in the knickknacks, the pictures, the piano. "Do you play?" he asked.

She shook her head.

"There aren't that many books, for a book person."

Marca shrugged. She didn't know what to say. She had been surprised when the cop leaned over and kissed her in the bar, and she wasn't sure what to do with him now that he was here. She didn't know what they were doing except that she didn't want to be here alone without Giorgio. Peter had sent her a text: "traffic ☹ home w/ Gio L8." It took her a moment to translate the message; it seemed so juvenile.

He walked toward her and bent down to kiss her again. He tasted like whiskey, and smelled, while not bad, as though he'd worked a full day. She imagined, while kissing him, his treading through the pond of porn at the old man's apartment, the pages fluttering out from beneath his work boots, resting on top of one another in all their airbrushed, oiled, distorted, distended glory. Was that what her subconscious looked like? A wasteland of glossy pages, boot-prints of morality kicking a path through them?

She opened her eyes to find the cop staring over her head at the watercolor portrait of Giorgio that hung behind the easy chair. "That him?" he said.

"Yup," Marca said. "You notice a lot. It must be your policeman's eye."

She was attempting flirtation, but it must have sounded more like assumption because he responded, "Nah, I'm not a detective."

"You know," Marca said, "you never gave me *your* name."

"Gabe." He kissed her again, and they moved over to the settee where she lay on top of him. He tried to free his arm to put it around her and bumped her so that she put an elbow into his abdomen.

"Sorry."

"My fault," he said. He kissed her again, and then attempted to roll them over. Marca's head hit the armrest and thudded louder than it felt. "Ow," she said.

"Oops." They continued kissing. Marca's skirt had bunched in such a way that it made an uncomfortable lump against her lower back. He had sharp pelvic bones.

Abruptly, he closed his mouth and her tongue met only teeth. She pulled back, and he had closed his eyes in a grimace. "I have to go."

Marca felt the hot flush of embarrassment crowd her face. "You should go," she said, as though it were her idea, realizing as she said it that it was true that he should go, imperative even. She stood up and rolled her neck the way she was taught in her ergonomics seminar at the gym. Then she let it loll all the way around, which she was not supposed to do, feeling the vertebrae skid and pinch each other.

At the door he said, "I'm not—I don't—"

Marca held up her hand and looked at her feet. She was wearing old tennis shoes, the tops permanently raised where her big toes had resided all these years. She was ashamed, both because she had kissed another woman's husband and because he was ultimately the one who rejected her. She wanted to crawl into the space above the toe in her shoe; into the smelly, canvas darkness she deserved.

"Bye," he said.

When the doorbell rang again a minute later, she was sure it was Gabe, having forgotten something in her apartment, and she swept it quickly with her eyes before answering. But there at the door were Peter and Giorgio. The dog stood impatiently, jogging from foot to foot to foot to foot, tail wagging as though he were a puppy let out of a cage, so strongly that his entire hindquarters shook with joy.

Peter took off his hat and gloves and stood in the entryway. He cleared his throat. Instead of alleviating Marca's distress, she felt another wave, like nausea, overtake her.

"I don't know how to say this," he said, "without coming off like a nut, but your dog and I want to be together."

Marca nodded, stunned. "What?" she said. Then she laughed.

"I'm serious," Peter said. He stood ramrod straight in her doorway, his plastic face mocking her with its solemnity.

"But he's my dog," she said in a small voice.

"I understand that. But I think we need to revisit ideas of ownership. He may be a dog, but he's not your slave."

"Now wait," Marca said. She found herself offended at being compared to a slaveholder. Her indignation quickly turned to anger. "You can't just take someone's dog—"

"I just meant," Peter said, "that Giorgio and I have a chance to be really happy. Don't you want that for him?"

There was a long pause broken by the sound of a siren as it wound its way down the street. Marca looked at the dog. He was sitting politely, waiting patiently for a treat, trying not to beg. His ears formed small triangles as though he were straining to understand. How could she have been so blind? And Giorgio could never explain what she did, or didn't do, to make him fall out of love with her. There was no answer. She reached down to pet him, and it was the head of a stranger.

After the holidays, the Former Fatties met to discuss *The Poisonwood Bible*. "Are you all right?" Mitzi asked. "You let Ayelet go on about malaria for hours."

"I'm fine," Marca said. "The holidays." Usually if she merely stated the obvious, people discovered a hidden meaning that she hadn't intended.

"Oh, I know," Mitzi said. "I gained nine pounds this month. Nine. How can that even be possible? That's like three pounds a week. You couldn't do that if you tried."

The doctors noticed Giorgio's absence (though not Peter's) when they met to discuss *Complications*. "Where's the pooch?" one asked. Marca looked around as though he had to be somewhere in the apartment before she remembered that Giorgio and Peter were probably in some fancy dog run uptown, happy, together, in love.

And when Merrill Lynch sat down with their plates of sparkle cookies and non-alcoholic eggnog to rehash *Into the Wild*, she actually began to cry, hiding it in a coughing fit.

In the Land of Cyberotica . . .

"That's Ms. Farmwell, Esquire to you, mongrel."

"You used to let me call you Elizabeth." And with that, he moved back and tore off his mask.

"You . . . ," she stammered. "But, how? Why?"

Dominic shook his head, loosening his long hair. "It was the money. They knew too much. They became liabilities, just like you."

"All of it? A scam?"

"No," Dominic paused. "My affection for you was real, if unrequited. And when I saw that I couldn't have you, then the only thing left to want was money. Lots of it. And if you didn't love me, you could at least help me to that."

Elizabeth was shocked. She thought back to every time they had held each other, every time Dominic had tucked her hair behind her ears, every time he'd come to her rescue. She should have put it together. He took the robe after he used its belt to kill the prostitute. It was he that day in the abandoned warehouse, and it must have been he who pulled the alarm at the symphony gala. All that blood, all those lives . . .

"Don't," she pleaded. "I promise I'll never tell. I didn't mean it—"

"You have nothing to apologize for," said a voice. And Elizabeth turned her head to see Officer O'Malley pointing a revolver at Dominic. "You were just being a good investigator. He's the scum here."

Dominic laughed and pulled a .357 Magnum from his waist. Elizabeth screamed and closed her eyes, hiding her head in her shoulder. She heard gunfire, and the expelled gasp of one who is breathing his last.

"It's OK." She heard Officer O'Malley's lilting voice. "It's all over now."

"Is he . . . Is he dead?"

"I'm afraid so," Officer O'Malley said. "But I can't say I regret shooting him. I've been following you for a couple of days."

Elizabeth began to cry as the policeman untied her. "But I knew him. I thought I did."

"*Sometimes, it's the people you think you know best that you don't really know at all,*" he said. "*And the people you don't know at all that you really understand. And who understand you back.*"

He looked deep into Elizabeth's eyes. And in his eyes the prosecutor saw the kindness nestled there, the comfort of their dark blue, and she knew, as he picked her up and carried her over the corpse of her former lover, that she was home.

In the Land of Cyberotica, this is what passes for a happy ending.

SOMETIMES IT'S LIKE THAT

The first time I told Paul that I'd tried to commit suicide, he looked immediately at my wrists. That's how I knew he wasn't an imaginative soul, and I tried to think about how that would make me feel, being married to someone who thought first about the most obvious explanation, who looked for permanent traces. I decided that it wouldn't be so bad, and it hasn't been.

"Not like that," I said, when he looked at my wrists, which were supporting my head. "There are other ways, you know."

"I know," he said.

There was a silence. It was early, and the diner was almost empty.

"That means, statistically, I'm more likely to try it again." We were getting married in a week. It felt like something I should let him know before he said I *do*, something like HIV status that required full disclosure.

Paul's eyes narrow when he listens to you, as though he's squinting to see the words. His eyes are brown, like his hair. He chased some eggs around with a crust of toast. "I could drive my truck off a cliff," he said. "You could die of breast cancer." He wasn't really looking at me, but over my shoulder.

"Is that supposed to make me feel better?" I asked.

He put down his fork. "I hadn't really thought about it that way."

I met Paul at my best friend Betsy's wedding. Betsy and I were the last bachelorettes of our friends from high school. It was the first wedding I'd been to in a while that wasn't a shotgun. She'd been waiting for love and she found Dave James. One of the things I remember my daddy saying was "You can never trust a man with two first names," and he was right because Betsy's got two kids, and where is Dave James now she can't tell you.

Paul was driving the rig west and gave Dave James's best man (a cousin from the East Coast) a ride to the wedding. He had obviously borrowed the suit, because the pants were too short and they were bunched at the waist by a belt so much that they looked like they might fall down if he unbuckled it.

The wedding was at The Mutton Chops, a medieval theme restaurant where Betsy's mother worked. I'd helped Betsy with her hair, braided it back off her face and stuck in a few flowers I took from the head table.

My mother was there too, already not feeling too well and she said how beautiful Betsy was. "Isn't there something about being a bride that makes them all so beautiful?" And I had to agree that Betsy had a flush to her cheeks, and an excitement about her that made her look like a cover model. "I want to see you safely married before I die," she said.

"Oh, Mama," I said.

I danced a little with Dave James, who was shorter than I was, and with the best man, and then with Paul, who stuck his thumbs out when he danced like he was hitch-hiking. It made me laugh. He stood next to me during the picture and kissed my cheek. It didn't feel bad.

I took him home with me that night. I was in a stage where I did that a lot, and it was fine. I was surprised to see him there when Mama's phlegmy cough woke me up in the morning. They didn't usually stick around for a cup of coffee.

"I'm a sound sleeper," he explained.

And that was supposed to be the end of that. But I ran into him a month later at the Safeway. He was buying sandwiches and chips. I was buying Bayer. And it happened again.

This time he took me to breakfast. "Twice might be my record," I said.

He shrugged. "Are you gonna eat that?" He pointed with his fork at my sausage.

My brother Vince was on his way to Alaska, said the letter. He'd heard that canneries paid really good money, and he thought he'd go up there for a year or two and try to get rid of his credit card debt. There was only one problem, he said. There was this girl he was sleeping with, this Delia, and she wanted to come with him. He wasn't sure that was fair, because he didn't love her and knew he never would, but she loved him and wanted to come with, and he had heard that women were really scarce up there and what did I think?

I read the letter and sat down and thought about it. Paul was running a gig, so he wasn't around, and the small house echoed with the creaks of the wind. I was surprised my brother was thinking about ethics, and even more surprised he'd asked my opinion. I sat down on the stairs outside the house and smoked a cigarette and decided that she was presumably a big girl, and what I thought was that if Vince wanted her around, and she wanted to come with, then it didn't seem too smart to question was it fair or not. Mama probably would have answered differently. She was a romantic that way.

It became a routine of Paul's and mine to hang out whenever he passed through town. Mama was getting worse then, and I was glad for the company. Vince had moved downstate to try to get a job to pay for Mama's treatment. Paul never asked what was wrong with her. In fact, until he said that about him dying in a truck wreck or me dying of breast cancer, I wasn't sure he even knew.

Mama seemed to like him. If she was feeling all right she'd cook waffles in the morning. I could hear her banging the pots looking for the iron.

"Tamara," she called, "where did you put the waffle iron away last time?" which I knew was just a ploy to get me out of bed.

I helped her blend the mix with milk. Her secret was to add it a little at a time; it eliminated the bubbles and the waffles tasted lighter that way. She wanted to talk about sex.

"Do you like the way he does it? Because if not, I read about some ways to do it differently, in a magazine. Your father, he was the one with the magic hands, you know? Although I think it's all in how you feel about him. If you put in crazy, you'll get crazy out. Now, that bastard never could light my fire." She was talking about my stepfather, Karl, who we always called "that bastard." No one had seen him for years.

"It's all right," I said.

"Just all right?" Mama sat down at the table. She slumped forward slightly.

"Yeah," I said. I ladled the first waffle onto the iron and closed it. It hissed. "All right is about as good as it ever is." Paul was in the bathroom, and I knew he could probably hear our conversation.

"Poor baby," Mama said. It sounded like a complaint, like she was talking about herself.

"You in pain, Mama?" I asked.

"I'd like to see you married before I die. It takes practice, is all. Before I go. Paul's a nice boy. I'd like to go to your wedding."

"Oh, Mama," I said.

"Paul's a nice boy," she repeated. " I want to dance at my baby's wedding."

A week later, Paul proposed to me in front of the television in the living room. The credits to the movie we'd rented traveled up the screen. I accepted.

I was sitting on the front stoop, smoking with my eyes closed, like I often do at night. That way it feels like I'm the only person on the planet. When I heard a car coming, I ran into the house and stood by the window.

Vince and Delia parked their beat up VW Rabbit on the street. From where I was I could see him standing on the grass, waiting, then throwing his cigarette butt into the street while Delia opened the back door. A couple of dark bundles fell out, and Delia bent over, stuffing them back into the car. She was wearing shorts, and they rode up the back of her thighs. She was skinny, but flabby; the skin hung loosely, bagging at her knees. She riffled through the backseat and came up with an oversized leather tote. Together they walked toward the house.

I let Paul answer the door. "Hello," I heard him say. "How ya doing, Vincent?" And then, "You must be Delia. Come on in."

The three of them walked into the small living room. "Hey." I hugged Vince and shook Delia's hand. She had feathery bangs that framed her face and stuck out slightly. Vince seemed bigger than I remembered. He had grown a beard and let his hair go long, and the result was a little like an ungroomed dog. "Looking a little shaggy there, Vince," I couldn't help saying.

He smiled, embarrassed, and looked at Delia, who gave him a pointed look back. She still hadn't said anything. "Oh yeah," Vince said. "Hey, can Delia use your bathroom?"

"Sure," I said. "It's around the corner on the right," although Vince could have told her where it was, since this was the house he grew up in.

Delia followed my finger out of the room.

"So, good trip?" I said.

"Yeah . . . yeah," Vince said.

"You, uh, want a beer?" Paul asked.

"That'd be great."

"Does Delia want one too?" I asked.

"Sure," Vince said. "Yeah, Delia drinks beer."

Paul left to go get us drinks and there was a heavy silence. I don't see Vince very much, and he has a sort of adolescent awkwardness about him. It wears off after a while, like he's trying to test me to see if I'm really his sister.

"Alaska?" I said.

"There's supposed to be some good jobs up there. I heard from this guy who says you can make fifty, sixty thou a year there."

"They pay really well, huh?"

"It's that and there's nothing else to do up there. You work fifty, sixty hours a week, and there's nothing to spend your money on."

"Just wine, women, and song," I said. It was an old expression of our father's.

"Just that, yeah." Vince smiled and I saw him relax a little bit.

Delia came back. "That's better," she said. "I had to go since Alba, but Vince wouldn't let us stop."

"Christ," he said. "We were almost there."

Paul came in with four open beers. We each took one and I held it up.

"To family reunions," I said.

"Amen," said Vince, and we all took a long swig. For a while there was just the sound of us drinking. I saw Delia's eyes wander around the room, taking in Mama's furniture. I wondered what Vince had told her, how close they were. If she had an opinion about how the room was decorated, good or bad, she didn't let her face show it.

"How's the rig?" Vince asked.

"Oh, you know," Paul said. "Actually, business is pretty busy. We're doing a lot for that online bookstore, you know, and people are ordering a lot more."

"You're off this week?" Vince asked.

"I asked for it off, you know, to hang out with you all."

"Thanks," Vince said. "That's nice of you."

"You guys hungry or anything?" I asked.

Vince looked at Delia and then at me. "We ate on the road, but yeah, I'd take a snack."

"I have popcorn," I said. "Or stuff for nachos."

"Nachos'd be cool."

"I'll give you a hand." Delia followed me into the kitchen. I love my kitchen—it's the only room in the house that's mine and mine only. It's just the way Mama left it. I don't let anyone in it. Paul even has his own mini-fridge on the back porch where he keeps his beer and the ice packs that keep him awake on the road. I just started to let Betsy James come in, and she's my closest friend from way back, and I only let her in if she'll sit on the bar stool, still. But suddenly here was Delia, straight off the road and in my kitchen.

I swallowed once and opened the refrigerator, setting some shredded cheddar on the counter along with some salsa. Delia opened the bag of chips and arranged them on the cookie sheet I put out.

"So, have you guys been together long?" I asked.

"About a year," Delia said. "Did he tell you he doesn't love me?"

"Umm," I said, not wanting to betray my brother's confidence. "He talked about moving to Alaska."

"He's afraid if I come with that means we're serious."

"Oh," I said. "I didn't realize it was a sure thing."

"It's not," Delia said. She was struggling to open a can of refried beans. "I mean, I might just drive him up there and leave. It's my car."

"Oh," I said again. I was sprinkling the cheese on top of the chips so that each chip had a little teepee of cheddar.

"I just think he's scared," she continued. "If he let himself, he'd be crazy about me. I've asked him. He can't come up with one thing he doesn't like about me. It's just the idea of me he doesn't like."

"I don't know him that well," I said. "I've only seen him a couple of times since he's been an adult."

"Am I the first girl he's brought home?"

The word *home* struck me funny. I hadn't thought about it, but I guess Vince and I are the only family each other's got. "You seem very sweet," I said. "You know what you're doing."

"Exactly." Delia brushed her bangs out of her face with the back of her hand. She took the spatula I offered and let clumps of beans drop onto the tortilla chips. "That's what I keep telling him. Life's not a fucking movie, pardon my French."

"Did you ever see *September Noon?*" I asked. Delia shook her head. "Well, sometimes it's like that, but you can't count on it."

That night through the wall that separated Paul's and my bedroom from the guest room, I could hear Delia and Vince make love. It wasn't exactly the sounds of sex I heard; there were no squeaking springs or grunts and moans, but rather an absence of noise, as though they were trying to be quiet. I could hear the rustling of sheets as they rearranged themselves, and then a small gasp followed by a stifled giggle.

I sat up in bed. Paul was sound asleep next to me. He always snores after a couple of beers. His noises were rhythmic and slow, and then he held his breath. I waited. He did this sometimes—sleep apnea it's called, I read it in a magazine. But still, every time, as ten seconds turned into twenty and twenty into thirty, I wondered and worried that he might never breathe again. And a couple of times, I'm ashamed to admit, I let myself think about what I would do if Paul died, if the silence that reigned when Paul was on the road were complete and permanent. If the loneliness that was alleviated by his presence would take over. Just a couple of times.

That night I watched as his mouth twitched slightly, taking in no air, as though directed by some inner puppet strings; I half thought I'd be able to see the breath when he took it. But of course he gasped at last, drew in air noisily through his mouth, and rolled over onto his side away from me, which stopped the snores, and left the house silent.

The next day was Sunday. Betsy James had worked as a 411 operator long enough to get weekends off, so she brought over Clark and Tanya early to see Vince. He and Betsy James had been friendly when we were all in high school. She was the only one who treated my brother like an equal instead of a bratty little brother. Vince and Paul were taking Clark fishing.

"Go get your stuff, little man," said Paul. "This truck is rolling out."

"Can we count on fish for dinner?" I asked, going through recipes in my mind that would hide the fishy taste of the seafood.

Vince looked skeptical. "Are the trout running for sure?" he asked.

"Oh yeah," said Paul. "Definitely. Last week, I pulled out three in an hour. Had to throw two back because I'd already fished my limit."

Clark came bounding back into the room. He had a miniature fishing rod and a hat with a wide brim.

"Put sunscreen on him," Betsy James said.

"Sure thing," said Paul, and he leaned over to kiss me quickly on the lips. "See you tonight."

"Bye," I said. Delia was standing a little in front of me, looking at the floor and playing with her fingers.

"Bye." Vince looked back as they all turned around, and he made a cutting motion across his neck which meant *Buy a lot of potatoes 'cause we're not bringing back enough for dinner.*

When the men had gone, Betsy James let Tanya slide to the ground. The little girl ran to the front door and pounded on it a few times before falling to sit and suck her thumb.

"There. Now the menfolk are gone," Betsy James said.

The three of us looked at each other expectantly. Since Dave James left, Betsy and I spent most days together. At night she was a telephone operator for directory assistance. Over the years, she had amassed an encyclopedia-like knowledge of states and their random cities. She knew What Cheer was in Iowa, and that No Name was a town in Colorado. We'd just go about our business together. I'd clean the kitchen or do Paul's laundry; Betsy'd play with the baby or darn Clark's jeans, or watch soap operas. We always watched *Jeopardy* together at 4:00—unless Paul was home, in which case Betsy James stayed away until he'd left again.

Not that they didn't get along, but there was some tension between them that no one ever addressed. I think Betsy James was jealous, in a way. Not that she wanted Paul for a husband, but that I had one who stuck around, and we didn't even have kids to glue us together. Maybe Paul felt sort of responsible or embarrassed about Dave James's leaving her, although he only knew Dave's cousin, not Dave, and then even as an acquaintance, not a friend. And maybe Paul saw something in Betsy James that he gave up when he settled with me. I try not to think about what that is.

But in front of us right now was Delia. Neither of us knew what to do with a third person, someone we had to entertain.

"Ma-ma," Tanya said from her post next to the door. And then came a volley of syllables that I couldn't understand.

"Not now, honey," Betsy James said.

The baby responded by bursting into a wail. Betsy sighed and put down her glass of water. "Excuse me, ladies," she said and went over and picked Tanya up. She stopped crying immediately and buried her head in Betsy's shoulder.

"Shh, shhh," Betsy said. "That wasn't a helicopter." She smiled. "She's been afraid of helicopters ever since Clark told her something or other about them. Somebody's a little tired, huh?" She looked down at the baby hidden in her arms. "I'm just going to go put her down, OK?"

I nodded. Betsy left. I looked at Delia. She was neater this morning. She'd put on makeup, but one eye had more eyeliner on than the other, and her lipstick extended above her upper lip.

"I'm, uh, going to go clean out the kitchen cupboards," I said. Delia followed me.

Betsy James came in behind her. "Kid went out like a light. Whatcha doing?" She eyed Delia in my kitchen suspiciously.

"I'm going to clean the cabinets today," I said. "Before we go to the grocery store."

"All right," said Delia. "We'll help."

I took the plates down carefully and started on the glasses while Betsy James wet a rag in the sink and stood on a chair to reach the insides of the upper cabinets. Delia stood a little behind her, watching.

"So," Betsy James said. "You're Vincent's girlfriend."

"Uh huh," Delia murmured.

"And you're going to Alaska?"

"That's the plan," said Delia.

"Can you get there by car? Don't you have to take a ferry or something?" Even though she knew about cities and their states, Betsy James always did terribly in *Jeopardy* when the category had something to do with geography.

"No, you can drive. Through Canada," I said.

"Oh," Betsy said. "I thought it was an island."

"No," Delia said, brightly.

"And what are you going to do up there?" Betsy asked.

"I guess I'll just get a job, you know, wing it."

"Oh." I could tell Betsy James didn't approve. She liked planning and responsibility and security. That's why Dave James threw her for such a loop.

There was a long silence. "So, did you guys sleep OK?" I asked, I'm not sure why.

"Yeah, totally," Delia said. "Hey listen, speaking of sleeping, can I ask you guys a kind of personal question?"

Delia took our silences to mean yes. "So, um, what do you use as birth control? I mean, as mature, married women and all."

Betsy James's jaw dropped. I could see from where I was standing next to the fridge. This was something we never talked about, ever. I never used any birth control. As far as I know, I can't get pregnant, because I've certainly had the opportunity, and it hasn't happened. Paul mostly leaves me alone since we stopped pretending we were trying to have kids. Usually when he came back from a long run, he liked to put me on top so he could fall asleep right after, but recently I'd been using my mouth instead. But there was no way in hell I was going to share this with Delia.

"Lord," Betsy spoke first. "I haven't been with a man since Dave left, and I don't care if I never see one again."

Delia looked at me, but I couldn't say anything.

Betsy James saved me. "Do you hear the baby?"

"I don't hear anything," Delia said.

"Mother's ears." Betsy stepped down off the chair.

Delia and I followed her into the bedroom where we stood on either side of the door frame in the hallway. Tanya had indeed been crying; she saw her mother and reached out her arms. Betsy James pulled up her shirt to expose her breast. Tanya took the nipple into her mouth, twisting her finger around Betsy's long hair. She was almost 18 months; she should have been weaned by now.

It was as though we weren't there. Betsy stared at the baby and Tanya stared back with a look of pure adoration on her face, all the rapture of a couple on their wedding day, when all the guests seem to disappear as the couple moves toward each other for the first conjugal kiss. There was a tension in the room, as though Delia and I were watching a movie, the slow-motion satisfaction of Tanya's desire. We almost had to avert our eyes, that's how intimate it was.

Delia turned to me. "No one's ever looked at me like that, not even my own momma," she whispered.

I despised the sour note of question in her tone, as though she was looking to me to agree with her, to admit that no one had ever cared about me that much either. What I couldn't tell her, or anyone, is that Paul looked at me like that. I could never describe the awesome sense of responsibility and dread that I felt as the object of that—the fear that I could never live up to that adoration. I wanted to hit Delia, slap some sense into her, tell her that there's no trick to getting someone to adore you. Any idiot who waits long enough finds that out. The secret—the challenge—is finding someone you can look at like that. How dare she, I thought. How dare she assume so much and know so little.

"I asked Vince if he would ever want to marry me and he said 'maybe.' What does that mean?"

"Look," I said, backing into the hallway. My voice sounded harsh. "Let me tell you something about Vincent and me. We don't fall in love; we're just not made that way. And any idiot who's known us for more than half a minute can see that. It might as well be tattooed on our foreheads. 'Maybe' is the best you're gonna get. Take it or leave it."

"Oh," Delia said. Her mouth snapped shut. "Oh," she said again. I was immediately sorry I'd said anything. All her brightness had fallen away, and I wondered what I could do to take back what I'd said, to soften it. While I was wondering, she turned and walked away.

The evening before they left, I gave my brother forty dollars. We were standing on the front lawn, smoking.

"What's this for?" he asked. He was already taking his wallet out of his back pocket.

"To take Delia out," I said. "Someplace nice."

"OK." Vince put the twenties in carefully. I noticed that the rest of the bills were ones and fives. "Why?"

"Because I'd want someone to take me out is why."

It was the best I could do. Delia had been cold, quiet around me. She tried to avoid me, going out on a long walk and accepting Paul's offer to teach her how to steer the rig. When she caught my eye, she drew back as though afraid of me. I considered apologizing, but for what? It was the truth and better she should know it now.

My brother seemed to accept this explanation. "Hey, thanks," he said.

The sky was dark and cloudy. Only a few stars shown, but the lights from the street were enough to see my brother's face, watch the smoke he exhaled climb skyward.

"So," he said. He put his left hand in his pocket and looked down. "You don't like Delia much, do you?"

"She seems nice," I said.

"Yeah, that's what I thought." He laughed. "That's what I thought," he repeated.

Another long silence took us. I watched his cigarette dwindle to the filter.

"So," he said again. "I heard from Karl."

Karl was our stepfather. We hadn't talked about him in years. He dropped completely from our lives one day, taking our father's bowling trophies, the bronze cast of Vince's baby shoes, and Mama's good silver serving dish.

"What'd he want?" I asked, as though it happened all the time that Karl called.

"He heard Mama'd passed away, wanted to *extend condolences*." Paul put on an exaggerated version of Karl's southern accent.

"After five years? Wanted to know about life insurance is more like it."

"Yeah," Vince said. He took out another cigarette, extending the package to me, even though I'd only smoked half of mine. "Yeah, umm, I just wanted to ask you . . . Did he ever, I mean . . . to you?"

"No," I said quickly, without thinking whether it was true or not. I wondered how Vincent thought to ask, and what that meant, and what good he thought that knowledge would do now. It was not something I thought about, ever.

I could see my brother's face, his concerned eyes close together, the shadow of his nightly beard. He looked like Mama, around the nose and mouth, with the cigarette dangling. They had the same exaggerated chin. We both looked a little like her; maybe that's why we didn't see each other too often.

"I'm going inside," I said. "It's getting cold."

"Good idea," Vince said, putting the unlit cigarette back in its package. "Late, too."

"Very late," I said. I held the screen door open, waiting for him to go inside.

That night Paul put down the magazine he was reading in bed. "Delia seems nice," he said. "She could be good for Vincent."

"Mmm," I said, noncommittally.

Paul paused a moment like he does when he wants to say something but doesn't know how. Usually the waiting doesn't do any good. I've gotten used to translating what he says into something I want to hear.

"Tamara," he said, finally. "Why'd you give them money?"

"Because I wanted to," I said. I was putting on my nightgown.

"We could have used that," Paul said.

"It's just forty bucks," I said. "Besides, it's my money." Which was sort of true. It was the money from Mama's life insurance policy. Small, but mine.

"To go in the vacation fund," Paul said. That's what Paul had started to call our savings account once the name "college fund" seemed too much like wishful thinking. I got into bed. "She reminds me of you, a little," Paul said, leaning over to kiss me.

"It's my money," I said again. I met his kiss with closed lips and moved away to turn out the light. I put my back to Paul and pulled the covers up high to my chin. "She's nothing like me," I said. "Nothing at all."

No one in my family is ever good at good-byes, so when the sun came up, Vince and I hugged quickly by the car. Then I went around to Delia's side. I gave her a hug, too. She hugged me back, limply. "Thanks for having us," she said. "I hope we weren't a lot of trouble."

"No," I said sincerely. "Not at all."

Vince started the car. "You know," I said, "I hope you'll come back and visit, on the way back. Even if it's just you."

"Oh," Delia said, surprised. "Thanks." She got into the car.

"No," I said. "I mean it."

Vince leaned over her. "Bye, Tam," he said, and they drove away.

Paul left right after that. He'd be gone a week. He kissed me on the forehead and took his cooler and drove down the street out of sight.

Then the house was quiet again. I spent the day in the kitchen, reorganizing. And then I washed the towels and sheets.

The following week, I was watching the soaps with Betsy James over the phone when a commercial for the Pill came on.

"That Delia girl was a talker," Betsy James said.

"Oh, I don't know," I said.

"Well, I do. I mean, how dare she ask us that stuff? Total strangers."

"Sometimes it's easier to talk to strangers," I said. "Strangers can't use what you say against you."

"Don't I know it?" Betsy James said. "At work, people want to explain, 'It's my long lost brother' or 'Grandma's sick and I need to call Johnnie and tell him' or 'I always wondered what happened to Joshie Western,' or something, and I'm like, Lady, what listing, for chrissake?" Betsy laughed, but stopped abruptly when the commercial ended.

"I wonder what Delia's last name is," I said. "I wonder if I could find her if I wanted."

"Shh," Betsy James said. "It's starting."

When night came I went out onto the front stairs and smoked a cigarette into the sky. I kept my eyes open the whole time, just in case I saw the VW Rabbit. I didn't necessarily expect Delia to come back, or even that she'd stop here if she did decide to leave Vince in Alaska, but I was half hoping she would. And so I kept my eyes open, just in case, and spent a good part of the night like that, lighting cigarette after cigarette, watching the smoke fade into the clouds until I finished the pack, stood up, and went inside.

THE JANUS GATE

What he noticed first was her misuse. He could teach her, then; he had to, it was a pedagogical imperative. You are not *dis*interested in Western literature, my dear, for that is a judge's attitude before a court of law, but rather *un*interested. And are you, *cara mia*, completely and totally uninterested?

It started with a list, a long tail of words, strung together by their common classification. Can we examine these? He asked her a rhetorical question, as if she could say no. Subject them to scrutiny, however misguided, misdirected.

Ma chère, he explained, looking at her face, at the strange scar which cleft her chin in two. Arguably, she was attractive. He tabled his work to attend to hers, to bring her project to the table. He was wretched, both to her and because of her, his temper flammable. Overseeing her project, he supervised blindly. Was it not awful?

Awful

It was not hard to teach a Jewish girl from Allentown, schooled in Slavic languages, the finer points of Romance tongues. My name is *Janis*, she insisted; don't call me *sweetie*. Sure, *cariño*. French, Italian, Spanish, Catalan, and the bridge which is Romanian. Hungaro-Finnish, his native tongue, they tabled. It took office hours, the door pulled to—not closed—heads conspiring over a book or at a computer.

At his insistence she spent hours in the library looking up etymologies in the *Oxford English Dictionary*, which was bound, he teased her, with the skin of former graduate students.

She wondered at his gallery, at the coterie of former students he had tortured in this manner. The number of PhD candidates he had stolen from other departments. He had a curiously self-satisfied manner, crossing his long legs and sitting back from the desk, one hand on each knee as a king, sated by the rightful regal repast. But when his eyes looked away, when they were not boring into her, into her cleft chin, they seemed sad, and the phone never rang, and whenever she called he was awake and alone. And when she drove by—the lights of her car dimmed, on the way home from the library, so late it was early—she saw the light on in his office, his silhouette with cigarette.

Flammable/Inflammable

What percent of the classes did Janis teach? The Professor liked to sit in the back of the class and watch her. He knew the teaching made her nervous, but really, all she had to do was deliver his lecture, his notes, provided by him. He fielded all questions afterward. What made her more nervous was his stare, he knew. He stared at her, always at her, with a conspiratorial wink if she added a personal flourish to his lecture.

Sometimes he stood outside the classroom and smoked a cigarette. He could see in the window, and watched how she didn't finger her Star of David, how she gestured with her hands instead of rubbing them along the seam of her dress, how she answered questions with the confidence and evasion of a practiced educator. It was he, then, who inspired the nervous twitching, the lilting of the voice.

He could throw back his head and cackle with the thought of what he could make her do with his glances and his fingers. He could touch her pinkie next to the computer and feel her stiffen. Repulsion, attraction, surprise, it was all the same to him, so long as he provoked in her a sharp, uncontrolled physical reaction. He could make her scream, he knew, during sex.

He did. Not knowing or caring whether it was out of pain or ecstasy, whether she craved him or hated him. Whether she did it out of duty or gratitude, desire or curiosity. She was unused to it, he could tell, and he liked to look at her, both of them with their eyes opened wide, hers sparkling with terror or suspense.

Their *real* work lay almost forgotten, his in neatly arranged computer files and a small desk pile at the Department. His home office—a large oak table surrounded by full bookshelves (a mini-library), an antique globe, and the dictionary stand he had always dreamed of owning—was laden with Latin texts, Xeroxed pages of the *Oxford English Dictionary*, lists of words, definitions.

The project progressed. Her list grew. Biblical references, courtly documents, Greek philosophers; her beloved Czech dissident authors discarded, her Tolstoy research abandoned. Sweetheart, he said.

What was this bond, this obsession? His hand on her knee, she had learned to stare back, to communicate without words, since words were contradictory, antiquated. But what did they say to each other? Did she know his favorite food? He her favorite color? How many siblings the other had?

And what did their frantic coupling prove? Not passion, for they rarely kissed. Not intensity, for they often gave up for lack of interest halfway through. They spent hours in separate rooms of his house, disgusted by the sight of each other, yet Janis rarely went home.

They had passed a point. They had opened a door to war, famine and flood, pestilence and despair, exaltation and paper, ink and paper, ink and paper.

There exist two lexicographic terms for words, whether through use or misuse, that have become the dialectical antonyms of themselves, walking contradictions. They are startling, for they reveal the general ignorance of both the speaker, who automatically assumes one definition, and the listener, who makes similar, but potentially opposing, assumptions. How ironic their speech when the sentence is flipped to a reverse exegesis, inverting the intended meaning. The linguistic terms which describe this phenomena are contranym, if a word has two contradictory meanings, and antilogy, if two opposite words carry the same mimetic significance("Antilogy" 578).

Boned and Deboned, Boneless

Over Christmas break she never left, and he did not wonder about this. There was no question that she needed to stay, that there was no possibility of leaving before the project was finished. They drank more now, all colored liquids. Brown liquid warmed in their coffee in the mornings, clear liquid on ice for lunch, more amber reinforcements in the afternoon, and red with dinner. Later, a creamy concoction.

He caught the flu Christmas day and took to their bed. She left him mostly alone unless he called to her, *Janis* instead of his usual Indo-European epithets, and she brought him a liquid with medication, doctor sanctioned, not their usual alcoholic panacea. She continued to work, wrapped in the spare blanket, his trouser socks pulled up high, her hair bound in rubber bands stolen from broccoli stalks. The paper progressed.

January occupies the unique position as the first month, the opening or head of the year. The appellation derives from the Roman god Janus, god of beginnings. In Latin, the word ianus means "gateway" connoting the gateway to the new year, the beginning of a new cycle (Booker 332). Let us not forget that each beginning is also an ending of the previous state, so that the word in itself is contranymical.

Excavators at the Roman site of Ephesus in modern-day Turkey have recently (1989) uncovered the believed-lost gates to the city. One should not be surprised to discover the likeness of Janus affixed to the gatepost. The body was portrayed (as always in antiquity) with two heads. One looked outside the city to the warring countryside, the other faced peaceably inside the city walls. Both faces were bearded, hiding the features, as if to suggest that Janus himself was stoically unable to decide how he felt about war and how he felt about peace. The two-faced figure took on two symbolic meanings in Roman mythology: one, hypocritical, betraying, deceitful; and another (contranymical significance), sensitive to polarities and dualities ("Digging").

Sanction and Oversight

The Departmental Head began to clap him on the back before faculty meetings, the jocularity a sure sign of dissension. Little else was talked about near the Xerox machine. The issues on the meeting agenda—parking (permit violations and scarcity of), coffee machine abuse, hiring woes, budget cuts—seemed banal in comparison. How many bytes of e-mail were wasted in speculation? The secretaries clucked, the tenured crowd shook their heads. Hadn't they seen this before? How could it possibly end without destroying someone? Hopefully her, and not this senior faculty member, who might drag the Department or the University down with him.

They disapproved, yet how much of their head-shaking was with desire? Nodding in an attempt to clear the fierce cloud of envy—that work could produce this bond, that a project could mean life and death, could be air and water and food. The women swooned to be Janis, while they didn't understand her and found her ugly and disheveled. The men marveled at his virility, for they smelled it on him, saw it in his hair follicles and his disengagement from faculty politics. Oh for these imperatives, just once in their lives!

He forgot to hand in grades. He did not fill out his Tenure Committee questionnaire. He didn't remember the Departmental Picnic. He declined the Faculty Retreat. He stopped attending lectures. He resigned from the New Hire Committee by default. He was overseeing something important.

She was sanctioned, shunned by the others at Friday night Hillel dinners. Her cat died of feline leukemia. She resigned from the Graduate Action Committee, stopped campaigning for animal rights. She neglected to vote in the plebiscite.

But the paper, the paper was going well. As soon as he recovered from the flu, he started on it in earnest as well, writing from the back, the conclusion first, to compliment her introduction, then the proofs of her theses. He stopped only to refill their glasses, to maintain their clarity.

Once he put down his pen to stare across the table at her. She looked up and smiled, though she was not happy, necessarily. He felt a sudden desire to wipe that smile from her face, to deepen the cleft in her chin, to rid her of her mouth and of the ability to speak, forever. He ran at her, she fled from him, and the union that ensued was violent and loud, their screaming far from the admission of vulnerability that shouts often reveal, but rather war cries, guttural fendings-off, repulsions as they climaxed simultaneously. And afterward they worked.

Antilogical words, on the other hand, grow out of usage. If boned, boneless, and deboned have logical exegeses, it is due to their contranymical nature. Remember that the act of boning is impossible, so the verb "to bone" ("to deprive of bone") is necessarily the polar opposite of itself: "to furnish with bones" ("bone"). However, the vernacular usage of "to bone" meaning "to copulate with" retains the original suggestion of the insertion of bones.

Flammable/Inflammable presents a similar conundrum. Both mean "prone to flare up or erupt into flames," while the prefix in-, in both English as well as other Romance languages, takes its definition from the Latin root "to have a negative or privative force." Inflammable, then, is contradictory in its significance, meaning, modernly, "capable of…being set on fire" and, etymologically, to be fire retardant ("inflammable"). To attract and repulse.

Wretch

He said nothing about the presentation of the paper, nor did he communicate it to her in his stares. He had the presence of mind, the autonomy to send in an abstract and a bio, and arrange for a plane ticket to the Conference.

After she found it in his files (did he think he could hide it from her, after they were working so closely that they were practically the same person?), she sobered up enough to do the same.

It changed slightly, subtly, after the first draft was done. They proofread separate sections, then switched, changing words here and there to promote clarity or directness, then changed the other's modification. They questioned; this was new.

They had sex once after printing it out, with a nostalgic sort of separation, as though they were already distanced from it, as though it were years from now and they were meeting at a conference and cheating on their current lovers. He bent to kiss her, *mon petit chou*, and she turned her head from him, showing him her profile. He put his thumb in the cleft in her chin and put his weight on his fingers around her neck, leaving little marks.

The last time they touched was on the way to the printer's, when their shoulders bumped walking from the car. He held the door open for her on the way in, but she was gone before the copies were ordered.

He was surprised to see her there, though he had sensed she knew about the Conference. Her name appeared alphabetically before his, and their paper had caused a minor sensation, not because of its content, which, really, was not so revolutionary after all, when looked at with perspective and distance, but because of the mystery of their relationship, about which everyone had heard, and which the paper veritably oozed.

His heart dropped and his knees fluttered when he heard her being spoken about, and when he saw her, he felt momentarily paralyzed. She had cleaned herself up, was wearing a dress, had cut and combed her hair, added highlights. She was wearing light makeup. He felt angry and guilty; he knew he had acted wrongly, done something to betray her. He felt unhappy, utterly miserable and pitiful.

She sat at a table with her legs crossed, her shoe dangling off her right toe. She was sipping vodka, neat, and chatting with the Head of Slavic Languages and Literature of an eastern university. One hand fingered her Star of David. She was telling the story of how her brother had attacked her with scissors as a child, creating the vertical scar down her chin. He had never thought to ask.

The fundamental conclusion one can draw from these apparent discrepancies is an important observation about the English language and perhaps the Anglophone character. English will accept multiple words, as well as unclear explanations. Do English speakers self-delude? Rather they are true to their origins, to the biracial nature of English words: the dueling Latin/Greek and Germanic roots. The flexibility to accept change, to incorporate difference, is historiographically the English language's legacy, as well as its future. English exemplifies and amplifies the two-faced nature of all language, the distance between intended and perceived meaning. English is the first Janus, duplicitous, betraying—as well as the other Janus, sensitive to dualities and polarities; the god of beginnings and endings.

Works Cited

"Antiology" *Dictionary of Literary Terms and Ideas*, ed. Lois M. Dherbin. New York: Binter Press, 1967. 598.

"bone, v." *The Oxford English Dictionary*. 2nd ed. 1989. OED online. Oxford University Press. 20 May, 1997 <http://dictionary.oed.com>.

Booker, John Smithe. *Roman Gods and Latin Roots*. Durham, England: Durham University Press 1904.

"Digging for the Future: Excavation of Ephesus." *Franco-Italian International Treasure Preservation Society*. Rome, Italy: Edizioni Romani,1991.

"inflammable, a." *The Oxford English Dictionary*. 2nd ed. 1989. OED *online*. Oxford University Press. 20 May, 1997 <http://dictionary.oed.com>.

To Cleave

He could not get out of the pattern. He looked at the definition of cleave: to adhere, to split. Contranymical. From the Greek, the Latin, the French, and the German. Four roots, a linguistic Chi square.

The mail brought a postcard. I'VE MOVED. An address: a hick university town in Louisiana somewhere south of Baton Rouge where she was undergoing her post-grad penance. No signature.

I'VE MOVED. A change of address card. He couldn't imagine that this postcard was engendered by real emotion, born of the loneliness of exile, the density of the cypress swamp.

I'VE MOVED. He wandered about the house, clutching the postcard like a talisman. What could have persuaded her to send this? How ridiculous, how betraying, how two-faced and cruel, to throw this at him. For what could love mean to Janis? What could love mean—but hate—to Janus? What if it were neither contranymical nor antilogical? What if it meant something in between, impossible to discern?

What, he thought forlornly, what if it means neither love nor hate nor something in between, but a third thing? Oh God, he thought, please, love or hate, but not indifference! If this is but indifference, if we feel nothing, if it was nothing! This he cannot bear.

WHAT WAS OVER THERE IS OVER HERE

Maximilian Savage stands in cargo pants: low rise, flat front, zip fly, straight legged, 100% cotton brushed twill. There's Max Savage crouching, squatting, standing, leaning, bending, lying down, and snapping. Crouching yesterday in Pittsburgh, he photographed an apartment complex surrounding a pool. He squatted in the ambient light so that he was even with the gas fireplace. Standing, he photographed ceiling fans. He lay down to make the living room look bigger. The photographs were like the "Find the Five Differences" drawings in the Sunday papers: variations on a theme.

The day before that was Baton Rouge, where he shot a new building designed to look old and weathered, venerated. He snapped the wood trim, nails hammered in like small erosions in a cliff's face. He's supposed to photograph these "touches" so that the rental property can be listed to advantage on the website. He's supposed to:

• arrive on time or call the contact number if late (anything over five minutes);

• smile, make eye contact. Do not eat or chew gum in client's presence. Do not use the garbage in the rental office;

• DO ask if the client has any special considerations to accommodate.

There are also instructions for complications, numbers to dial for equipment failure, for client dissatisfaction, for rental car problems. Like a climbing buddy, RentWithUs.com will belay you; RentWithUs.com has got your back.

Today Max Savage is lost. He has never been to Miami; he always vacationed in the mountains. He is—was—a climber. He has *Astroman, Hall of Mirrors, Lost in America* under his belt. But that was not a profession; that was a hobby. Photography is a vocation. He married the two and for three years he scaled cliffs to photograph tourists rafting down the Colorado River. He free-soloed, not bothering to rope in. He didn't have to; he did this every day. But he always climbed carefully, no dyno moves, no unnecessary risks, camera banging against his hip with every move.

The day before Baton Rouge was Sacramento. Hot. Lizard-on-a-rock-in-the-sun hot. Max got lost in the California capital. He drove the rental car by a football field where a team of cheerleaders practiced the pyramid. The top girl somersaulted, was caught by her teammates and set carefully on the grass.

Now Max is in Miami. When he gets out at a gas station to ask directions, the cargo pants sit low around his hips.

Side pocket, left:	cell phone.
Side pocket, right:	crappy light meter; what's left of a pack of Certs; pocket knife (edge dulled by hours of useless whittling while waiting for tourists to raft by).
Back pocket, left:	memory cards.
Back pocket, right:	wallet.
Thigh pocket, left:	bandanna (rolled); Pepto Bismol tablets (pink), some out of their plastic wrapping and crumbling.
Thigh pocket, right:	brochure on Pittsburgh apartments (with client's home phone number), folded; carabiner.
Around his neck:	the good light meter; braided leather necklace with a shark's tooth pendant.

The gas station is blaring salsa music and the attendant is speaking Spanish rapidly and loudly to himself. Then Max sees the earpiece. He decides not to ask directions.

Max's fingers are callused from climbing, still. Clients approve of this, as though it were a sign of hard work. Max has no tip to the pinkie of his right hand, though he could climb just as well without it. Max is also missing his incisor tooth on the top right, and Max is missing the use of his left arm. It hangs from his shoulder like an empty banana peel, like a wet bandanna, like the tail end of a rope.

At the gas station, Max buys:

- a liter of water;
- a value pack of Hot Tamale candies;
- green Pepto Bismol tablets;
- a plastic-coated, easy-fold map of Miami.

The clerk eyes him suspiciously; he has never seen cargo pants used to carry freight before. He checks the fridge over Max's shoulder for a missing forty-ouncer.

In the car, Max is able to locate neither his current location, nor his desired one. He wants Xavier Ct., and though incarnations of Xavier multiply like plastic saints before his eyes, there is no Ct. Down the index: Ave., Blvd., Pl., St., Terr., Way. If Max consults the Operations Manual, he will see that this is the recommended occasion for cell phone usage. In Sacramento, he was nearly two hours late to the property, a new record. Max photographed the apartment building and paid special attention to the laundry room per the client's (a skinny woman in an ankle-length, butterfly-patterned sundress) instructions. Max:

- smiled;
- did not chew gum;
- DID eat a sub sandwich offered to him by said client.

The last was counter-indicated by the RentWithUs.com employee manual, but Max has a weakness for Italian cold cuts.

Max is three days up the Shield Route, bivouacked on the side of the cliff face. His polypro is torn at the knee from when he fell scrambling up the scree. Not even on the rock yet, he should have taken it as an omen. In his tent Max swings in the wind like something adjunct. He never sleeps when bivvy-ing. He's not sleeping now, but still he's dreaming of falling, unable to gain purchase in the sheer rock, the boulders tumbling down after him like spilled popcorn. When he wakes up from this dream-that-is-not-a-dream, Max has the use of only one arm; the other is shriveled like a lizard left sunning too long.

Cargo pants are a variation on the denim jean, invented and patented on May 20, 1873. The six pockets are designed to hold gear, gear, gear, gear, gear, gear. Either photography equipment or carpentry tools or simply vestigial climbing equipment so that the wearer can finger carabiners open and closed—a nervous habit—in his pocket. With his good arm.

Max is a half hour late when he finally asks directions from a little Hispanic kid who stares at the shriveled arm while he answers. Max goes right, then left, around one of those roundabouts. He continues straight until he spots the street he thinks he wants, only it's Xavier Pl. He is turning the wheel in preparation for a U-turn when he sees the statue.

DOLORES DE LEÓN, reads the large plaque, A GUACATA INDIAN, WAS THE WIFE OF EXPLORER JUAN PONCE DE LEÓN. SHE AIDED THE MEN IN THEIR SEARCH FOR THE FOUNTAIN OF YOUTH AND DIED OF SMALLPOX IN 1532. She is more than fifteen feet high, constructed of bronze made green by oxidation and guano. Out of place amid dilapidated plywood houses, in the middle of the cul-de-sac, she stands on a large raised mound of brown lawn surrounded by a thin moat of wilted magenta impatiens. She is wearing a loose robe which is falling off her shoulders. Her arms are outstretched. Her face, looking downward, is contorted in compassion, in the immense sorrow of her futile quest.

Max stops the car, and without thinking about what he is doing—how he will have to download the images later onto his laptop and how he will then send them to the office, and how he will have to explain the statue-in-the-slums-of-Miami digression, as well as his tardiness and the client's dissatisfaction at his distraction and dishevelment—Max begins to photograph the statue. He climbs onto the brown mound and snaps away, looks up at her concentrated, downturned face, unclouded and still bronze. She has a thick nose with no nostrils, big parted lips that reveal no teeth, wide, pupil-less eyes that, though crying, shed no tears. Max suspects that her pity is directed at him.

Max hangs the camera around his neck where it bumps against the light meter. Putting one foot on top of her sandal, Max uses his right arm to grab at her knee. He hoists himself up, placing the other foot into the slight hold between folds of her robe, slipping off. Max re-places the foot, jamming the toe of his shoe into the crevice, and then he is in the air, climbing again, the camera and his arm banging against each other on his chest like tom-toms.

The metal is hot in the sun. Max pushes off with his foot without planning the move, courting a fall until he grabs at the polished indentation between her breasts, a smooth, perfect hold, an invitation. His feet find purchase on her waist. Again without thinking, Max swings his bum arm around her neck, grabbing the wrist with his other hand and letting his feet swing. Max dead-hangs, using his worthless arm as a harness, holding his weight until his feet find holds above her waist. He presses against her cranium, cradles it against his stomach, the heat of the metal making it feel almost real.

From here it's an easy adjustment to sit on her shoulders. The top of her head is as hot as a skillet. His cargo pants ride up, exposing his scarred ankles. He can see the outline of the useless carabiner against his thigh. Now Max can see from Dolores's perspective the brown mound of earth, the line of dead flowers, his rental car giving off shimmers of heat. His left arm throbs with the memory of the strain. Above Dolores's gaze now, up in the air, Max no longer feels that she pities him.

Max watches the blackness of the asphalt, magnified in his zoom so that it appears as pocked and dented as the surface of the moon. The heat makes it almost liquid; it gives off waves of fever; it seems to move, to soften under Max's gaze. Max thinks that if he fell he would be absorbed into the asphalt as though in a pool of water, or quicksand. Then he sees a gecko making its slow way across the road. The lens draws the image close to him; what was over there is now over here. Max photographs the lizard, capturing the image in his camera— the monochromatic ridged back, the shrunken, wrinkled skin. Max snaps the shutter on a pivotal moment in its methodical trajectory.

HOW MUCH GREATER THE MIRACLE

"Joanne," I yell. "Eight o'clock tee time, forty-five minute drive."

"I know, I know," my wife calls down from upstairs. Since the kids have grown we have taken to golfing together on the weekends. "I can't find my visor. Can you wait one fucking minute while I find my visor?"

"Just once," I say. "Just once in my life, I'd like to hit balls before we play. Just once in my life, I'd like to be warmed up when I hit the starter's post."

There are things I could do while I wait. I could start the dishwasher, but the pile in the sink is discouraging. I could go around and collect all the loose change and put it in the jar our daughter has set out to save the souls of whatever African nation is in peril this decade. Instead I turn on the television. Golf may have eclipsed baseball as our national pastime; there is always golf on one of the ESPNs.

The soul and golf are interrelated. I try not to wax too philosophical, but the soul is like a golf ball. If you want to make it to the hole, it takes a lot of technique. Swing big, lay up, stroke softly across the green.

These were things my father taught me, when he took me to the range. In those days, golf wasn't as popular as it is now and the chance to play a real course didn't come for me until I was eighteen, but even then I knew I loved it. What a sense of accomplishment I felt then, a sentiment I've since lost in the frustration of swing-tips videos and pricey pro lessons. How a little piece of graphite (well, iron in those days) could make the ball soar into the heavens, infinitely farther than I could make it travel with my own appendages. How in three shots I could make that round, dimpled victim reach a hole so small I couldn't see it until I was practically on top of it.

With my father there was no cheating, not the way I let my kids cheat when I taught them to play. No "hand wedges," no mulligans, just stick and ball. They didn't even have to carry their own clubs, since our course subscribed to a scholarship fund and hired inner-city kids with college aspirations to caddie. Hey, if golf can send a tiny ball to a distant hole, how much greater the miracle if it can send a black kid to college?

"I'm ready, OK?" Joanne rumbles down the stairs. She's wearing plaid shorts with a white collared shirt. The trim around the collar matches the checks on her shorts. The shirt has no sleeves, and the fat around her upper arms jiggles as she struggles to support all the items she carries. Most of these are attached to her waist by various clips: mountain-climbing carabiners, plastic rings, tied around the belt loops. The buckle on her belt is shaped like a frog. "Did you pour me some coffee?"

"No, then you'll have to go to the bathroom." I struggle to see which button on the remote will turn off the television.

"I'm a grown woman; I'll decide if I have coffee or not." She drops a hat, some sunscreen, and wraparound sports sunglasses on the table to grab a Kleenex and a handful of tees from the basket we keep on the counter next to the phone. "Besides," she adds, "I'll have to go to the bathroom anyway."

When we pull off the expressway to stop at a roadside gas station, I finger the golf balls in my pocket. I use Titleist now, exclusively. I used to use X-outs for water holes, but now I think that balls are the symbol of how seriously you take golf, and I take it extremely seriously. I don't know when golf became so important, but it seems to be both the reward and the goal. Golf itself, not the score. When I stand on the tee box, my right hand wrapped around my left, my hips loose, my head focused on the uppermost white dimple, and maybe a corner of the "T" that is showing from the brand marking, I feel a slight nervousness. In a good way, letting me know that this is something important, and something I can control. Sometimes.

"Thanks," Joanne says, getting back into the car. "Whew, that feels better."

"Coffee," I say.

"Fuck you," she says. She says this so often, it's almost an endearment.

Why am I still with my wife, I wonder? I can't imagine being with anyone else, I guess, in anything but a fantasy sort of way. We're getting old together. That's what I swore we would do, I believe, when I proposed, one thousand years ago. I know we're getting old because we don't talk anymore. It's all been said between us.

Our youngest, Natty (short for Natalie), says we're so ecologically conscientious that we recycle conversations, and it does appear that way. We have settled on two topics: health and golf. They are interrelated.

Joanne hates our doctor, but he's a specialist in heart trouble, which is something Joanne and I share. In me, it's inherited; my father died of a heart attack at sixty, almost the age I'm at now. Joanne has high blood pressure and an astronomical cholesterol count. My back bothers me sometimes. Joanne has tendonitis in her left elbow, which she should be keeping straight anyway when she swings.

We talk a lot about golf courses. Which ones we've played (together), which ones we fantasize about playing.

Joanne plays Cog Hill in her mind when she can't sleep at night. I can hear her counting yardage softly to herself when I wake up to turn over or get some water. I have golf on my PC at work, and I waste a lot of company time playing it. I'm a senior partner though, so I suppose it's my time to waste. The other thing I do a lot of is write e-mail to Deidre (our oldest). She's in college, and she only occasionally responds. Usually I describe in detail the way I played our course this weekend. She knows the course intimately too. I taught her to play and dragged her out there many a weekend in junior high. She's the only one who pretends to be interested in golf. The other two hate golf now. They refuse to play. They hate the whole "bourgeois, eco-destructive capitalist system" (Natty's words) that we subscribe to. Now when I play, I consider that I'll have to write Deidre about it on Monday. Do I lay up? Will Deidre think me a coward? Am I really reading the green correctly? That's what Deidre is good at: reading greens.

Joanne is moving her lips next to me, and I can see her thinking. This is something her mother did, too, think half out-loud. It strikes me as slightly insane.

"What?" I say.

"Nothing. I didn't say anything," Joanne answers.

"Yes you did, out loud," I lie. She'll believe me.

"Oh. I didn't mean to, Walter. Sorry to disturb your precious silence."

The word silence makes me think of the radio, which I reach over and turn on. I have a Spanish learning tape in the deck; I eject it and turn on the CD player. There is a six-CD changer in the trunk, although I can't remember the last time I was in the car for six CDs.

"No Tom Jones," Joanne says. She is rummaging through her fanny pack, looking for something.

I don't say anything, but hit the forward button until the changer reaches the African drum CD that Leonard sent us. He's a freshman at Emory this year, and he hasn't called in two months. That means he's happy.

I pull off the highway, and we head east through the wheat fields until I can see the gates with the manicured lawns, the long driveway leading up to the clubhouse. I have done well for us, I think. We're of a certain class. My father would be proud. Well, confused, but proud of a son who drives a Lexus and belongs to a club where the club boys call me "sir." This should make me happy.

"Sir, are you walking or riding?" I look at Joanne, who is struggling to get out of the low bucket seat. She has pushed some of her belongings out in front of her so that the sidewalk next to the car looks like a mini bazaar. I can't take five hours of this, I think. "We'll ride," I say.

We've missed our eight o'clock tee-time. I'm surprised the starter hasn't started scheduling us a half hour later than we sign up for. The Millers have already teed off. "Morning, George," I say, trotting over to the tent where George and his omnipresent clipboard reside.

"Morning, Mr. Simons, sir. I'm afraid the Millers are already out."

"That's OK, George. I couldn't get the old lady out of the house this morning. Do you have anything for us later?"

"Ten minutes OK? With the—I mean, with Doerr and Allegro?"

"Sounds great."

I jog back up to the car, which Joanne has already parked. "We're playing with some couple with two names. Ten minutes."

"All right." Joanne is sitting in the backseat with her feet out the door, changing into golf shoes. "Soft or hard spikes?"

"I think it's going to be soft all summer," I say. "I think the whole world's going soft."

I get a plastic bag out of the trunk and start to collect Joanne's belongings. "You need this?" I hold up a mostly-empty package of travel Kleenex.

"What are you doing?"

"Getting you organized."

"Give me that, I can do that." Joanne snatches the bag away from me. She hates to think she's deficient.

The loudspeaker announces, "Porter to the tee, Simons, Doerr and Allegro on deck."

I start toward the first tee to stretch before we're up. I haven't even swung a club yet this morning, damn it. My back feels stiff. I take out the Super Big Bertha and swing her around. I put one hand at the base and one at the grip and lean forward, letting the club stretch my triceps behind my back. Then I turn from side to side. I feel my back loosen slightly.

I take a couple of practice swings, then switch to a short iron and take a few more. I've created quite a hole here on the practice tee. I look around for my divot, but I've shredded the sod.

I hear a large crack as the last person ahead of us hits, and then George calls our name over the loudspeaker.

Where the hell's my wife? A cart rolls up behind me. I can hear the rubber scrape along the paved path as it brakes.

"Hi. Winston P. Doerr." A callused hand extends toward my right shoulder. I take a step back and grasp it firmly. Winston P. Doerr is an older man, close to seventy, with a full head of gray hair. He has a round face and carries his weight on his sides, his hips and thighs, so that his stomach caves in behind his Bobby Jones patterned shirt. He wears a Nicklaus hat sideways like his hips, and pushed-down kneesocks. He takes his left hand from his pocket, dropping some change, a tee, and a divot tool. "Whoops, shit," he says.

"Here let me," I say, and as I bend over, I see that he has custom golf shoes. You can never underestimate a golf player who has invested in his sport. Equipment isn't everything, but it certainly helps, and like I said, serious equipment equals serious mental attitude. Serious equipment also means serious money, which means serious leisure time. Leisure time is golf time. My father played golf the day before he died, eighty pounds overweight with a hip replacement and a bum knee. Shot three over.

Next to Winston P. Doerr's specially made footwear arrives a pair of Foot-Joys, off the rack. Attached to them are anklet socks hugging shapely ankles, tanned muscular calves, and lots of thigh. Shorts too short for this course (though probably no one will say anything), collarless shirt—transparent mesh down the sides revealing a lacy bra—blond hair in a ponytail out the back of a visor. "Hi," I smile. "I'm Walter Simons."

Winston P. Doerr clears his throat. "Most people call me Junior. This is Cicely Allegro."

"Pleased to meet you," I say.

"Hi," she says. She has bad teeth, I notice, and perhaps the slight hint of an accent. Where is my wife?

"Do we have a fourth?" Junior asks. The name is slightly ludicrous on him, considering his age and his size.

"Supposedly my wife will be joining us," I say, "but . . ." I let the sentence trail off.

Junior steps in back of his cart. "Well, I guess I'll tee off then. Championship tees?"

"Sure, whatever you usually play," I answer, looking over the landscaped embankment for Joanne's tottling form.

Cicely puts a manicured hand on my forearm and stage-whispers conspiratorially. "I'm a beginner," she reveals. "I hope you'll be patient?"

"Of course," I say. "We were all beginners once," and think that this will be a long, long day. Beauty is not a commodity in the golf world. Just look at Laura Davies.

Junior addresses the ball, wiggling his enormous hips from side to side like a belly dancer. He takes the club face back halfway, stops a second, draws it back farther and shifts his weight, grunting as the club swings toward the ball, ending in a satisfying and resounding crack. He must put all his weight in the swing somehow, because the sucker travels a good two hundred yards, dead straight. Amazing.

I take a deep breath and pick some grass to test the wind. Light, straight in our face. I tee my ball up and he chuckles. "Love it when I nail it in front of the starter. Audience loves me. Cigar?" He pulls a thin wrapped one from his lapel pocket.

"No thanks," I say. This is a pretty straightforward hole. Sand on the left, trees on the right. Pin back today, tricky green especially with all this rain. Concentrate, I think, concen—

"Walter, you hit yet?" My club is halfway back.

"My club is halfway back, Joanne, no."

"Oh, sorry," Joanne says.

"Joanne, my wife," I announce. Her lipstick extends beyond her mouth on the right side, balanced by a higher left sock. "Winston P. Doerr, called Junior, and his friend Cicely-the-beginner."

Junior and Cicely laugh and extend their hands. Joanne shakes them. Both her hands are gloved.

"Let's move along gentlemen," George nudges.

I close my eyes when I hit. It's something I've always done. I have to trust Joanne to watch the ball, which she does properly about fifty percent of the time. After I make contact, in the second before I open my eyes to see where my shot has gone, I visualize where I want it to be. As if this helps; as if in that small moment my shot can be perfected. I close my eyes now. My swing is a little stiff, but when I open them the shot is straight up the fairway.

"Nice, honey," Joanne says.

"Better if I'd warmed up," I say. I can't let it go. This is one of the bad habits you pick up in twenty-five years of marriage: sticky grudges.

Cicely approaches the tee. Junior comes up behind her and leans into her bottom. He wraps his hands around hers, and together they take a couple of practice swings. Then he steps back and picks up the cigar he left lying in the grass.

Cicely swings and whiffs. "It's going to be a long day," I mutter to Joanne, who nods, watching. Cicely finally makes contact and the ball sputters, a low grounder about sixty yards.

"Right-o," Junior says.

"Great!" Joanne yells.

Cicely looks proud as she walks back to her bag, then comes to stand between me and Junior. "Nice shot," I say. "You'll be a good golfer." Cicely flashes me a closed-lip smile and blushes slightly.

Joanne swings madly at the air; then she approaches her ball. It falls off the tee and she grunts as she bends over to replace it. She stands with her large bottom out, powerful shoulders facing us. I can see the backs of her strong calves.

Joanne's shot slices far right. She hits the lone tree separating the two fairways and ricochets off the tree, hitting the cart path. The path slopes downward here, and the ball bounces off the cement a half dozen times before coming to rest in the short rough off the side. She's lying perfectly, her ball even with Junior's.

Cicely miffs the second shot, too, and plays field hockey to the hole. I get stuck in the sand, but it's packed down from all the rain and I get out easily, leaving myself an eight-foot putt, which I knock down in a respectable two.

Joanne comes up from behind the green with a blind chip shot that hits the flag and comes to rest about three feet from the cup. Junior chips in from the edge of the green.

The front nine slide by. Joanne is taking target practice; she hits every possible obstacle on the course. Even the storm shelter from whose gutter the ball rolls onto the fairway. Still, her ball finds Junior's wherever it is. He's playing cart golf, and puffing on the cigar (he finishes the first one at the fourth hole and lights another immediately).

While Joanne hits, I watch Junior and Cicely. It isn't hard to imagine their story. Is he married? I wonder. I assume she's in her twenties, just a couple of years older than Deidre. Would Deidre settle for this existence, the high-priced whore of a golf junkie? No, be fair: the trophy wife of an older businessman.

I feel the ache of jealousy in my arms. Junior is a caricature of the successful golfer. Straight down the middle, pars on the fives, splits the fours, one under on the short holes. Overweight. Cuban cigars, a foreign girlfriend.

Joanne is talking to herself again on the golf course. I'm not sure if I can hear her or just see her lips moving: "C'mon, Jo, focus. Face falls first, elbow straight. Visualize the hole," she mutters.

Sometimes I hate my wife.

Our son Leo is the most like her, happy-go-lucky. He likes the outdoors. He's strong in an oafish way, athletic, but not disciplined. He has Joanne's thick black hair, is quick to anger, and forgives, like a dog, seconds later. The girls started calling him early, middle school, and he was uniformly nice to them, flattering and funny. He has an ease with the opposite sex that I have always aspired toward, something innately comfortable and inviting.

Deidre is my child. Yesterday she wrote me that she is starting the interviewing process at school. She wants to go into consulting. She has had the same boyfriend since freshman year of college. We met Bill last Thanksgiving—a nice boy who wore a suit to dinner and stammered nervously when I asked him what he planned on doing. We had retired to the living room to watch the Bowl game, and we sipped brandy from snifters.

Bill wants to be an investment banker, like I am. He dreams of joining one of the large firms, paying off his student loans, letting the company send him to business school. There was a touchdown, and I took a long sip of brandy to hide my tearing eyes. Was this scene not what I had worked for? A frame from the idealized cartoon of my life? So why did I feel as though I had invited a car salesman to dinner, as though Deidre had coached him as to what to say to ingratiate himself to me?

Natty, meanwhile, is the child we didn't mean to have. Neither my wife nor I can account for her—neither for her conception nor for her anger. She is the product of our rancor, and she is indignant and stubborn and often mean. She's a pro-choice feminist vegetarian demonstrator; she condemns so vehemently, I don't need a conscience anymore.

Thinking about Natty's anger brings tears to my eyes. One thing I've been doing a lot lately is weeping. Sometimes I close the door to my office, and when the computer golf no longer works to calm me, I'll hide my head in my hands for a half hour. I feel better after that. I don't know why I cry; I've never been a crier. I used to be angry; the kids were scared of my temper. And now I weep. This is something I don't write Deidre over e-mail.

And now, on the ninth hole, a short par three with water; a shot I will write her about. A solid, straight hit which carries the pond. I have chosen the right club, a seven-iron, made the proper adjustments to the wind, felt a momentary dissipation of the pain in my back, and I when I open my eyes I see, as though in a slow-motion dream, the ball sail to the green and land lightly like a leaf abandoned by the wind. My three-foot putt clunks soundly in the cup. I place this hole in my mental Greatest Hits file. Deidre will smile when she reads it, write me back "Congrats Daddy!" and tell me how her classes are going, how her thesis simply refuses to research and write itself, how her advisor is helping her find a job.

At the halfway house at the tenth hole, Joanne stops at the bathroom and I go in to buy us sandwiches. "Anybody need anything?" I call. Junior is on his fourth cigar. He has bought three beers from the floating drink cart. "I hate to interrupt," I interrupt. He and Cicely are parked in front of my cart. Their heads are together and Junior's hand is out of sight in Cicely's lap. "But does anybody need anything?"

Junior and Cicely look at me. "I'll go with you," Cicely says. We walk into the shack. "Two turkeys and cheese on rye," I order. "And for you?" I ask, as though I were the sandwich kid.

"A cookie," Cicely says, pointing a long red nail. "That one, and a bag of chips. An iced tea."

The sandwich kid looks at me. He makes me a turkey sandwich every day, but now he is wondering where my wife is. If Leo were here, I think, he and the sandwich kids would make hubba hubba noises and snicker when I left with the sandwiches. I stand a little straighter. I'm not embarrassed to say that the idea of a pretty woman on my arm thrills me.

Most of my friends have trophy wives. My successful friends, that is, who can afford alimony and shopping trips to the city, and therapy for the younger kids, and college tuition for the older ones. Usually I make fun of them, congratulate myself on my fidelity. I have cheated on my wife only once, after Deidre was born, when I bedded the stripper from a college buddy's bachelor party.

The sandwich kid hands me my wrapped sandwiches, two cans of Diet Coke without being asked, and Cicely's cookie, drink, and chips. He catches my eye, and I see why my friends have these wives who look like store mannequins. It's interesting how the attractiveness of one partner reflects on the couple as a whole.

Joanne comes out of the bathroom in time to see me pay for both meals. Cicely thanks me with a gloveless hand on my forearm.

"Here, I'll take that," Joanne says.

On the tenth tee, Junior hits the fairway as though his ball were guided by a magnet. I hook into the woods on the left and swear, audibly.

Joanne shakes her head as she removes her driver from her bag, but she has little to feel superior about; her shot slices right, careening off a signpost into a wheat field. "Did you bring your scythe?" I ask her.

"You bring yours, asshole?" she retorts.

Cicely is hitting by herself for once. She wiggles a few times at the tee and her shorts climb up her thighs. "Oops," she says, and her ball bounces left into the forest with mine.

"Here, we'll switch carts," Junior says, "and I'll help your lovely wife locate her ball, if you'll help Cicely out of the woods."

I climb into Cicely's cart with my wedge and a three-wood, and we drive off toward the woods. I can hear the reverse whine of my cart as Joanne and Junior head off in the opposite direction.

As we reach the beginning of the growth, Cicely says, "Let's find yours first, and I'll watch how you do it." Her mouth stays in a slight smile while she says this, so I can't tell if it's a suggestive statement or if she's making fun of me.

I tramp around in the forest for a while, using my three-wood as a divining rod. I can hear Cicely's breathing as she searches ahead of me. "Not long," she says.

"I'm sorry?" I say.

"We haven't been together long, if that's what you were wondering. About three months."

"Oh."

"Here you go," she says. "A Titleist, that you?"

"Yup." She is pointing to my ball which is teed up nicely on top of a pile of leaves. I have no clear shot out to the fairway unless I poke it back a little. But maybe golf is little like football, you have to drop back to advance. What would Deidre want me to do?

"Will you show me what you're doing?" Cicely asks. This is definitely suggestive, an invitation. She is almost whining when she says it.

"Sure," I say. I feel my face flush and hope it's hidden by the trees' shadows. "I don't want any height on it, so I'll use the wood, and just try to knock it out straight through the trees." I line up with the ball to show her, pointing out with the three-wood. I leave the wedge on the ground. "Now, I don't want to get under it, so I'll leave my hips loose," I wiggle a little for show, "and relax the shoulders." I have a choice here—play the game of amateur country club golf, or swing for the bleachers, take a risk.

"Ahh," Cicely breathes. "Let her rip, right?"

"Right," I say, and I hit the shot, which does exactly what I want it to, non-spectacularly. It loops out onto the fairway. Hardly the impressive shot, but the safe one, the right one, the one I can write to my daughter about.

"Oh," Cicely says simply. She is kind enough to raise her voice as though impressed. She moves closer and smiles, and suddenly the manicured golf course is gone and we are bodies alone in the woods. I close my eyes as though setting up for a swing, as if this will hide my embarrassing erection. "Oh," she says again, sharply this time, with no pretension of being impressed. Then, like a whip, I hear a crack, and a ball careens over my left shoulder. I move away from Cicely and turn to pick it up. Titleist. It's Joanne's.

Without speaking, I walk slowly back to the cart where we left it at the edge of the forest. I wait until I hear the weak contact Cicely makes with her ball and watch it bound in front of mine onto the fairway before I climb into the passenger seat.

I throw Joanne's Titleist onto the fairway for her and she walks quickly up to the cart. I always wear events on my face—my bad days at the office, my surprises for the kids—and Joanne can see what has happened as clearly as if it had been sky-written against the deep blue cloudless firmaments above. Cicely emerges from the woods, examining her golf glove as she walks purposefully back to her cart.

Joanne releases a series of insults directed at the fact that I had the audacity to remove her ball from its rightful lie in the forest. I am powerless to defend myself against the logic that this game cannot now be counted toward her handicap, tainted as it is by my filthy meddling hand. She spits while she screams, and her eyes bulge, and she raises her arms threateningly so that I flinch. I have to admit I feel guilty. More about moving the ball than about Cicely, which is feeling more and more like a blip in my space–time continuum, like an imagined par.

The four of us return to our conjugal carts and play in silence, not even pretending to congratulate the other on a fine shot or a good chip. On the sixteenth tee, Joanne swings hard and misses completely, spinning on her heel. Usually I would say something sarcastic like "Next time swing a little harder, why don't you?" but today I hold my tongue.

Joanne's anger spews in my direction. She screams, "This fucking shithead game. Goddammit fucking hell."

I look nervously over at Junior and Cicely, who have averted their eyes. Then Joanne takes her driver and hurls it at me. I am protected by the frame of the cart, but as it hits, Big Bertha's head flies off and pops up in the air, denting the cart and finally coming to rest precariously on top of it.

Usually, I would scream back, lecture Joanne about responsibility and acting like a grown-up. I'd probably even invoke Natty's words and call her a maniacal raving bitch. But today something is different. Today I am sorry I moved her ball, and I know I should take her in my arms to stop her flailing, calm her down and take her home. Instead, I feel the tears start to well up in my eyes, and I hide them in my hands.

There is a moment of silence when even the wind dies down, and the only sound on the course is my crying. A minute passes. Joanne calms down and she starts to laugh. "Can I borrow your driver, Walt?" she asks, contrite, and her laughter, although I know it is directed at me, is infectious.

"Go ahead, Rambo," I say. "But with my clubs, you break 'em, you buy 'em."

"Fair enough," Joanne says, and takes my driver out of my bag. She reaches up and retrieves the head of the club from its perch on top of the cart. It has broken off right where it used to meet the shaft. "Think they'll fix this?"

"It's worth a try," I say. I wipe my eyes on my handkerchief. My face is dirty.

"We've shocked our companions," I say, a little loudly so that they can hear.

"They don't know about twenty-five years of marriage."

Junior and Cicely look at each other, then at me. They smile nervously, together. Joanne lines up and tees off well.

Mercifully, the game ends. I score under my weight, and hopefully under my IQ, which on some days is all you can ask for. We don't count Joanne's score, seeing as how I've moved her ball. Junior finishes three over.

Junior and Cicely shake hands with us warily. We've scared them silly, and I have no doubt we're dinner conversation around the club tonight. This bothers me, but there's nothing I can do about it. Joanne and I wisely decide to go home, though we haven't eaten our monthly club minimum. We'll order a pizza from the car when we hit the turnpike, so it will be waiting for us when we get there, and we can eat and shower and watch the news and fight a little with Natty before bed. It's Sunday, so maybe Leo will call (there's always hope).

"Sir, your wedge?" says the boy wiping down my clubs.

"What?"

"You're missing your pitching wedge." The boy speaks softly and looks at his shoes, as though I'll get angry at the news and punish the messenger.

I think about where I last used it. "Shit, I must have left it in the woods off the tenth hole." I feel Joanne stiffen.

"I'll send someone to get it," the boy says. "Will you wait?"

"Sure. It's about a hundred yards up on the left, twenty yards in."

"You forgot your wedge in the woods?" Joanne asks.

"Yes."

"What else did you forget in the woods, Walter Simons?"

"Nothing," I say. I look Joanne in the eyes. She is squinting back. "I forgot nothing else in the woods." Joanne walks away. I can hear the car door slam. When I get in next to her, she leans away from me against the window.

In the car, Joanne snores in time to the rhythm of Leo's African drum tape. Her upper arm weighs on her left breast, and under the cellulite I can see the bulge of her bicep. The afternoon light glints off the wheat stalks, sending shimmering lightning bolts as small as slivers into my field of vision.

There are windows in my life, maybe it's the same with everybody, through which, briefly, unexpectedly, I can see myself with clarity and honesty. And I look at myself from above: two sets of clubs in my trunk (wedge safely re-turned and nestled between the sand wedge and the nine-iron), and suddenly I know that golf is just a game of sticks and balls, and I could never be the kind of man who has a Cicely and a cigar, who shoots par at sixty-five years old. Because in my world, golf is not about the score but about the excitement, the joy that the backswing inspires. The closed-eyed moment of possibility, the struggle to concentrate, to control the club, knowing the shot will not be perfect, but relishing the challenge of the next one. Almost one hundred opportunities per game to fine-tune, to adjust, to get it right.

AND THEN THERE WAS CLAIRE

Funerals ought to have invitations was Garvey's first thought. Embossed ones: Dr. and Mrs. Herman Stoltz request the honor of your presence at the funeral of their daughter, Claire. 1:30 PM Steinberg Memorial Chapel, Washington D.C. But instead, of course, there was a phone call—a calm, pretentious phone call from Buddy, that old son of a bitch, all Hello, how are you? How's Cleveland working out for you? Are Midwestern chicks really that ugly, and do you fuck them anyway? And oh, by the way, Claire's dead. Yeah, Primatene Mist, same as killed that model. You know. Some congenital heart defect thing reacted weirdly to the inhaler. Boom, her ticker just stopped. They found her on the floor of her apartment, that one on the Circle. Life is short and all that. Listen, the funeral's the day after tomorrow, if you want to come.

No, he probably didn't want to come, but he scribbled down the address anyway, on the company non-sticky notepad by the phone. THIS IS SO IMPORTANT THAT I'M WRITING IT DOWN ON A SMALL PIECE OF FLY-AWAY PAPER read the top; the bottom contained a childish illustration of a Post-it with wings. Claire Stoltz. Jews bury their dead so fast you didn't have time to decide whether or not you wanted to take the plane to D.C., see those people, get back into that scene.

He looked around his office, somewhat stunned. His desk was neat, with just enough studied clutter to look as though he frequently used it, which was an exaggeration. His name was painted on the glass door like the set of a 1970s TV detective show. Andrew Garvey Masterson—his full name, not Garvey, what he'd been called since the first day of first grade, when, with parents present, blue-haired Mrs. Griffin said there were three Andrews in the class, and who would like to be called by a nickname? Garvey's mother raised her hand and spoke up for her son, deciding he should be called by her maiden name, condemning him to years of ridicule as Gravy Garvey, or, worse, Groovy Garvey. Until that radio personality Garvey Wanna came along, galvanizing suburban Chicago and catapulting Garvey into coolness, a throne he still occupied today—blond hair, toned body, gift of the gab.

So Claire was dead. He could hear the whirring machines below, the presses stamping messages onto cards. RSVP Josh Weinstein Bar Mitzvah; Mr. and Mrs. Kenneth R. Churchman request the honor of your presence at the wedding of their daughter Julie to Connor McGuell; and the birthday cards, condolence cards, thank you cards that were the backbone of their operation. Presses printing what should have been a news bulletin: Claire is dead.

A phone call—that's how things happened now. Now he would start dreading phone calls the way his parents did. Now his heart would start beating harder every time the phone rang. Garvey picked up the pen and traced Claire's name on the paper so that it was in boldface. What font would that be? Garvey probably should have known, but he left the day-to-day business, the actual printing, to his cousin, concerned himself with making sure everyone reported to whom they should, and that everyone knew his/her job. Not so different from the government job he'd held in D.C.—a lot of futile paper-pushing, a lot of lunches;

vapid, encouraging words, posturing, and perky ass-kissing. When he'd arrived in wide-eyed innocence in Washington, he'd asked the secretary what exactly his boss *did* for a living. "He delegates," she answered, her eyes remaining on the computer screen where she was transcribing dictation. "He's excellent at it."

And now Garvey was in Cleveland and had a dead ex-lover. She's the first one, he thought; the first of us to die. The first of my lovers I'll outlive. How dramatic. He'd imagined a time when firsts would be less frequent, even non-existent—a time after the first apartment, the first investment portfolio, the first wedding, the first custom suit—but they continued, and would, he now knew, until his death; his first (and only) death. Aside from the usual car accidents and suicides of distant acquaintances, he'd been left relatively untouched by death: his uncle Nick from cancer, a grandfather who'd kicked the bucket, but one he barely knew who left the entire family business to cousin Tate.

And then, back then, there was Claire. There was D.C. And now there simply wasn't anymore, not Claire. D.C. was still there, of course, but so distant as to be non-existent. Do places exist if you're not there? And was it that strange, really, that Claire no longer existed when she hadn't anyway, not really, for two years? Not since he'd left that fictional place called D.C. for Cleveland, another planet?

He should go and say good-bye to Claire, good-bye to D.C. He buzzed Laurie, who buzzed him back. It gave him great satisfaction to have a secretary of his own at age thirty-two, to buzz her and give her instructions like book a flight to D.C. tomorrow, and she'd comply and wonder why. Why D.C.? Why suddenly now? And he owed her no explanation.

Garvey could see through the glass walls overlooking the factory floor that Tate was not in his office. He was down there with the masses, so to speak, fiddling with something while the maintenance guys stood watching. Tate was wearing another loud, passé sport coat, no tie, and Doc Martens.

Garvey banged, but there was no way Tate could hear him with the racket on the floor, and Garvey straightened his tie in the weak reflection in the glass before heading down the large metal stairs to the factory floor.

"Tate," he screamed. The din was deafening. "Tate." He tapped his cousin on the shoulder. Tate turned around suddenly, hands cocked in a karate pose.

"Hai-YAH!" he said, giving Garvey a fake chop.

"Tate, listen, I'm going to D.C. for a couple of days, OK?"

"You're going to the sea?" This was one of Tate's stupid games, pretending to mishear because of the noise. He turned his head, leaning his ear toward Garvey, and smiled goofily.

"No, D.C. Washington."

"Watch the sun, great."

"No, it's my old . . . girlfriend, Claire." Garvey tried to infuse his words with solemnity. He found no humor in Tate's juvenile stand-up routine, but at least Tate was consistent in his sophomoric responses. He respected Tate's stability, his predictability. He knew there would never be a moment of self-doubt in Tate's life, no crying into his beer, no might-have-beens.

And he didn't fail Garvey now: "What about her?"

"She's dead."

Tate nodded. He paused. The hair he combed over his bald spot toward the front of his forehead fell a little. He pushed it back absently. "Sure am sorry. Hey listen, the cylinder's broken again."

"Bummer," Garvey said, delegating. "I'll be back Friday."

"No rush, partner. I'll hold down the fort." Tate turned back to the press.

Garvey bought a paper and draped it over his knees as the plane took off for Dulles. Claire Stoltz. He could summon her face only vaguely now, the eyes a little too close together, the small button nose. Her memory provoked only that terrible feeling of loss from two years ago when he stepped onto the plane for Cleveland and she waved good-bye to him from the gate, her right hand in her pocket fingering, he knew, one of those cigarillos she liked to smoke, waiting for the plane to take off so she could step out of the airport into the unclean capital air and light it up. Little Claire, waving fervently, guilelessly, and that heavy nauseous feeling that he never took for grief or emotion but rather dismissed as indigestion, or nervousness. They'd eaten ribs at one of those places on the way to the airport where they tie plastic bibs around your neck. Amicably, they'd eaten three whole slabs, tearing into the flesh (Claire, too, stuffing the food into God-knows-where on her five-foot frame), messy with the grease and sauce, eyes stinging from the spicy barbecue, and laughing so hard that other tables turned to stare. They forked cole slaw at each other, retreated into the plastic bib armor, and stuffed whole unbuttered rolls in their mouths, wiped their faces with the backs of their hands, washed it all down with large Cokes, refilled. He asked for the check and paid it with the newly acquired company credit card.

Amazingly, when the bibs came off and their faces were wiped clean with warm lemon-scented towels, they looked presentable. A sidelong glance at his watch told Garvey they were late, and they took off in her unreliable Cabriolet which for once (miraculously, fatedly) started right up.

Now, on the plane from Cleveland, the stewardess came by and asked Garvey what he wanted to drink.

"Gin and tonic—no, just tonic," he said, remembering the hour.

("How can you drink tonic, plain like that?" Claire had asked. "It's like that stuff they put on sore muscles, what—Ben Gay. It smells like a boxing locker room."

"You, Queen-of-Logic-and-Cigars, asking me how I can stand a smell?"

"They're *cigarillos*, thank you very much," she said and sparked one up right there in his Dupont Circle apartment. The cockroaches never returned.)

He sipped the tonic slowly, not sure what he was supposed to be feeling. Cleveland was good for that, for numbness: its industrial skyline, its small pond status. He was named most eligible bachelor by *Cleveland Weekend* magazine the month after he moved there. "Andrew Garvey Masterson, bachelor, hails most recently from our nation's capital, where he held a job in the high reaches of government. A Georgetown University graduate, 'Groovy Garvey' as his friends call him is also an avid mountain climber who enjoys cinema and Asian cuisine. Garvey will use his business savvy as Vice President of Cleveland's own Masterson Stationery, founded by his grandfather, the late Nathan Masterson. Welcome to Cleveland, Garvey!"

Welcome to Cleveland indeed. Low rents, decent sports bars, lonely women—it was as though Cleveland stretched out the red carpet for him. If he wasn't happy he was, well, comfortable, which was the word his father always used to describe his living. Comfortable living: central heating, dry cleaning delivery, premium movie channels. Comfortable, but not permanent, not forever. The future was, of course, unknowable, but it was never supposed to include Claire Stoltz. Now it couldn't include Claire Stoltz.

D.C. *looked* unchanged during the slow, traffic-snarled ride from the airport to the hotel. It was hotter here, and humid, making him sweat. He could have stayed with Buddy or someone, but he had decided that a hotel was the way to go; he could afford it, and he wanted the vacant luxury of air-conditioning, a clean bath and a minibar, a basement workout center and a small shoe-shine kit. But of course D.C. had changed. Cities change faster than interest rates; stores are built, restaurants go under, streets are torn up, renamed. If he stayed longer it would be like visiting a foreign town—he'd make wrong turns and feel the continual disappointment of unfamiliarity.

Garvey watched out the window as the car wound through the busy city streets. Washington looked so different from Cleveland with its rows of endless museums, green parks, Victorian buildings.. The monuments and the Mall lit up at night in a perpetual Christmas for tourists. D.C. was always "on," always showy. And it was true that at any given time, heads of state were deciding the fate of the nation, major drug deals were going down, intrepid reporters were uncovering corruption. And the streets were swept clean, whitewashed almost, by street sweepers who were armed only with brooms in the fight against filth, who wore wires and sold stories to the *Enquirer*. You had to be on your guard in D.C. It could catch you unaware and sweep you away into the Potomac. Garvey felt that old tension coming back, the clenching of the jaw and of the gut. He never felt that in Cleveland. Cleveland had no aesthetic pretensions, no premeditated urban planning. It just was.

After he checked into the hotel, Garvey traveled to Claire's parents' house in Virginia in a taxi with torn vinyl seats and Islamic prayer beads hanging from the rearview mirror. He asked the driver to wait for him in the Stoltzes' long driveway while he ran up and rang the doorbell. He could hear the ancient dog barking inside. A black woman in a modified maid's uniform answered the door.

"Hello," Garvey said. "I'm Garvey Masterson. Are the Stoltzes at home?"

"No," the woman said. She stared at him. "They've lost a child."

"I know," Garvey said. *They've lost a child*, as though they'd simply misplaced her. *Now where did I put that Claire?* "I'm an old friend. I came here once, for dinner, do you remember me?"

"I haven't been working here long," the woman said, and Garvey realized with embarrassment she didn't look familiar at all. He wasn't sure what he had come to the house for, but there was something satisfying about the rows of neat begonias outside the front door, the tidy chaos of the flagstone walk and the pale symmetrical columns holding up the second-floor porch. He noticed a small dandelion growing among the begonias and thought immediately of Claire's sunflower dress: a huge, gaudy, yellow housedress she wore all summer. He wondered if she was really as small as he remembered. She was shrinking in his memory, dwarfed by the dress and by the amount of time that had passed.

"Right, sorry," Garvey said. "I'm sorry to have disturbed you." He turned and walked toward the waiting taxi.

"It's all right. Would you like to leave a note?" the woman called after him.

Garvey stopped and looked at her. She was young, probably not much older than he was, but fat with neglect, or maybe indulgence. He thought about leaving a note, but what could it say? "No. I'll see them tomorrow at the service."

Garvey got back into the taxi and gave the address of Steinberg's funeral home. Parked outside the austere building was a Lincoln Town Car with Virginia plates. Garvey paid the cabbie and walked toward the entrance. He pushed the door in and smelled the thick scent of air-freshener and shag carpeting masking a deeper, more pervasive odor. What was he doing here? He wanted to see her one last time, see if his memory of her size was correct. The casket would be closed at the funeral.

He could hear voices down the hall—a woman's, distraught, and an older man's. He walked toward them and was unsurprised to see Claire's parents. Mrs. Stoltz was crying into a handkerchief.

"Hello, young man," said the doctor, something Claire had told Garvey he always said to people whose names he couldn't remember. It was how he had addressed Garvey when he came to dinner that once.

Mrs. Stoltz looked up. "Oh Gravy, I'm so glad you're here." She rushed toward him and fell into him, waiting to be embraced. Garvey obliged stiffly. He didn't correct her use of his old nickname. Mrs. Stoltz was small like Claire. She barely came up to his chest. The sharp corner of her purse, wedged between them, pressed against his leg. He felt awkward and intrusive. Mrs. Stoltz squeezed Garvey's arms against him with a strength that surprised him.

Then, just as suddenly, she stepped back. "I wondered if anyone called you. I was going to do it myself, but I just couldn't bring myself to. Do you want anything?" she asked, reverting to hostess mode though she was in a funeral parlor and not in her own home.

"No, thank you, Mrs. Stoltz. I just wanted to pay my condolences."

"Thank you, darling. You know, I always thought, the way Claire talked about you, that you'd be the one—"

"Dolly," Dr. Stoltz cautioned.

"This is Gravy," Mrs. Stoltz gestured to Garvey. They had always called him that, fondly, he supposed. "You remember him."

"Of course I do." Dr. Stoltz put his arm around his wife's shoulder. She disintegrated into sobs. "I'm sorry," he apologized. "It was so sudden, so unexpected."

"Hmmm," Garvey made a sympathetic sound.

There was a long pause. "Do you know where Claire might have left her high school diploma?" Dr. Stoltz asked suddenly. "We've been looking for it everywhere."

It was a bizarre question for which Garvey had no answer. He looked around the hallway, which offered no help. Funeral homes were always so tacky, he thought; the carpet was red plush, as was the wallpaper. There was a cheap oil painting, a solemn plains landscape, on the wall above a cherry wood table with fake lilies in a vase. "Umm, no, sir, I really don't know where she would have put it. She didn't really have places for things . . ." Garvey trailed off, remembering an afternoon spent looking for his keys, tearing apart her chaotic, crowded apartment where she insisted nothing could be misplaced because nothing *had* a place. She sat on her bed smoking, watching him and laughing. Garvey wondered why he had ever wanted to see her corpse in the first place, what peace he'd imagined the sight of her dead body would bring him.

"Oh," Dr. Stoltz said. His brow furrowed. If he'd been crying, his face didn't show it. "I think I'll take Dolly home now." He looked down at his wife, shuddering into her square of cloth.

"Of course," Garvey said. "I'm so sorry to keep you. I'm sorry. Claire was . . . ," he started. Claire was unknowable, un-articulatable. "I'll see you at the service tomorrow."

Mrs. Stoltz was buried in her husband's shoulder; he had his arm around her. Garvey stepped back to let them pass and watched them, crippled by the differences in their height, hobble to the front door.

When he couldn't reach him at home Garvey thought he could probably find Buddy at their "local," as they called it in the English manner. It was Wednesday, and Buddy usually went out Wednesdays, or used to anyway. Garvey left the name of his hotel on Buddy's answering machine. The room was growing oppressive, small, and sterile. Garvey thought he should probably go out for a good piece of fish, since he was in D.C., and he walked to a restaurant he knew near the hotel, which, to his relief, was still there, though they'd changed the menu substantially. He brought along the paper from the plane.

Garvey really didn't like to eat alone, but he didn't feel like calling any of the old gang. He would see them tonight, or tomorrow at the funeral. He ordered Chilean sea bass and tried to read the paper, which was a little unwieldy for a dinner table. He thought he could sense pity in the waitress's officiousness.

Afterward, he walked to the pub though it was hot still, even at night, a two-mile stroll which made it late enough to possibly find some people he knew. The bar was almost empty, the large television sets playing soundless sports events, including a strange feed from Asia broadcasting an Indian version of what looked like that old schoolyard game, Smear the Queer. Garvey looked around. He didn't know any of the people in the booths or at the bar. He didn't like to be alone at bars; often he went out of his way to pick friends up in his car just so he wouldn't arrive first. He sat down at the bar, and he and the bartender nodded at each other in vague recognition.

"Yes?" the bartender asked.

"A gin and tonic," Garvey said. He had thrown away the newspaper on the way over and now he was sorry. He watched Indian Smear the Queer while the bartender poured his drink. There was some sort of safe zone the player could take refuge in, and a no-man's-land where it was fair game to pin him to the ground until the fat referee blew his whistle. The bartender placed Garvey's drink on a napkin in front of him with a lemon wedge.

"Four fifty," he said.

"Do you still see Buddy Nothern and those guys in here ever?" Garvey asked.

"Tall blond guy? Kind of loud?"

"That's him," Garvey said.

"Sure. Sometimes." The bartender took his white cloth to the other end of the bar. Garvey sipped the drink and swiveled around to watch some people play pool. Two couples, on a double date it looked like. The men typical D.C. liberals, early thirties, government guys probably. The girls were thin, with long blond hair that draped down their backs and swung when they laughed. They'd been drinking awhile and were giggling, playing sloppy, interminable pool, accepting flirtatious instruction from their dates: "No, now line it up like this, and softly, but firmly, you know how I like it . . ."

Claire used to sit on the pool table while they were playing. He'd pick her up and move her like patio furniture when she got in the way, and she'd continue her monologue, moving through the air in mid-sentence as though it were normal to levitate while conversing.

Garvey watched NASCAR races for a while on the TV above the couples, and when his watch said midnight he left the bar and caught a cab to his hotel.

Garvey was a little early for the service, but most of the mourners had already arrived. Claire's relatives he could discern from their Eastern European hips and outmoded clothes—exactly the bumpkins Claire had painted them as. The Stoltz parents stood toward the front near the coffin. A large, youngish, well-tailored group was standing over on the right side of the large room. Garvey moved their way.

He shook hands with Peter and Josh and pecked Julianne on the cheek. Georgia had been crying; she had mascara tracks down her cheeks.

"Groovy Garvey, man, nice to see you," Buddy was in front of him suddenly, a little happy for the occasion. "So bad it had to be for this."

"Yeah," Garvey agreed, accepting the handshake and the left hand pat that went with it. "How are you?"

"Good, really good. Hey listen, where were you last night? I tried your hotel a hundred times. We were all going to go out."

"I turned off the phone," Garvey said. "I was really tired."

"Well, after the service there's this reception thing in Virginia and then we can catch up. I want you to meet—here, honey." He tried to get the attention of the wiry brunette behind him. "Rhina, meet Garvey."

"Nice to meet you," they both said simultaneously. She was pretty, with green eyes and a long nose. She had on a short dress that just barely won the fight between risqué and appropriate.

"I've heard a lot about you," Rhina said. "From Buddy."

"Oh," Garvey said. He didn't really want to be making small talk. He wanted to be sitting, looking at the coffin, listening to those Jewish dirges. He wished, suddenly and violently, that he and Claire had been engaged when she died so that he could sit up in front with her parents and hand Mrs. Stoltz fresh Kleenexes, maybe shed a few tears himself, at least put his head in his hands, grieve publicly.

The lights dimmed, and they all took seats. From where he was seated on the aisle, Garvey could see the

Stoltzes, rocking in time to the litanies. He understood little of the service. The rabbi gave the eulogy, and it was short, talked about the mysteries of God's ways, and proved, through the citation of various Old Testament passages, that the test of death was for the living, not the dead. When Garvey looked over once, he saw that Rhina and Buddy were holding hands and Buddy had tears in his eyes. Buddy had never dated anyone as pretty as Rhina, and he didn't usually like brunettes. Garvey tried to concentrate on the service, tried to drum up tears in his own eyes, but they seemed to all be located somewhere under his rib cage, attached to his sternum maybe, in a sac he couldn't dislodge.

There was a lot of standing and sitting and standing again and then suddenly it was over and everyone was filing past the Stoltzes telling them how sorry they were, and Garvey took his place in line. When he got to Dr. Stoltz, the older man looked at him blankly. "Thank you for your sympathies, young man." Mrs. Stoltz was sitting down, her eyes covered by the handkerchief.

Buddy and Rhina drove Garvey to the cemetery for another short service and the lowering of the coffin. It had started to rain, and Buddy offered Garvey a part of the newspaper to put over his head for protection, which Garvey accepted. They all took turns shoveling dirt in the grave. Garvey took a large bladeful of dirt and followed it with his eyes all the way down until he saw it land like hard rain on the coffin's surface. He gave the shovel to Josh behind him, and he and Buddy and Rhina made their way to the Stoltzes' house in Virginia.

He was surveying the dining room table laden with food, and contemplating what to eat when a tall, dark-haired woman stepped up beside him. She skewered a mini hot dog.

"Jews serving hot dogs at *Shivah*," she sighed. She looked at Garvey. "Of course, I guess they could be kosher hot dogs." She narrowed her eyelids, gave him a look that Garvey could only describe as lascivious.

"Are you a *Lansman*?" the woman asked. She spoke softly and with her mouth full of hot dog he could barely understand her.

"A linesman? What?"

She held up one finger as a time-out and swallowed patiently. "A member of the tribe. Are you Jewish?"

"Does it matter?" Garvey was taken aback.

"Well," she considered. "Yes, I would say it does." She was whispering; he couldn't hear her above the din, so he leaned in close, as though he were the one making the pass, an admirable ploy on her part.

"No. I'm not a linesman. I don't even play football." Seeing the joke fall flat he added quickly, "No. I'm not Jewish." Christ, he was sounding more like Tate every day.

"What are you then?"

"Like, what religion? I don't know."

"What do you mean you don't know?" she asked sharply.

This was getting weird. Garvey speared a cold cut with a green sword toothpick and put it in his mouth to discover it was a small pickle surrounded by roast beef. He didn't like pickles, but felt obliged to swallow it. The sodium rush made him gulp down his gin and tonic and hang on to an ice cube to suck. Any port in a storm, he thought, then wondered if the port was the ice or the girl.

"I mean, I don't know. I wasn't raised anything. Episcopalian, maybe." He picked a religion at random.

"Episcopalian? Christ!" She threw back her head to laugh at the private joke that was Episcopalianism, but Garvey didn't get it. The room seemed to stop for a moment to listen to her laughter, a guttural rushing sound, like an avalanche.

He studied her now that she was at a distance. She had a pageboy haircut, wide brown eyes and a loose-fitting suit that exaggerated her shoulders. The pants hung loosely at her hips.

"So what are you?" he asked.

"Oh, I'm Zoroastrian." She set her glass of white wine on the table in order to place some melon balls on a napkin. The living room seemed to Garvey remarkably like a cocktail party all of a sudden. The woman busied herself with her food. Garvey thought she'd moved on, that he'd failed the religion litmus. He went to refill his glass at the self-service bar, tonging more ice in the cup.

"Are you from Cleveland?" she asked suddenly, holding out her glass for him to refill.

"Yes," he said. "How did you—"

"You're Gravy Masterson."

"Garvey," he corrected, extending his hand.

"Diane Cristals."

"Nice to meet you," he said automatically.

"I was Claire's lover, when you were in D.C."

If his life were a movie, this would be the place where he'd spit gin and tonic all over the room. Except his glass was still empty. "Impossible," he stammered.

"Not really," Diane said. "What did she tell you she was doing for a living?"

"Playing accompanying piano for a ballet studio."

"Not a total lie. I do live in a studio." She paused. "That would make me the piano." Diane popped a melon ball into her mouth.

"I don't believe you," Garvey said, although it made perfect sense when he thought about it. It was something he could have expected from Claire: the unexpected.

"No? She had this strange thing about her breasts." Diane turned her back to the bar and looked around the room as though searching for someone in particular. Her finger traced the rim of her wine glass. "She loved the left one, but if you touched the right one she'd have conniption fits." Diane's voice was louder, now that the conversation had gotten more intimate. Garvey could hear her clearly for the first time. He remembered looking at Claire, naked above him, and then some perverse instinct inserted Diane in her place in his memory.

"The sex was terrible," Diane continued. "In case you were feeling jealous, don't. The worst I ever had."

"She was date-raped in college," Garvey said softly.

"I know. That explains the frigidity, I suppose, but not the breast thing. What do you think?"

"I think I don't want to be talking to you about this here," Garvey said. He shifted his weight, feeling very uncomfortable.

"You still don't believe me, do you?" she asked. "I can tell you don't. Let's see. She liked to sit on your back and smoke cigars while you did push-ups. She said it turned you on. Maybe it's a guy thing," Diane continued. "I have to admit I don't really get it."

"It's complicated," Garvey said. He couldn't believe Claire had told anyone. He felt betrayed, and stared into his sympathetically watery drink with self-pity. He sloshed it around twice and downed the meager liquid left in the bottom.

There was a moment of silence. "Time for a refill," Garvey said.

"Here, take my card," Diane said. She handed him a small business card which had her home address, an apartment not far from his old one in D.C. There was no profession listed. He put it in his jacket pocket and poured some Tanqueray into his glass, watching the ice cubes crack with excitement. Shame to dilute it with tonic, but he didn't like straight gin, so in it went. He thought he could taste the filtering process, which was bullshit, he knew, but once he'd gotten the idea in his head he'd developed an aversion to the straight stuff. When he looked up from his potion, Diane had disappeared.

It was the kind of relationship Garvey had never thought existed. One he'd never read about, one he'd never talked about with the guys or seen on TV. One that Buddy wouldn't ever understand. It wasn't that Garvey *liked* Claire that much—that wasn't the right word—or that he *disliked* her at all, but once they met there was never any question that time spent would be time spent with her. Comfortable, like his maternal grandparents who were so close they spoke in a patois that only they could understand.

There were aspects of a mother/child connection in their relationship, though neither Garvey nor Claire was the clear offspring of the other. It was just that natural, that imperceptible, that mundane. The small weight of her lying on his back as he did his push-ups; her cigarillo, asthma be damned, sending the smoke rings up to the ceiling like distress signals. Garvey moving up and down with the strength of his arms, the colossal power he contained.

And their two successful lovemaking sessions, after they'd tried everything for months—talking and electronic aids and doctor visits (physical and mental), alcohol and pornography—and it had been repeatedly disastrous. Even Garvey couldn't come, and he didn't tell Buddy because he was afraid he knew what it meant; something about a place he didn't want to go unless Claire came with him. She was so little in bed, so easily reduced to tears, uncharacteristic (impossible even) when she was clothed. And then one Saturday afternoon she clipped the cigarillo and tapped Garvey on the shoulder midway through the push-up routine. He rolled over and it was just, well, the only way Garvey could describe it was right. It just was right.

Now it was ruined by Diane's revelation. If it had happened with Garvey, then it must have happened with Diane too, he reasoned. How many times? It killed him to think that Diane might have reached Claire in a way he was unable to.

Not that he wasn't seeing other women, too. There was Heidi, and Jennifer and Lana from work, and Micha, and a couple of dates with Celeste, which was weird because that was his mother's name and it was a rare enough name that he associated it only with her. But it was the mid-nineties, and after sex no one actually wanted to sleep together—the actual physical sleeping being too intimate—and Garvey itched to call Claire when it was over, like a post-coital cigarette, and tell her nothing about it, not a word, but just let her ramble on to him about the guests on the late-night round table discussion she was watching or her theories of meditation and redemption, her voice as elemental as breathing or bread or water.

What was he to her? He couldn't know, didn't want to, couldn't even articulate her place in *his* life, suspected (arrogantly, he knew) that it couldn't be categorized, had never before been experienced in the however-many-thousand years of human history. He didn't bother to search for the words, to perform the existential honing in on accurate classification. It would have boiled down to something existential and banal.

And in Garvey's life things were changing. Senator Jordan was indicted for embezzling campaign funds, and the Republican congress vetoed the president's welfare bill. And then Garvey's grandfather died, and the phone call came from cousin Tate, encountered for the first time in twenty years at the funeral in a shiny black tuxedo jacket and faded black Dockers (*again*, no tie), asking would he like to join the family business. And change, Garvey realized, was the only thing life was sure to bring you, *fuck* death and taxes. And the firsts would continue, always the firsts. You could never get too comfortable in a life with firsts. And so he thought about moving to Cleveland.

They all went back to the local in reminiscence of the good times. A different bartender was working, a new one, but Buddy knew him and laughed loudly with the man about something or other. The bar seemed brighter than it had the night before, and he found the source: an enormous lit plastic advertisement in the shape of a bottle of Zima, a drink no one in the place would have been caught dead with a couple of years ago. He ordered a gin and tonic—no, wait, two. He'd just get two now and save himself another trip to the bar. It was getting to be a few too many, but Garvey wasn't sure he cared. He was getting that pleasantly buzzed feeling for the first time since he'd left Cleveland, and it was a welcome one.

Buddy and Garvey retreated to a tall table for two. Garvey sat on the stool; Buddy remained standing and poured himself a glass of beer from a pitcher.

"How are you, man?" Buddy asked. "I'm terrible about the phone thing, and it's not like I'm coming to Ohio to visit you."

"Don't worry about it," Garvey said. "But it's really not so bad."

"I can't believe we're here after a funeral."

"Me either." They took a long sip of their drinks.

"What a way to meet up again," Buddy said.

"Yeah," Garvey said. He hoped that Buddy wouldn't try to pat him on the back or offer some sort of greeting-card consolation. But Buddy didn't try.

"We didn't see a lot of her after you left. A little bit, but you know, we started going to that new titty bar on Connecticut. Hey, if you're still around this weekend, we should check it out."

"I'm leaving tomorrow," Garvey said, a little unkindly.

"Oh, well, next time then maybe." Buddy took another long sip, finishing the beer. He poured himself another glass and held it up to clink with Garvey, who downed his first drink and picked up the second.

"To old friends," Buddy said.

They watched the basketball game on the TV. Buddy finished his glass and poured another. He had gotten significantly older in the two years since Garvey had seen him: more jowly, the extra skin looser around his face, the hair thinner at the crown, and Garvey wondered what changes the years had worked on his own face.

"Can I tell you something, Groove?" Buddy asked suddenly, his eyes wide open. He wore a confessional look that Garvey dreaded.

"Yeah . . ." Garvey froze. What other revelations did this day have in store?

Buddy took a deep breath. "I'm going to marry Rhina."

Garvey felt a wave of relief followed by the sharp jab of envy. "You, Mr. Good-Morning-Sweetheart-Last-Night-Was-Great-What's-Your-Name-Again is getting married?"

"Happens to the best of us." He looked over where Rhina and the others were laughing at a joke near the pool table. He winked and Rhina tossed her hair, blowing him a kiss.

"Wow, that's—that's just great, man. Who knew?" Garvey stood up and gave Buddy an awkward hug. "Hey, I should buy you a drink."

"I'm doing OK for right now." Buddy pointed at the quarter-full pitcher. "You get the next one."

"You are aware I have a moral obligation to tell embarrassing stories at the wedding?"

"I fucking hope so," Buddy said. "Why do you think I did those things? Just for fun?"

"I just thought you were an exhibitionist."

"You know me." The two men laughed.

Garvey fingered Diane's business card in his suit jacket pocket. There was an awkward silence. An image flickered into Garvey's mind of Diane and Claire together in bed: Diane's dark head on Claire's chest, her hand resting on Claire's hipbone.

"What's wrong, Groove?" Buddy asked. "You look like shit."

"I'm just a little freaked. I thought you were going to say something else is all."

"What?"

"No, forget it, it's stupid."

"Nah, what? Tell me."

"I just, I thought you were going to tell me you slept with Claire or something."

"Me?" Buddy asked. "Sleep with Claire? Come on, dude, you are not that deluded."

"It's not that ridiculous. She wasn't ugly or anything."

"Nah, she was cute, but I mean, it was all about dry ice, man."

"What?" Garvey wasn't following the coded slang.

"Cold fish. Terrible lay. She had it written all over her. I don't mean to be vulgar, but all that year you had that tight look around your eyes, like it wasn't working out so good between you."

"A tight look?" Garvey asked.

"Worried, whipped, like I'd never seen you before. I was glad you were moving to Cleveland, getting out of here."

Garvey just stared at Buddy. He never thought Buddy noticed anything, least of all subtleties in Garvey's physiognomy.

"Don't look so surprised. I'm not a total meathead. Cheers, bro!" Buddy raised his glass, and though Garvey's was almost empty, and it was bad luck to clink with water, the glasses touched, making a low sound like a quiet gong.

"Come on, let's join the gang. Enough of this bonding shit." Buddy poured another glass of beer, draining the pitcher. Garvey stood up and felt a little dizzy from all the alcohol. He took his hand out of his pocket and left Diane's card on the table before following Buddy to the bar.

One other memory: Claire was lying in bed with that flu that was going around, her face flushed by a fever, her breathing labored. She coughed weakly, more for show or out of habit than because of any physical need.

Garvey set the tray of chicken soup down on the bed next to her. She looked even smaller when she was sick, as though he was looking at her through the wrong end of binoculars. The tray must have been a gift from her mother. Its design—flowers pressed beneath glass—clashed with the art deco dishes Claire used.

"Here, try to eat something, honey," Garvey said. He lifted her up under the arms, like he would a child, and fluffed a couple of pillows behind her back ineffectually.

Claire reached for the spoon. Her arms were heavy, to let Garvey know she was going to eat just to humor him.

"No, let me," Garvey said and took the spoon from her hand. He dipped it into the soup, searching for a small piece of chicken floating near the top. He balanced it carefully, concentrating on keeping it level. He had heard that if you hummed while carrying liquids they wouldn't spill, so he hummed now, a low purring.

Claire looked at him. Her eyes were glassy, her face blotchy with sheet creases down the cheeks like surgical scars. Garvey was suddenly scared, terrified even, and his heart beat quickly. He continued to hum, louder now, around the growing lump in his throat. Claire opened her mouth and Garvey placed the spoon lightly on her tongue, waited for her to close her lips around it, felt the slight pressure of her tongue, the rim of the spoon touching the ridged roof of her mouth.

He removed the spoon and Claire swallowed, smiling weakly. "Good girl," he said, and reached down for another ladleful when Claire began to cough for real. The fit got worse, and she leaned forward to ease the racket in her rib cage. The entire bed shook as she coughed. And then she gagged and vomited on the tray, just bile, mostly, and the bite of chicken.

"It's OK," Garvey said. "Do you want the nebulizer?"

Claire shook her head and the coughing stopped. Garvey went into the bathroom and wet a washcloth in the sink. As he let the cold water run over his wrists he looked at himself in the mirror. He didn't look much better than Claire: hair uncombed, pale and haggard with those black bags under his eyes that he was more accustomed to seeing on his father's face. What was he doing here?

He returned to the bedroom where Claire was settled, her chest still moving with the enormous effort of drawing breath. He wiped her mouth, then turned the cloth over and placed it on her forehead. "There, isn't that better?" She leaned back and closed her eyes; she sighed.

"Why are you being so nice to me?" Claire asked softly.

"Because I love you." He said it quickly, matter-of-factly, with the ineffable, unarguable "because it's there" logic of Everest climbers. It came from a place Garvey didn't recognize, and he was almost as surprised as Claire at the words.

She shook her head three times slowly. Then she rolled over onto her side, away from Garvey. Then he knew that there was no feeling better for Claire. Life held no low hope of comfort, of solace, of palliative de-sensitivity, just a series of unpredictable firsts. An awful moment passed when Garvey realized what his earlier fear had meant—that he wasn't afraid so much that he would lose her, but rather that she would lose him. That this much was inevitable.

Garvey could go now. He could clean up the flowered tray and turn off the stove and walk the half-mile to his own apartment. He could call Tate and say, "Yes, cousin, yes," and make plane reservations, hire movers, a realtor. It could be so easy, comfortable. He could do what Claire probably wanted him to do. He could just walk away.

ACKNOWLEDGEMENTS

I wish to acknowledge and express gratitude for the kind support of the following individuals: Gina Frangello, Stacy Bierlein, Allison Parker and Lois Hauselman of OV Books; Dan Wickett, Steve Gillis, and Steven Seighman of Dzanc; my family: Jim, Sheila, and Anthony Amend; the Delta Schmelta Sorority: Sheri Joseph, Dika Lam, Margo Rabb, Lara JK Wilson and Andrew Beierle; Hannah Tinti; Susan Aurinko of FLATFILE galleries; Nancy Racina Landin; and also Margot Grover, Thisbe Nissen, Lynn McPhee, Lindsey Marcus, Stephanie Pommez, Duncan Smith, and Sarah Tombaugh.

I'd also like to thank the following conferences, organizations, and residencies:
Djerassi Resident Artists Program
Gibraltar Point Centre for the Arts
Fundación Valparaíso
Maria and Peter Matthiesen Long Island Idyll
Saltonstall Foundation
Sewanee Writers' Workshop
The Jack Wettling and Mitch Karsch Home for Hungry Writers
The Corporation of Yaddo
Tin House Writers' Conference
Vermont Studio Center

Finally, I want to extend my appreciation to the literary magazines in which these stories first appeared.